VALENTINA GOLDMAN SHIPS OUT

A Novel

Marisol Murano

A Hipso Media Book

Copyright © 2015 by Marisol Murano.

All rights reserved. No part of this publication may be reproduced, distributed or transmitted in any form or by any means, including photocopying, recording, or other electronic or mechanical methods, without the prior written permission of the publisher, except in the case of brief quotations embodied in critical reviews and certain other noncommercial uses permitted by copyright law. For permission requests, write to the publisher at the email below.

HIPSOMEDIA
info@hipsomedia.com
www.hipsomedia.com

Publisher's Note: This is a work of fiction. Names, characters, places, and incidents are a product of the author's imagination. Any resemblance to actual people, living or dead, or to businesses, companies, events, institutions, or locales is completely coincidental.

Quantity sales. Special discounts are available on quantity purchases by corporations, associations, and book clubs. For details, contact the "Special Sales Department" at the email address above.

Valentina Goldman Ships Out / Marisol Murano. — 1st ed.

Paperback / ISBN-10: 098873947X • ISBN-13: 9780988739475
eBook / ISBN-10: 0988739488 • ISBN-13: 9780988739482

Drive carefully. We'll wait.

–LAWN SIGN ON FUNERAL HOME

The sole cause of Man's unhappiness is that he does not know how to stay quietly in his room.

−BLAISE PASCAL

(Dear reader: Apologies for this second quote. It is—as some people like to say these days—Pascal's bad. Apparently, Pascal was so busy with his math that he didn't have a chance to discover women. So I've taken the liberty of rewriting his quote below. See what you think. I think when you repurpose it to include women, it becomes a little charged. But *you* tell me.)

The sole cause of Woman's unhappiness is that she does not know how to stay quietly in her room.

−MARISOL MURANO (as Pascal's interpreter)

(What do you think? Doesn't Woman come across as a super-meddler who can't leave well enough alone? Here's a hint: the main character in this novel wanted to stay quietly in her room, but another character wouldn't hear of it. Now you get to see what happens when a woman who's minding her own business does something against her will and goes halfway across the world to appease her mother. That's the plot in a nutshell.)

PART I

LANDLOCKED

PART II

ADRIFT

PART III

THREE SHEETS IN THE WIND

PART IV

ANCHORS AND TIES

EPILOGUE

PART I

LANDLOCKED

CLINICALLY

"I'm not depressed. I'm not depressed. I am telling you, Mamá: I am *not* depressed."

What line of defense are you supposed to use when your mother is both your mother and a psychotherapist? When she's simultaneously accusing and diagnosing you?

"The reason I know I'm not depressed is because the doorbell rang, I got up to answer it, and here you are."

"That's precisely why I know you're depressed, Valentina. Because I found you here."

"Where else would I be? I live here."

"At ten in the morning?"

"I live here at all hours of the day."

"Getting cute won't help your case, Valentina. By the way, you look dreadful."

"*Gracias*, Mamá. Please make yourself at home."

Did I mention that possession runs in the family? My mother flew in from Venezuela and in less time than it takes to say "How was your flight?" she took possession.

"*Hija*, when was the last time you saw the inside of a hair salon?"

"No need for that in the desert, Mamá. The minute you go outside your hair gets crispy. So I'm saving my money."

"You're evading an important question. That's a sign of depression."

After setting down the matching Gucci bags that gave her so much balance, my mother set out to confirm her diagnosis.

"When was the last time you dusted?" she said, running her index finger over one of the tables. She then walked to the kitchen—a place she herself never visits—and opened the fridge.

"When was the last time you bought milk?"

"I don't drink milk."

"And where are the ashes? I thought you told me you kept them in the fridge."

"I moved him to the bedroom; it gets too quiet in there sometimes."

"So now you're talking to the dead?"

"You talk to the dead every Sunday. And Christ has been dead a lot longer than Max."

After her brief survey of the kitchen, my mother reached inside her purse, put on her sunglasses, and went outside. "When was the last time you cleaned the pool?"

"I don't plan to go swimming anytime soon."

"That confirms it. You're clinically depressed."

So that was her final diagnosis. I wasn't just depressed. Or a little depressed. But *clinically* depressed. Somehow the word *clinically* made me feel terminal, a hopeless case. But how would my mother know whether I was depressed or not? Had she been married three times to three men who had nothing in common? Did she have three stepchildren who didn't speak her native tongue? Had she ever been a hapless widow in a foreign country?

No. Other than in her therapist's couch, where a parade of certifiable *locos* carried on about stuff she should have sold to the tropical tabloids, my mother had never faced anything extraordinary. For as long as I could remember, her chin-length auburn hair had been tucked behind her ears. She owned a husband who didn't speak until spoken to, and had two perfect grandchildren—my sister Azucena's little brand freaks; peculiar young people who considered Tommy Hilfiger a relative. My mother was a woman who spent the better part of her days gaining from scrutinizing people far less put together than her. Now I was one of her patients.

True. I had not dusted in a while. So what? I still folded the towels in perfect rectangles, the way she taught me before I even learned to speak. The folded towels in the linen closet proved that despite everything, I was still attached to order. And isn't attachment a kind of passion? And doesn't passion cancel depression?

Pouting, hiding in my room, or running away were desirable options. But this was my house, after all. She should be the one to leave. But faced with a woman who told her assistant, "Milena, my daughter won't answer the phone; please book me on the next flight to Scottsdale," my little runaway fantasies didn't stand a chance. On that bright Arizona day, I was unsuspecting of what was coming my way. As it turned out, my mother's visit was merely a courtesy consultation. She had big plans for me. Worse yet, she had plans for us!

I'd be lying if I said her sudden appearance at my doorstep wasn't a little alarming. She was, after all, a professional. And there was enough truth in her diagnosis to plant the seeds of doubt. That's one of my mother's talents, or maybe that's just a trick she picked up from her schizophrenics: making people uncomfortable enough for doubt to start seeping in. Seeping is always dangerous. She almost made me believe that hating the world and every single last one of its occupants was not normal. But I didn't let her get to me. Not just then, anyway. But only because I had no idea that when she showed up at my doorstep without an invitation my mother already had a plan to get me out of the depression she had already diagnosed long-distance from Caracas. I knew I wasn't depressed. But to tell the *generalísima* Serena Serrano that the Buddhist calm had not settled in me since my late husband committed suicide in his ex-wife's kitchen was a waste of time. The only person in our family ever to win an argument with my mother is my sister Azucena. Only Azucena has what it takes to hold a stare and make people feel like solid waste without wasting a single word.

INCARNATIONS

Before I met Max, I used to believe that the secret to happiness was to keep moving. Since Max's early departure the year before, I had rarely moved from the same chair, except to go through the routine motions. I went to get the mail, though I hardly looked at it anymore. Better to let the bills pile up somewhere where I wasn't. The bills were safe in the study. I took to wearing Max's watches and dragged my feet in his shoes. From time to time, I visited the grocery store for Kleenex and Special K refills. Truth be told, it wasn't that special. But making my way through five cereal aisles only to arrive at the checkout counter with a different box of sugar became so daunting a task I just grabbed the one with the simple logo and the colors I recognized.

It wasn't until my stepdaughter, Emily, left for Ecuador, though, that it hit me like a tsunami: I was alone, alone, alone, all alone in a foreign country. And Max was to blame. But I wouldn't stay mad at him much longer. Any day now I might open the door and find Max standing there saying, "Hello, my name is Lazarus." But if there was a way in which my little fantasy was flawed, it was this: Max wasn't Catholic. There was no way he would come back as Lazarus. To my way of thinking, though, if miracles are truly miracles, shouldn't they work, regardless of denomination? Even so, I would have settled for reincarnation and set aside my beliefs on resurrection. I would have taken Max back as a porcupine. But I was pretty sure suicide carried substantial penalties for reincarnees, even for the all-forgiving Buddhists.

To add insult to misgivings, I had left my promising advertising career in New York and moved to Arizona to help Max raise Rosemary's babies. (The ex's name isn't Rosemary, BTW. But she would have easily won the part).

Now Max was gone and I was "clinically depressed" in a desert house stalked by coyotes. I wasn't depressed. I was horrified. Thanks to my brother-in-law, the banker, one banker led to another and the house was no longer foreclosed. It was now in my name, which meant I could sell it. According to my neighbor and Realtor, Marilee Lewis, selling the house would help me move on. Maybe. Maybe not. But who wants to move on when suffering like Christ can get you so much attention? It is true that most of the attention you get after a suicide is unwanted. But it is attention nonetheless. And who can trust a Realtor, anyway? Even through the hazy curtain of grief I was able to catch the occasional whiff of greed. The only reason Marilee kept telling me to sell the house was so that she could get her commission. And besides, I had more pressing worries than getting rid of a cactus-ridden house. I had to find a job, and pronto. The problem was that after a few years of playing tropical stepmother in the desert, I had no clue where to start. What to say to the HR robot ready to pounce at a missing comma on your resume: "How do you explain the gap in employment?" In the many imaginary job interviews I conducted inside my head, I always played my trump card: "Did I mention I'm bilingual?" But whenever I did, inevitably, I heard the Inhuman Resources representative say: "We now have Google Translator for that."

Some days I was mad enough to scream at Max's ashes.

"I can leave, too, you know. I don't have to sit around waiting for the mailman to bring any more bills!" But I was too exhausted from arguing with the neurotic digital cashier at the grocery store. "Unidentified item. Please place your item in the bag. Unidentified item. Please place your item in the bag."

I heard you the first time, you fucking avatar!!

No doubt my mother had misdiagnosed. I wasn't depressed. I was bitch angry.

OPEN to INTERPRETATION

Morning arrived, obnoxiously bright and obnoxiously early as mornings tend to arrive in sunny Arizona. My first thought on remembering I had an unwelcome guest in the room adjacent to mine was, *At breakfast, I'll tell her I'm selling the house.* As far as driving somebody away it wasn't a terrible idea. No one likes helping people pack. But selling the house might take a while. More to the point of the unexpected visit, though, was the fact that I've never enjoyed a day that's open to interpretation. Nor do I have what it takes to cope with anything that insists; whether object, animal, or person. I kept a running list of peeves about things that made themselves redundant by repeating themselves, which included, but was not limited to: digital cashiers, the blinker in my car, the whiny refrigerator alarm, and the maddening cooing issuing from the desert at unpredictable intervals. To that list, now I had to add my mother who walked around the house insisting: You're clinically depressed. You're clinically depressed. Give me a hammer, already!

In the month's following Max's death, sleeping until noon became so unremarkable that I got used to it. Let a few more months go by this way and pretty soon your whole perception of time begins to shift, until one day it has shifted so completely that you hardly notice it anymore. Now you're living in a different time zone. And the next thing you know, your mother is ringing the doorbell, accusing you of being clinically depressed and sitting in your living room, ready for the next level of evaluation.

That was where I found her when I came out of my room, still sleepy-eyed, wearing Max's robe. She was sitting on one of the living room chairs, poised as a tulip, dressed in yacht white from head to toe.

"I'm taking you to breakfast," she said. "Put on some nice clothes."

After some wasted resistance on my part, we ended up at a cozy French bistro not too far from my house where my mother ordered two perfectly poached eggs and a croissant. But the most impressive thing about her eggs wasn't that they were perfectly poached. It was the fact that she managed to eat them without spilling any of the yolk onto the white plate, a feat she handled effortlessly and also with the silent underscoring that is her hallmark: that everyone should eat their breakfast without messing up a perfectly clean plate.

After years living in the States the fog was starting to lift a little. On seeing my mother's clean plate, it began to dawn on me that I wasn't all that different from those prisoners of war who had spent years in the dark with mild levels of amnesia. That must be what happened, I mused. I must have run way. I must have left my country, my native language, and my friends behind to run away from the impossibility of not breaking the yolk while eating the egg. Once, as an experiment, I tried tipping the plate and swallowing the egg whole. Unfortunately, it landed on my shirt. There were more epiphanies to come. But the morning was still young. For now I had to remain sharp for my mother's next set of leading questions. So I took a sip of my coffee. A jolt of caffeine always helps when trying to outsmart a therapist.

"Haven't you always wanted to see the world, Valentina?"

"Who, me? No. I love postcards, Mamá. I want to see the world without having to strip for TSA agents."

Perhaps I should mention that this was one of my mother's better tricks, one she must have used time and again against her patients—inserting ideas in their heads and making them think they were *their* ideas.

While I pushed the ham and cheese omelet around my plate, I could almost hear her: "Mario, haven't you always wanted to stop beating your hamster?" Or, "Yolanda, haven't you always wanted to quit smoking?" The trick being all the more clever because who's dumb enough to say: "As a matter of fact, Doctora Serrano, I've always envisioned a future that includes coughing up blood. Don't you just love Camels? I only wish they came in menthol."

It was as she casually allowed the idea of seeing the world to float around like a colorful air balloon that she reached inside her Louis Vuitton bag and produced a series of brochures so bright it was impossible not to want to pick one up.

As the cliché lament goes . . . if only I had known then what I know now. It turns out there's only one way to explore this world in all its watery glory. Mariners have known this for centuries. Columbus knew it. Magellan knew it. Captain Cook knew it. And that is by taking a plane to a sleazy port somewhere and plunging into the roiling seas for a bit of seasickness. Brochures, even the best ones, cannot do justice to the many intensities of blue to be experienced in the oceans of this world. I didn't know what I was missing yet.

For now, though, I just said, "There's no way I'm getting on anything that floats."

I happen to like my freedom. And to me, freedom involves walking on terra firma, or driving on solid ground. At all times, though, there has to be land involved.

"You have to trust me on this, Mamá. If I had wanted to go on a cruise, I would have done it by now."

As if she gave a whook!

After my brief embellishment on the subject of travel by water, my mother didn't insist. She's a trained professional. She knows how to be persistent without pushing herself on people. So she put the brochures away and didn't say another word. Instead, for the better part of two weeks she took to following me around, if quietly, around the house. Then, at random—yet calculated intervals—she disappeared, no doubt so I'd wonder: Where is she? And then, when I least expected her, she materialized by my side like a ghost. And thus, by appearing like the ghost of Christmas past, present, and future, my mother meant to send me a simple message. You can remain on that chair. You could move to Patagonia and set up an igloo with penguins and seals. It doesn't matter, I will hunt you down!

For now, though, at the cozy French bistro where she took me for further observation, she just said, "Do you know where the restrooms are?" as if nothing odd had transpired between us.

"I've never been here before," I said, tersely.

During her too-brief absence, I thought about how many people—former coworkers from New York, for instance—used to pine, or whine, "Oh, if only so-and-so would surprise me for my birthday [or Valentine's Day, or whatever] and take me on a cruise . . ."

As for me, I couldn't shake the feeling that I was being cleverly manipulated. So when my mother returned from her pre-scheduled restroom break I said, "It's not as if I'm free to come and go as I please, anyway."

It was barely out of my lips and my on-the-fly excuse already sounded lame.

"I'm not sure I follow, Valentina."

"Emily's in Ecuador now. But she might come back. Who's going to let her into the house? I just got a postcard from her, as a matter of fact."

"Remember when you used to call and tell me you were just the 'guest mother' and you didn't count?"

"I do."

"Guess what? You are *still* the guest mother."

Later that night Azucena called so that my mother could talk to the children. After issuing a series of unrecognizable coos and oohs to Sofía and Lucas Enrique in a tone she never used with either Azucena or me when we were kids, my mother reclaimed her aloof therapist voice to say, "Your sister wants to speak with you."

No sooner had she handed me the phone than Azucena—with that empathy that keeps her getting promoted at work—said to me: "I guess I have to have a dead husband for her to take me anywhere. Greece is on strike again, you know."

Azucena's mention of Greece could mean only one thing. My mother knew exactly where she planned to take me. The brochures were a ruse! I was being humored by a professional. For the second time in my life I was speechless. The first time was when the police officer called to ask if I was Mrs. Goldman. But even then, right after learning that Max had taken his own life, I still managed to say to the officer, "No one calls me Mrs. Goldman. It's not something I think I'll ever do, the Mrs. thing."

I didn't mean it as a political statement. I'm just one of those people no one will ever feel moved to call Mrs., madam, or grandma. It's like blood type. I just don't have those titles in me.

That night, I also didn't have it in me to keep talking to Azucena, or to start an argument with my mother about the dangers of manipulation. My mother was armed. And by this I don't mean armed with the glossy brochures where everything was pictured in every hue of Santorini blue.

DARKNESS VISIBLE

The reasons we weren't leaving right away soon began to reveal themselves like cards in a poker game. Not only had she pre-calculated the time it would take to wear me down. She had already bought the tickets for something called the "Majestic Mediterranean Voyage." But to her way of thinking there was much to be done before embarking on this majestic adventure. Or perhaps I should clarify and say there was much to be done to *me*. After all, you can't just snag your recently widowed daughter and take her on a cruise just the way she is—what with the fried hair, the tired goat eyes, and the scaly skin. Fellow cruisers expecting the vacation of a lifetime might take offense at the sight of someone who belongs in a fish stew. Ultimately this would turn out to be the spirit of the entire cruise as well. Nothing bad, ugly, or sad ever happened on a cruise. It was strictly forbidden to die, to have a terminal illness, to be about to be divorced from your spouse. All those depressing things happened only to people who were dumb enough to ignore the glossy brochures and to stay on dry land. But someone did die while we were at sea. And in the most creative way, too. But that was still in the future on the day my mother announced that we were going to the spa.

"Which spa?" I was eager to know.

I'm not a spa connoisseur by any stretch. And there won't be a shortage of spas in Scottsdale anytime soon. The only reason I asked was that I could not fathom how my recently arrived mother knew where to go. There was, quite literally, an entire ocean between her and such knowledge. I shouldn't have worried, though. When it comes to luxury, my mother and Azucena are naturals. They would know, simply by smelling the air around them, where the nearest spa was located, even if they had been dumped by a helicopter in the middle of Kosovo.

In the end, we headed to a place where two enormous, building-size lions guarded the entrance and where the only accepted brands of cars ware Bentley, Jaguar, or Mercedes. My poor little Miata looked like a limping scarab on the double-wide circular driveway.

What passed for the "spa lunch" was a small revelation. It involved a bonsai forest of miniature unrecognizable greens on tiny plates that reminded me of a tea set I used to have as a child. I might have had the mimosa that was included with it but was afraid that my stomach needed something more substantial to accept the alcohol. After our doll lunch, we were escorted by an attendant into a dark and meandering place where we were to put on robes and get ready for our treatments. The darkness was meant to be relaxing. But as I followed the uniformed attendant through the cavernous surroundings I half-expected to bump into other people walking in the dark, or to run into furniture. When I finally sat before the woman who was to turn my calloused feet into the envy of the Mediterranean I wondered how she was going to find her tools in the dark. I prayed to the spa lions outside that the woman wouldn't throw a chunk of one of my toes into the water.

"Is the water too hot?" she asked in a practiced lilt and handed me a magazine.

Has anyone ever heard of a lightbulb around here? I wanted to ask. But already I was exhausted from the comings and goings of a relaxing day at the spa. Instead, I closed my eyes and conjured images of Max and I dancing in a Gypsy cave to the beat of Zambra music on our wedding day. I remembered jumping onto the stage with the *gitanas*. I remembered grabbing Max's hand and belting out over the music, "*Diosito*, make this moment last forever." The ruffled red skirt I wore on my wedding day was still hanging in the closet. Maybe I should have worn white. Maybe it was the red skirt that jinxed it.

While the woman massaged my feet I could almost hear the finger cymbals echoing inside the cave. Now I was grateful it was dark. Shedding tears during a hundred-dollar pedicure could be easily mistaken for being spoiled. So I willed my eyes dry, which isn't as mysterious a thing as it might seem, because back then I still had a double. I was both, the one shedding the tears and her companion, who observed everything from a distance with detached curiosity as her twin struggled to stave off the incoming waves of intolerable panic.

My mother opted for a massage, presumably to get some distance from her clinically depressed daughter.

COLOR BLIND

The next day over coffee my mother announced that we were going shopping.

I went up to the kitchen drawer where I kept the car keys and pushed them ever so gently in the direction of her empty coffee cup. That's when she said, in that tempting tone oftentimes used by serial killers, "Oh, but you're coming with me."

Shopping is my mother's nirvana. At one point in my life, when I still lived in Venezuela, it had been my nirvana, too. But after moving to the United States, where towers and towers of jeans at Costco are usually eclipsed by mountains of blue tortilla chips and ten-gallon bottles of salsa, the sheer excess of it all had turned shopping into a revolting experience for me. Going shopping now felt like when you've eaten way too much and the only image your mind can bring forth is the lining of a cow's stomach.

Revolting or not, we ended up at the famed Arizona Biltmore. That was where my mother's little plan began to reveal itself, one shop window at a time. Very little had changed during the year I'd been holed up pining for a life that had gone the way of smoke in a tipi. The nail salons were still there. Acrylic nails were still fashionable, but now there was something sturdier, yet more natural, called lacquered nails. Orange was now the color in season. Every single window was featuring something or other in orange. If my eyes rested a second too long on any given window my mother was quick to say, "Should we get that for the cruise?"

"I told you I'm not going on a cruise."

Quite deftly she changed the subject.

"Is red still your favorite color?"

"Nothing is my favorite anymore!!!" I yelled, causing passersby to stare.

My mother can bear a great deal. But if there's something she cannot, absolutely, beyond all doubt, tolerate, it is unwanted attention, especially the embarrassing kind. Who knew this would be the last drop to cause the glass to overflow?

Once onlookers went back to minding their own business my mother approached, breathed out slowly to make sure I understood I was being tolerated, and, when she was certain I had her full attention, lowered her chin while simultaneously raising both eyebrows, a complex expression of disapproval that left zilch for doubt.

"That was unnecessarily dramatic," she said, and walked away.

It crossed my mind to run after her, if only to ask her when being dramatic was an absolute necessity. Now that we had reached an impasse, no doubt some kind of a truce had to be worked out. So from that point forward I vowed to say yes to everything she proposed. Oddly enough, not having to argue made the shopping expedition go by a little faster.

By late afternoon we arrived at the house carrying bags full of outfits that my mother had deemed essential for cruising connoisseurs: sandals, bathing suits, hats, bracelets; all in sunny colors. Never mind that she herself had never taken to sea. Or that she had spent an entire lifetime dressed in various shades of brown. Her yacht-white outfits were reserved for shopping and other special occasions.

That night I lay in bed thinking of ways to turn my feelings into elegant words that would not offend. "No fucking way I'm going on a cruise" needed a little massaging.

I was almost falling asleep when the phone rang. Rarely did anyone call anymore, so I was startled by the ringing. And also by Emily's voice. She sounded agitated.

"What's the matter, Emily?"

"Mom and I got into a big fight."

What's new? I wanted to say. Instead, I went for the less accusatory "Long distance?" And refrained from adding: "Your mother spoiled for a fight while you're away in another continent?" But I bit my tongue. By then I knew that no matter how abysmal the insult, the person who doesn't want you is the one you always want. That's how Helen roped in Emily again and again. She was awful to her, so Emily craved making up with her mother. It was deviant behavior as there ever was. But I never forgot, not even during these briefly confessional outbursts of Emily's, that I was the guest mother.

"It's so good to hear your voice, Emily. How's Ecuador?"

"That's kinda why I'm calling."

She didn't have to say another word. Whenever Emily used the word *kinda*, what she really meant was: "If I told you the truth, you'd go ballistic."

I was pretty sure she was coming home. That's just what I needed; a confused eighteen-year-old texting around the house to help me cope. On the other hand, I now had a tangible excuse to offer my mother for not joining her on her seafaring adventure.

Whenever I spoke with Emily, I felt a raking sort of guilt that felt like a crack in the windshield. Should I have tried to counsel her, rather than playing it safe by changing the subject? In no time her wasted future was swimming around my head, splashed with thoughts of not being a good stepmother.

Since the day I met Emily when she was nine years old she had dreamt of being a dancer. Her dad's unexpected departure had been as much of a detour as if she had broken a leg. I was there when those bright blue eyes became bloodshot and stayed that way from dawn to dusk. I could understand a year in Ecuador; I could understand running way, even if I had chosen to attach myself to a chair instead. But it was time to stop running away, though I was hardly qualified to lecture anyone on moving on. The only thing I knew for sure that night was that I didn't want to go on a cruise.

"Max," I whispered in the dark. "That was Emily. I don't think I handled that very well."

to BURN, OR NOt to BURN: tHAt WAS tHE QUEStION

In the end, Max and I chose to elope because, after taking stock of our different orthodoxies, prior relationships, and temperamental offspring, we were certain that a blended wedding would have to involve more alcohol than we could safely enjoy. Somehow, step-flower girls failed to evoke the idyll promoted by bridal magazines everywhere. You also ran the risk of a bridal shower that might feature a mailed-in virus sent by a borderline ex as a gag gift.

When Max and I decided to get married, we were also unsuspecting about how quickly the blended family would start to bleed outside the circle of our nearest and weirdest. We couldn't have known, for instance, about Emily's Chinese girlfriend whose parents forbade her to sleep over at our house because the blond girl with the Latina stepmom was too painful a reminder of a rotten Kung Pao Poodle they had once eaten near Beijing.

If those were the challenges in life, imagine the reminders in death, that the mingling of all these subspecies had been an error of Darwinian proportions from the start? Among other things, I remembered being plagued by doubt. But what I doubted most was the wisdom of getting everyone together at a standard funeral service; that is, the only funeral service I knew—a protracted affair involving opinions from every last known relative, burning candles, sad music issuing from an organ, a man in robes drinking wine, and the nauseating smell of incense. Having been raised Catholic, I was already a little overstimulated by visions of hell and a guy dressed in red Capezio tights holding a pitchfork by the door. There was no way around it. A room in Dante's inferno already had been reserved for me for marrying outside my faith. But these were really moot worries; a traditional burial after a suicide simply could not happen anywhere in the vicinity of a Catholic church. The priest would just as soon mix Red Bull into his communion wine before forgiving such a travesty. God's mercy can only extend so far. And if you're stubborn enough to insist on treating your life as if it were your own, then you were on your own *per secula seculorum*, which in Latin means: You're fucked.

So what to do with Max?

If coping with death is difficult under normal circumstances, when you're straddling two worlds, plus trying to grapple with the unexpected, mapping the edge of things can make you feel as though you have a serious bout of split personality disorder. As I prepared to knock on my neighbor Marilee's door, I wasn't just weighted down by the suddenness of everything, I was also dragging along a lifetime of expectations, which included something my parents had once called "our values."

In an unprecedentedly long family meeting of long ago which ran for a couple of hours, my parents, after grounding me for lying to them, proceeded to go on and on about "our family values." The gist of the one-sided conversation was something close to this: "There are values," my father said—while my mother looked on enraptured—"which we have, which many people have, which everyone should have . . . and which . . . we should all respect. Your mother and I . . . that is, all of us in this household . . . we believe . . . that all decisions in your life, Valentina, should come as the result . . . should arise from a foundation—that is, in any case, our hope after having this conversation—of certain core values, which we, your mother and I ... uphold ..."

I had no idea what my father was talking about. But my mother's eyes were fixed on him as if he were Reverend Papi. She even gave him a rare smile of approval.

"So can I go out this weekend?" I asked.

"No," said my mother.

"Why not?"

"Because, Valentina. This is a test of our values. And, as your father just explained, we don't approve of lying."

We don't approve of lying. The phrase kept ringing inside my head as I prepared to ring Marilee's doorbell. She had already agreed to come with me to the funeral home. Still, I had a sinking feeling in my stomach, and the urgent desire to run. It's the burden of what you know; the visions of your hair burning in glowing red that are hard to get out of your head. My parents didn't approve of lying. In taking his own life, had Max been lying? Were I to give him a traditional burial, would that mean lying by association? Should my parents' values become my own by some sort of familial osmosis? The first time you're confronted with actually having to put a belief into practice is a form of birth. Disregarding the beliefs honored by the people who raised you is like tiptoeing around the home of your childhood and stealing from your parents. I might not have understood a word my father said on the day that I was grounded for lying.

But I remembered the entire conversation; that is, not word for word, but as an event. Why, of all the times in my life when I had faced struggle, should that conversation choose to return at the precise moment when I was about to ring Marilee's doorbell?

It's impossible to understand all the causes behind everything, including why Max did what he did. We don't approve of lying. We don't approve of suicide. We especially don't approve of lying to your wife by going to your ex-wife's kitchen and doing it there. Were there to be no exceptions when it came to upholding a belief? I wanted to disappear, and not just from Marilee's front door. I felt like running to a place far, far away; a tiny country without a name where no one could find me. When is it okay to disregard the pulling forces of the values you uphold; to set them aside on behalf of an event that demands to be obeyed in equal measure? In leaving the way he did, Max was forcing me to veer from the truth of things as I knew it. Was I supposed to do to Max what my parents had done to me that day and say, "I don't approve of suicide," and have the people who collected our garbage haul his body to wherever garbage was hauled? My neighbor's front door wasn't the ideal place to realize that the rules of my childhood home could not be the rules of my life going forward. I didn't know what hurt more: betraying my upbringing, or the realization that Max had been lying all that time.

I wished I didn't have to be there. I wished Max hadn't left. I wished the happy part of my life had lasted a little longer. I wished I didn't have to ring Marilee's doorbell. Why involve yet another person in this? I could go by myself. Except, I didn't trust my car to take me all the way to the funeral home, where cremation was one of the options. That's not how we did death where I was from. I needed Marilee for more than just the driving. I needed her to help me stay steady on my feet. It's like pulling stitches, I told myself. One last yank and you'll be done. When Marilee came to the door I felt I might throw up the lining of my stomach.

"Let me grab my purse," she said, in that chirping tone of hers. Chirping was good. I needed chirping.

The reason I asked Marilee and not Ann—who was married to Max's business partner, David, and who, unlike Marilee, was practically inaudible—was that Marilee is a little daft. And daft can go a long way when the going gets sticky. For one, daft people don't want to "go deep." Daft people don't ask you if you have "closure." Daft people have the same kind of compassion as an innocent child. When I had called to ask her if she'd come along, I knew that during the prickly car ride through cactus and shrubs Marilee wasn't going to further poke me with questions, such as "What are you going to do now? Do you have any plans?" As if, as if I had any other choice but to clean up the ever-sprawling spill that Max had left behind.

As it turned out, I worried for nothing.

Save for the missing orange apron, the heartache representative at the funeral home was not all that different from the color consultants who help you pick out wall paint at Home Depot. During the initial "discovery interview," which included loads of euphemisms such as "untimely departure," which did nothing but make me think of Max as a train, my mind became wrapped around a loop of silly thoughts, the most insistent one being: Otto, were you the only boy in your school who *didn't* want to be a fireman when you grew up? I wish I knew why all these trivial thoughts came to me at such a terrible time, except maybe there comes a point after the tick tick ticks of terror, after the bomb has already blown up, when you realize you're solo dancing in a burning house and the tick tick tick has lost its clout. It's also possible that my brain was just doing its job, wisely distracting me from the heartache ahead, lest I short-circuit.

"All our caskets are lined," Otto said. "And the pillow is included."

"A pillow? How about . . ."

I was about to ask Otto about other options when Marilee interrupted me. "Those caskets are tremendously marked-up, hon. I'd say by at least two hundred percent," she said, with alarm.

Is it right to make a profit from death? And what recourse do the living have for poor customer service at a funeral home? Evidently, Marilee had touched on a sore point with the mark-up issue, because, as befits a trained death consultant, Otto changed the subject while casually brushing imaginary lint from the sleeve on his jacket.

"Have you thought about burial garments?" he asked.

"Excuse the ignorance," I said. "But why can't he wear his own clothes? He won't be using them anymore."

By then Otto was standing on my last nerve. It was at the tip of my tongue to tell him that the need for the dead to wear branded apparel and bring trinkets along had died with the Egyptian pharaohs. How did they plan to try these clothes on, anyway? I was going through enough as it was, never mind having to worry about fashion statements in the afterlife.

In the end, it boiled down to being broke. So I chose the ashes.

tHAt SUCKs

By the time my mother appeared at my doorstep I had already moved the ashes from the fridge to our bedroom. Maybe the temperature change in balmy Arizona didn't agree with the box, because the box eventually broke. Actually, there were two boxes. The outside box made of something lacquered or other, and the inside box, which was made of wood. Cheap wood at that, because when I went to take the smaller box out of the lacquered one, it fell apart and Max's ashes spilled all over the carpet.

"I'll be right back," my mother said.

At first I thought she couldn't bear looking at her daughter crying over spilled ashes. But then I saw her standing by the door with the vacuum cleaner. That's when I lost it a little.

"Don't you dare vacuum him!!!"

My mother gave me that calm look that therapists reserve for their worst cases, the ones that belong in the asylum. And then she said, "Valentina, please don't turn this into an Electrolux commercial."

"Can. You. Just. Please. Wait. Can you please wait two seconds, Mamá?"

Before there was Dyson, there was Electrolux. And before there was Amazon.com, the people living close to the real Amazon used to buy their vacuum cleaners from door-to-door salesmen. My mother remembered a time when the Electrolux salesman clad in brown polyester from head to toe would ring the doorbell at my grandmother's house and shamelessly interrupt their wordless family dinners. My grandmother, a true old-fashioned lady, would invite the salesman and his vacuum cleaner for a *cafecito*, after which there followed a demonstration of the sucking prowess of the latest Electrolux model.

Sometimes, I can't help being from South America. I can't help having been conceived in a continent where vacuum cleaner salesmen suck and where superstition runs rampant. I can't help being superstitious, any more than I can help having been raised in a weird hemisphere. It was inevitable that I would see the spilled ashes on the carpet as a sign.

Was Max trying to tell me to dust and clean up? Or was he telegraphing that I needed to stop wearing his robe and put it in the wash? Even if that had been the case, I was afraid that if I washed his robe, I'd wash him away forever. Or maybe it was Max trying to tell me that a woman dragging her feet in his expensive Italian shoes wasn't what he had in mind when he bought them in Rome.

Meanwhile, while I pondered hidden meanings, I could tell that my mother was horrified at my outburst. She was calmly horrified, which is to stay stone-faced, which is so much more effective than being hysterically horrified. I could also see a kind of relief start to descend on her face after the spill. The ashes called attention to themselves and also to the deteriorating situation at hand. The spilled ashes demanded, from that point forward, that something be done. They forced me to move; to get back into my own clothes and to stop dragging my feet around a dust-infested house in shoes that were too big for my feet. My mother was as happy about the spilled ashes as she was about writing prescriptions to keep people like me under control. But lest I brand her as an ice queen, the swift sucking of the ashes didn't mean she didn't care for Max. She actually adored Max. But my mother had a genius for making the unpleasant disappear from view. The proverb "Out of sight, out of mind" had a nearly holy meaning for her.

REASONS to WORRY

I didn't just fear going on a cruise. I feared being stranded at sea with someone with my mother's history.

When Azucena and I were enjoying an otherwise peaceful adolescence, my mother (just like other parents who enjoy tormenting their innocent children during this delicate passage) decided to renovate her office. Temporarily, she moved her practice to a room in our house. But this wasn't just any room. This was the room where Azucena and I used to listen to American music and lip-synch to Chicago's "If You Leave Me Now," as if our lives were over. We wouldn't have cared one way or the other who my mother's patients were. But because they stole our music room and snatched our American idols, Azucena and I began to refer to her patients as my mother's schizophrenics. Two of them, in particular, remain vivid in my mind: the stutterer and the snake charmer.

We needed to meet people like her patients and listen to the messages they left on our shared answering machine to know that we were really normal. In a few short weeks what was considered normal at our house had gone the way of our Chicago music. Our beloved cozy couch in the former music room was now where due to anxiety, stress, and stars being aligned the wrong way, my mother's steady supply of perverts *royale* proceeded to lie back.

As for their messages, Azucena and I would be innocently putting our finger on the "play" button to see if a girlfriend or boyfriend had called, only to find urgent messages that included words like *necrophilia* and remarks such as "I can't help myself. Please call me back." That's when I began to learn details about the life of a woman named *señora* Ruiz, who should have not been called *señora*, given she could not stop herself from copulating with her pet snake. Apparently, hard as she tried, there was nothing my mother could tell the good *señora* Ruiz to kick the slimy habit.

There was no avoiding these messages. The idea of a second phone line is still revolutionary in a country where getting a single phone line can take upwards of five years. This meant strange people with strange philias phoned Doctora Serrano and in desperation left voice messages as proof of how vital their urges were.

Given the sinister Caracas traffic, many times my mother had to conduct business over the phone. So while her office downtown was being remodeled, we overheard conversations such as "*Señora* Ruiz, how about you bring in the snake next time? After I meet him, we can discuss why you keep assigning human qualities to a reptile. Then we can begin to address your phallophobia. Does that sound like a good plan?"

Azucena has always had the gift of tuning people out. But I've never been so lucky. I really, really wanted for the painters and the decorators to be finished with my mother's office. We never actually met the snake charmer. But we did meet Luis.

The reason Luis had the pleasure of our company was that he made the mistake of making his appointment for a Saturday morning when Azucena and I were not in school. Azucena was on her way to play tennis when the doorbell rang. For a while, people used to think we were twins. But that's unfathomable. Twins read each other's minds, have the same hobbies, and play the same sports. If Azucena ever read my mind, it would be to say that I was about to lie. And if I ever were to hold a tennis racket, it would be to smack somebody, not to waste a beautiful Saturday morning chasing a ball in a courtyard.

Impatient to get to her tennis match, Azucena beat me to the door. The three of us were speechless as we took in each other's presence. There stood Luis, the stutterer, eighteen or nineteen at most, wearing his sad plaid shirt and frightened stare.

"May we help you?" said Azucena.

"Bu bu bu bue bu buen bue u bu bu bu bu bue bu buen bue u buenos..."

"Oh, I can't stand this!" I blurted out, further proof that we were not twins. For her part, Azucena was already in training to run her future staff meetings. Because when she said, "Would you mind getting to the point?" I thought Luis was going to tumble down the stone steps in front of our house.

That was, in part, why I feared going on a cruise with my mother. I was worried. I didn't want to appear anywhere nearly as incompetent as her worst case. Let's face it, wearing your dead spouse's collection of watches would never compare with a boy who couldn't spit out a simple *Buenos días*.

CONTAIN YOURSELF

"Okay. I'll go on your cruise. But only on one condition."

"I'm listening," said my mother.

"If we can bring Max."

"You mean his ashes."

"What's *left* of his ashes."

"How impractical."

One thing one has to admire about psychotherapists is their restraint. Rather than saying, "That's insane," my mother opted for the less confrontational "How impractical."

That's how we ended up at the Container Store. We were shopping for a discreet container in which to take Max to the Majestic Mediterranean.

My mother approved of the aqua dress and sandals I was wearing that day. She said I looked refreshed, though I can't say I was thinking refreshed thoughts when we crossed the threshold from chaos to the promised land of order that was the Container Store. I was thinking something along the lines of: Had I ruptured this woman's birth canal during childbirth for revenge to involve taking me on a cruise?

My impure thoughts were interrupted by a not-quite-male voice that sang: "Welcome to the Container Store. My name is Virgil. What are we shopping for today?"

It was difficult to put my unusual request into words.

"Well, Virgil, I'm not sure where..."

"I know what you mean, doll. The place is a little overwhelming at first. Were we looking for closet, kitchen, or office? By the way, I love, love the aqua. And I *love* off-the-shoulder."

"Urban Outfitters," I said. "It also comes in purple."

Only because I'm her daughter did I notice the ever imperceptible stiffening of my mother's neck.

As for Virgil, all he might have noticed by way of disapproval were my mother's lips, which curled into an aboriginal snarl after I told him where he could find a dress like mine. I briefly considered getting her a subscription to *People* magazine so she could see for herself that compared to other people—say the cast of *Topless Prophet*—Virgil was not all that bad. He was even a little classy. It's true that he wore a little rouge and lip gloss. And that he was wearing falsies. But they looked good on him. The dark lashes gave his beautiful eyes depth. And besides, his skin was flawless, so he could get away with it. But so as not to continue offending my mother's homophobic sensibilities, I blurted out, "Closet."

When Virgil offered to walk us there, I knew my mother would need a horse tranquilizer if I said yes. So I told him we could find our way there by ourselves—you had to be blind to miss the signs.

Now I was really looking forward to our cruise. Despite my mother's excellent English I was pretty sure she had missed the line on the back of one of the brochures that read: LGBT-friendly. I only hoped that if there were any transvestites in the Majestic Mediterranean voyage, that they would feel inclined to flaunt it—say spike heels to the pool and teased wigs with matching bathing suits. Or perhaps the nightly entertainment might be themed? Deep inside, I knew my mother had good intentions; that what she wanted above all else was to help me move on. What I resented was the manipulation.

Our arrival in the closet section of the store made me think of Azucena. If there existed a heaven my sister had dreamt about it was inside this model closet where shoes, sweaters, and identical wooden hangers were lined up like soldiers. But I didn't see many boxes there that fit our purpose. So I asked my mother—in jest, of course—if we should go ask Virgil for help. My mother shook her head.

"Did you really need to encourage his behavior by telling him where you bought your dress, Valentina?"

"Mamá, it's not a behavior. It's a lifestyle. Think of gay as the new black."

But my mother wasn't the type to laugh at dumb jokes just to lift my spirits.

CURL UP AND DYE

One thing for another: bringing the ashes in exchange for color and cut. Ahhh... the lost art of compromise.

    The Saturday before our grand departure for Athens we arrived at the hair salon with a purpose. We were there to trim my shredded wheat hair down to shoulder length and color it into something reminiscent of a lavish burgundy. When I protested about the color, my mother, who during our adolescence had pronounced dyed hair to be "only for whores," said I looked like a widow.

    "But I *am* a widow."

    "You're too young to be a widow. We need to change that."

Let it be spoken. Let it be done. With her powers of persuasion and a bottle of dye she was going to change my status. But could she change my heart? While the young woman with the spiky blue hair shampooed mine I played with Max's watch, the black and copper one with the square face that he had bought during a business trip to Switzerland. Back then, he had gone on and on about Swiss movement versus whatever other movement there is. Now I wished I had held that moment for how precious it was. I wished I had been paying attention when he told me all about the watch museum in Zurich. Now all I had from that wasted conversation was a watch that was too big for my wrist. But what was really bothering me was the impending haircut. Little by little, in just a few days, my mother had managed to chip away chunks of the person who had shared a life with Max. Pretty soon, all of Valentina Goldman would be gone. And who would I be then?

I had no clue. All I knew by the time the woman wrapped the thick towel around my head was that I had to run. Run fast and find someplace to hide. It was the only way to keep the shards of my crumbling life from flying all over the place.

"I'll be right back," I said, and proceeded to run toward a nearby door that appeared to be a restroom. It turned out to be a supply closet. I wouldn't recommend sobbing while inhaling dye fumes.

PART II

ADRIFt

IMAGINE EVERY REASON

After twelve hours sandwiched between a man who took snoring to new heights and my mother, we finally arrived at the bustling port of Piraeus, near Athens, in Greece. There was chaos, there was the crushing noise of traffic, there were colossal containers being lifted up in the air by equally enormous cranes. There were no Greek gods that I could see.

    The ship was so large that at first I missed it. Standing in front of it, you could only see a portion of one of the blue letters, which made it seem you were standing in front of a large blue wall. One had to stand back in order to grasp the actual size of the giant mass of steel.

We went through ship security, which really meant trying to discern a series of grunts by a couple of Greek thugs in uniform who were smoking something potent. When this dubious process was finally complete, we were greeted at the base of the ship's gangway by a band playing "Here Comes the Sun." Was it the jet lag, or were the Beatles in Athens? For reasons only explicable by immigration officials and world economists, all the band members were from the Philippines. For the most part the jolly band members tried to remain faithful to the song's original spirit. We would hear from them night after night at the various lounges around the ship. I took to drinking martinis, if only to be able to stomach "Imagine" sliced and diced into "Imagen all thee peeeple."

At the top of the gangway we were welcomed aboard by the cruise director, who introduced himself as M.C. His real name was Michael Coin, but we would soon discover that almost all crew members had stage names because by night they doubled as entertainers. When his voice wasn't piping through the intercom system upon arrival at a given port of call, M.C. was a dancer with the ship's dance troupe.

No sooner had we been given our cabin number and a map of the boat than M.C. invited us to the sail-away party at Five. On. The. Dot. I was feeling very special until M.C. repeated the exact same thing with phony ease to the next set of arriving guests. Michael Coin wore his pants a little on the tighter side and his smile had Crest Strips written all over it.

The minute we entered our cabin I knew that truth in advertising hadn't reached the high seas yet. As promised in the brochures, our room had a view. It was a view of a painting that looked like a porthole. On closer inspection I realized that the painting, along with everything else in the cartoon room, was bolted. Was there thievery in the high seas? Or was the promised Mediterranean rough, rather than majestic?

The queen-size bed was actually two twin beds pushed together and wrapped up as one. The thought of sharing this tiny space for the next twelve days with my mother gave me a touch of claustrophobia—a feeling that intensified when I opened the closet. Who needed to unpack? I could pretend I was still in college. I could pretend it was spring break and that I was ready to live out of my suitcase just for the fun of it. I had no idea how much this seafaring adventure had cost. But whatever it was, the number was too high.

The only thing I wanted to put away in a safe place was the Advil bottle that contained what little remained of Max after my mother's vacuuming frenzy. In the end, we had not been able to find a suitable vessel at the Container Store to carry the rest of Max to the majestic Mediterranean. It wasn't until I was packing while nursing a headache that the idea had come to me.

The handful of ashes I had rescued from the vacuuming fiasco was now inside the bottle of Advil. Max was probably as jet-lagged as I was, so I took the bottle out of my purse and set it on one of the bathroom shelves. My mother's raised eyebrows were perfectly framed in the tiny bathroom mirror. I was about to tell her she could have the closet and the five hangers inside it when the first announcement startled us, making us turn around. For a beat there, it sounded as though the voice from the intercom was someone inside our cabin.

"Safety training at sixteen hundred hours," said the heavily accented voice. Was this a former Russian spy? The voice then proceeded to tell us that safety training was mandatory, that it needed to be done in a certain order, that he would call our numbers in such and such a way, and to please bring our life vests with us.

I've often found airplane safety procedures unnecessarily dramatic. Do the flight attendants really need to throw those alarming-yellow jackets over their heads and pretend to blow on that red inflator? Is it really necessary to drop the oxygen mask to give a proper visual that we might asphyxiate? Compared with safety training at sea, airplane procedures were a breeze. The sea of fat orange life vests with giant black numbers affixed to their backs with Velcro, made the possibility of going *Titanic* suddenly real. I looked around to see if everyone was experiencing the same anxiety as I was.

That's when I first spotted Ethan. Of course I didn't know he was Ethan then. I just spotted a tall man wearing a white shirt rolled up to the elbows, and a pair of deeply set philosopher's eyes wandering in our direction. It was hard to tell whether he was looking at me, or at my mother, though. Sometimes people stare at me because of my height. But the sexy philosopher and I were at eye level. So I doubted height had any effect on him. Who could know why, amid a sea of orange vests, I was the one chosen for inspection? For all I know, he could have been fantasizing about the "LGBT-friendly" line in the brochures.

Whatever the case, I looked away and tried to concentrate on the Russian spy in the white uniform. On observing the people around me I had the impression that many of them had done this before and that my mother and I were among the few rookies. Pockets of murmurs floated around the safety officer's instructions; hardly anyone was paying attention. Ultimately, the main difference between ship and airplane safety was that here we actually had to perform the motions. We had to wear the life vests. We had to adjust the tricky belt around our waists while the Russian spy with the bald head admonished us to "Please save the chatter, or the captain might not give us the green light to sail away." The threat was now standing between these seasoned travelers and their first blue drink. Suddenly, everyone went mute.

The only sounds that reached us over the terse commands were the swishes of seagulls and sloshing water.

STEEL ON THE SURFACE OF WATER

It had always been an unspoken desire of mine to hear the sound of a ship horn. It sounded like God blowing his nose very, very loudly while fighting a bad cold.

During the much-anticipated sail-away, all passengers were outside on the various decks, leaning against railings and looking out to sea as the captain began to turn the ship around. Gliding alongside us in a tiny green boat, the pilot guided us out of port until his boat became a ripple and the bustling port of Piraeus flickered in the distance.

In a little while there was nothing before us, save an infinite expanse of water.

I knew nothing about ships or life at sea. Though I must admit that when I finally apprehended the proportions of the ship at the port, I found it exotic. It wasn't the traveling. It wasn't the adventure at that point. It was both the simplicity and complexity of a massive mass of steel parked on the surface of water. Before long we were the only object in the fluid expanse of green marble that is the Mediterranean. And then, as if Merlin the magician had touched us with his wand, water and sky became one and a swirling fantasy of peaches and blues was suddenly lit. The splendor of that sunset felt like a personal discovery. Perhaps there was something to this. I leaned against the railing and as the misty breeze caressed my cheeks, I wished with all my heart that Max were standing by my side. My mother's brown eyes rested softly on me. Here was a woman who advocated we rise above ourselves. Despite vicissitudes; despite laziness, or lack of will, one must get up and press on, even if it becomes necessary to tread ever more carefully as life threatens to crush us to a pulp. Despite the unwelcome detours that had got us to where we were, I was grateful for her.

WAS IT A FAKE?

Standing beside us on the deck, drinks on hand, were Larry and Alastair.

Anyone wishing to know what cruising was really about should have texted these two in advance of booking their vacation. As it turned out, not all was aboveboard in the high seas. But that was yet to surface in the days to come.

After making small talk about the colors of the sunset and the shocking beauty of it all, Larry, the taller of the two, told me he was the CEO of a head-hunting firm in San Francisco. There was something of the loose-limb quality to him. And he seemed a bit self-conscious in his starched white polo shirt and black shorts. I had the impression he had bought these new clothes after losing his luggage and was still trying to get comfortable in them. I tried to listen to what he was saying, but there was so much wrangling for my attention. For one, there was my mother. I wanted to include her in the conversation, but she seemed content to stare into the ocean. Then there was the water, which made a constant whooshing sound as the ship appeared to slice through it. And then, there was Larry's gorgeous watch.

Compared to Max I was hardly a watch connoisseur. But I knew from having gone on numerous watch-shopping expeditions over the years that Larry was wearing the real deal. I now owned Max's considerable watch collection, and took turns wearing them based on my shifting moods. For the first leg of my high-seas adventure, I wore a Modify watch that Max had given me for my birthday before leaving for good. The two happy feet that dangled before the bluest ocean were, on the face of it, nothing if not ironic—life as a beach. Really, Max?

By the time I met Larry and Alastair the sun was taking its leave behind the horizon, which is to say that I couldn't make out the face of Larry's watch. Still, I knew that if he were to turn it around, the back wouldn't say, "Made in China." He caught me staring, so he did something that might be explained as generosity, but which, given what life had dealt me so far, I could hardly be expected to take as a random act of kindness.

"You like it?" he said. "Here."

At this, he took off his watch and offered it to me, I thought, so I could have a better look at it. Alastair, who had been quiet up until that moment, turned to me and said with a pinch of cynicism in his voice, "Larry thinks he's the Godfather," and proceeded to take another sip of his drink.

I took the watch and carefully examined it, turning it this way and that, the way Max used to do when admiring superior craftsmanship. The watch had what's called a skeleton face, meaning that its parts were exposed—that such was the craftsmanship, its makers were proud to display it to the bare bones. On seeing that it was a Tag Heuer I returned it immediately for fear that it would fall into the ocean and that I'd have to hand Larry five thousand majestic dollars I did not have.

"It's yours," he said.

"Is it a fake?" I said, though I was fairly sure it wasn't.

At this, Larry coughed up a disbelieving laugh and said in a thick southern accent I had not noticed before, "Why would ah give you a faike?"

"Why would you give me your watch at all? Did you win it at the casino, then?"

Despite his imposing boardroom height, Larry now looked as deflated as a boy being sent to his room for no good reason. As for Alastair, who was younger than

Larry by at least a decade, what emerged at that moment was a cool, seasoned appraiser whose tenderness had been spent long ago. He was dressed in linen from head to toe and his hair was grayish around the sideburns. The sharp haircut made sense once I discovered what he did for a living.

In just a few short days I would learn that Alastair was with Larry to take a break from women and to give men a try. Observing drama, a spectacle of any kind, made Alastair come to life. He seemed to relish the exchange; the moment when someone's eyes either glinted with greed, or widened in disbelief. By then, even my mother was curious about the watch. Rather discreetly, she had turned her slim body around against the railing and was now supported by her elbows. She was no longer the tourist on holiday staring into the ocean; the observant manner of a therapist in session was very much on display as she proceeded to dissect the baffling transaction.

My eyes darted from one man to the other, trying to assess whatever can be assessed on the surface of things. Was I unwittingly auditioning for the naïve part in *Dirty, Rotten Scoundrels at Sea*? Was there a bet hanging in the balance?

Alastair took another sip of his drink, and then he said, "If you really hate it, you can always sell it on eBay." Nothing seemed to escape Alastair's cynical appraisals. I wondered if there were any hidden cameras on deck and if the trials of the past year of my life were playing exclusively for everyone's amusement. For his part, Larry was still holding the watch, shaking his head ever so slightly. He might have said, "I was just joking," and withdrawn the offer. But no. It seemed he was willing to stand by it and would only feel vindicated when a private long-running argument about the nature of humanity was finally settled in his favor.

What to do? Of course I wanted to keep the watch. But only so that I could show it to Max. My beach-feet Modify watch, with its changeable wristband meant far more to me than the brutally-expensive Tag Heuer. On second thought, though, I wouldn't have to wear it. What about Alastair's idea? Selling a Tag Heuer might solve some real problems. Were material possessions nothing to Larry? Did he enjoy catching strangers off guard? Or was his aim to charm people with unexpected gifts? Not knowing what to do about the watch, I opted for introducing myself.

"I'm Valentina, by the way. And this is my mother, Serena. It's nice to meet you both."

"Same here," said Larry, putting on his watch.

"We'll see you around," said Alastair, walking away.

EXIt SIGNS

I didn't have the courage to do it myself. I couldn't explain it. I didn't understand it. It's not that I don't understand that for some people the fierce decision to revolve in endless nothingness seems the only relief, the only absolute assurance that no more pain will follow. Life is, among other things, an act of intention. I can understand someone losing the will to keep hauling the weight around. What I still couldn't understand was why Max would stop at his ex-wife's house on his way to work and choose to offload it there, especially when he loathed the woman. Did he go there to warn her and things got out of hand? That made no sense; it wasn't like Max to give anyone ultimatums. On the other hand, it was like Helen to rail and rant, to revile someone until the person was fulminated and tripped forward into temporary madness. I had watched Emily pull off chunks of her hair after hanging up the phone with Helen and then collapse on the nearest surface until she passed out from crying. I had overheard the otherwise unflappable Zack screaming with hurt and frustration, "You just don't put your son on an egg timer, Mom! That's not how you get someone to talk."

Was it possible that Helen had pushed Max to the point that the only way to shut her up was to put a gun to her head? There were people like that; experts at standing on people's last nerve. To my knowledge, though, Max never owned a gun. And why he would turn it on himself? The most unsettling thing of all was to discover this in an autopsy report.

"Why, Max . . .? Why were you so unhappy? And how come I didn't know?"

I sat on the bathroom floor holding the bottle of Advil. By then I knew no answers would be forthcoming. By then I was exhausted by the dread of tears, tired of being undone, of conjuring up an imagined scene, of posing theoretical questions of a theoretical past fraught with the unknowable, a past I wanted to but could not commit to forgetting, because I knew, I knew that even contemplating letting go would mean that I would have to move forward and plunge headfirst into a future that included unwanted watches and which at the moment seemed more perverse than the few details of the past I could not know.

"Anyway, Max . . . I was just offered a skeleton Tag Heuer by a stranger. I really wanted you to see it. You would have—"

"Who are you talking to?" my mother asked, startling me.

"I thought you were at the library," I said, hurrying to my feet.

"And now I'm back."

I set the bottle back on the shelf and came out to greet my mother.

"Any books worth reading?"

"Mostly mysteries," she said. "In several languages, I might add."

"Was there a librarian there and everything?"

"No. Books are stamped with a note to please return them before disembarking. What should we do tonight?"

During the next two weeks this apparently innocuous question would turn into a recurring nightmare. For starters, the world *should* has always given me the creeps. For those who wanted to do it all, though, to wring the most out of this majestic adventure, the question became a preoccupation. People walked around the ship asking one another: What should we do today? One overheard strangers in the elevator asking other strangers as if in chorus: What are you guys doing tonight? And God forbid someone volunteered they were going to that Art Appreciation class, or some such. At this, a passerby might stare at them with the eyes of a hurt bunny and ask: Where was that posted? How come I didn't know about it?

The possibilities, though finite, seemed endless, if only because of the fact that when you're at home you don't have access to someone like M.C., whose voice was now booming through the intercom, letting all eight hundred of us know that right this minute we could all be enjoying the cocktail of the day at Neptune's lounge, the Sky Lounge, or the Pool Bar. The choice was ours.

At the conclusion of M.C.'s brief announcement my mother picked up the calendar of events placed daily on your bed by the room's steward, in our case, an emaciated young woman from Estonia whose name was Ina and who looked on both resentfully and forlornly as passengers headed to dinner while she was left behind hauling heaps of wet towels and emptying trash. Ina and others like her performed these soul-crushing chores day after day, night after night, month after month, for months on end without a break.

Larry, whose business was finding people—albeit on a higher pay scale than Ina's—would offer a few days later that he didn't know how his room attendant managed not to lose her mind from being quasi-imprisoned at sea.

"Oh, but she already has, dearest," said Alastair. "Didn't I just tell you she put my dry cleaning in someone else's closet?"

In the meantime, our evening was yet to be decided. According to the calendar of events my mother held in her lovely manicured hand, tonight's dinner attire was to be "resort casual." And in case anyone had missed the fashion seminar, the pamphlet specified: "Slacks and blouse for ladies. Trousers and short-sleeve shirts for gentlemen."

I wanted to have nothing to do with any of this. I especially didn't want to share defrosted food with strangers. But with that sixth sense my mother had picked up from her schizophrenics, she read my mind and repeated the question as if I hadn't heard her the first time.

"What should we do tonight?"

"I'm no—" I started.

"You're not staying in your room," she said.

It was the exact same tone—even if the exact opposite message—she used to use when I was in high school, when the words had been "You're staying in your room." I knew that if it were up to her, my mother would probably order room service and stay in bed watching a smart film. So when she handed me the pamphlet and offered to go along with whatever I proposed, I willed myself to find something we would both enjoy and to stop being a troll; even if I my resolution had an expiration date of one night.

In addition to shore excursions, every single day the activities were broken down on the back of the events calendar as follows:

- Early morning (for sleepwalkers, insomniacs, and people who like running in circles)
- Daily service (Mass for Catholics, yoga for Buddhists, hiding for Muslims)
- Lunch (self-explanatory; even if some food was unrecognizable)
- Tea (for people of British origin and those who couldn't wait to eat again)
- Cocktail hour (always 5 p.m. somewhere)
- Dinner (Same as lunch)
- Entertainment (where you might run into a sword swallower)
- Late Night (for heavy drinkers, swingers, and drug dealers)

In a special corner of the calendar titled FRIENDS, the following curious headers were printed: Friends of Bill and Friends of Dorothy. Who was Bill? And who was Dorothy? Soon enough, I would find out about all these "friends." For now, I had to vote on our evening plans: eat, drink, or gamble?

"I've never seen a juggler," I said, studying the young juggler's photo. "He seems sweet."

"The juggler isn't till nine," said my mother. "What should we do *before* then?"

Jumping overboard crossed my mind.

HoW Is It HaNGING?

Dear Helen:

 How is it hanging? I know. I know it's been almost ten years and we haven't said word "boo" to each other. But with Max choosing your kitchen, instead of mine, for one last cup of coffee, I've been almost possessed by the idea of texting you about it; a simple text, mind you, a one-word text, asking: Why? But seeing as I'm from Venezuela—I know you thought it was Argentina. I accidentally overheard you at Emily's recital that time when you said, "There's that bitch from Argentina." To put your mind at ease, that's a fairly common mistake, confusing Argentina and Venezuela. Why the two words almost rhyme! But here's a way to help you remember so that you won't make the same mistake again. VENEZUELA = MISS UNIVERSE. ARGENTINA = MALBEC. Now we can move on. Now we can let bygones be bygones.

Where was I? Ah, yes, this text. I know it's a bit longish for a text message, but seeing as I'm from Venezuela, and all of us in the Southern Hemisphere—not just people from Argentina—owe a debt of gratitude to Gabriel García Marquez, I'm going to elaborate a little. But not to worry, this text won't even come anywhere near *Love in the Time of Cholera*.

Okay. Okay. Okay. I'll ask you one last time: Can we please talk? Quite frankly, I'm jealous. Or is the word *envious*? The only part I'm not envious about is the cleaning part. I hate cleaning. Max said you weren't too fond of it, either. Do we detect a pattern here, Max marrying women who hated to clean? Speaking of marriage, are you seeing anyone? In case you are, I've heard match.com is really good at pairing up people. Psycho seeks psycho, and so on. The only downside is that you have to upload a photo. And that can be such a drag, choosing a photo of yourself to send to someone who doesn't know the first thing about you. I, myself, am a terrible photographer. But anyway, back to Max. The last I heard, the two of you weren't exactly on speaking terms. So I'm curious: Did he go to your place to ask you about our flower urns? For a long time after you came to our house and kicked the flower urns, the question has been floating around my head: Did you hurt your foot? That has to have hurt. Ouch! Now that he's gone, I should probably tell you that hurting you was the furthest thing from Max's mind. In fact, he had wanted to get the lighter urns in case you came to kick them one day. Really, it was my fault. I'm the one who talked him into the iron ones. I always go for the solids. That's because never in a million years would I have dreamt that someone from a civilized country would come to our house and forget to ring the doorbell. That sort of thing only happens to people who live in trailers, which is understandable. I've never visited a trailer, but *you* tell me, Do they have doorbells? So that's why I'm asking about your foot after all these years. Just between us wives, though, isn't it about time we moved on with our lives? The way I see it, I can either live in the past as a bitter Venezuelan whose husband was stolen from her, or I can live in the present as such.

Now, where was I? Ah, yes, how is it hanging? When I first moved here from Argentina—sorry, it's been so long ago, even I forget which country—I overheard two construction workers at a sandwich shop. One said to the other, "How's it hanging, buddy?" For a while, I, too, used this charming expression to greet everyone I met. I liked the ring of it so much that I tried it on store clerks, flight attendants, even baristas at Starbucks. But now I know better. It's taken me all these years to realize it didn't mean, Let's hang out.

Hanging out is something else altogether, isn't it? In order to hang out with someone you have to actually like them. I, myself, rarely hang out with anyone these days. And I'm going to take it that after all my letters, messages, and phone calls you don't want to hang out, either. I understand. Really, I do. You're probably still in crutches after hurting your foot on those flower urns. I'll bet even the few steps to the phone must feel like the Boston Marathon. But still, how about a quick call back sometime? I can only imagine what it must be like to clean a kitchen on crutches, though. So don't strain yourself, dear Helen. And keep icing it. Ice is good for certain injuries. Make it a block of ice while you're at it. Just watch your head. You don't want to make it any worse.

Now where's the damn "send" button? I should get a smarter phone.

CURL UP AND DYE: THE SEQUEL

Going to the hair salon on the boat was a big mistake.

The floating beauty parlor was located on deck 6, next door to the workout room. Strangely enough, this was where I learned what everyone was truly being fed on the majestic Mediterranean. I gained this valuable intelligence from Adna, the hair stylist from Bosnia. After scanning me for weapons from head to toe, Adna offered me a strained smile. Right away I could tell that smiling wasn't in her nature and that she had been trained to do it as part of making people feel "welcome." Unfortunately, Adna's teeth looked as if they had been tossed on a gaming table and returned to her mouth.

As a general rule, it is the customers who ply hairstylists with their constant, inane outpours until the stylists opt for burning themselves alive with the curling iron. As for Adna, she decided to take revenge on me for having had to endure hundreds of chatty customers in the past. In the fifty-four minutes—I counted every single one of them on the wall clock above the mirror—that it took for her to dry my hair in the damp Mediterranean air, Adna told me that she loved her job. She also told me that she had been doing hair since she was twelve.

"*Twelve*," she said, for emphasis. "Can you believe it?"

Seeing as she looked eighteen, I was tempted to tell her that six years wasn't a lifetime. In any case, in the course of our appointment Adna went on to tell me that she loved, absolutely loved, seeing the world. She had been to Antarctica. She had been to Hong Kong. She had been to Singapore. She had seen South America. The only thing she didn't like—she repeated at least three times—was the food on the boat. She then proceeded to catalog her personal famine for me. But before going on about majestic malnutrition, Adna turned off the hot blow dryer and dumped it on my lap without warning. Good thing I was wearing pants. Otherwise, my legs would have burned. For a minute there, I thought she had had enough. Most hairstylists won't see me twice. I have simply too much hair, and more often than not, stylists pass, the second time around. But this was the first time someone gave up while half my hair was still wet. As it turned out, I had Adna all wrong.

Just when I was about to jump off the chair and run around the deck to let my hair dry naturally, Adna stopped me by pushing me back in place with a firm hand.

"Do you see my arms?" she said, staring into the mirror.

"I do."

"Do you see something wrong?"

"I do not."

To be perfectly honest, I really didn't see anything wrong with Adna's arms. But being a woman, and knowing what it means to ask: "Do these pants make my butt look too big?" even if Adna had had a bulging scar from the Bosnian war running along the side of her arm, I wasn't going to say anything. I'd just as soon go to confession with Friends of Jesus down by the casino for lying to her.

"So you see nothing wrong?"

I shook my head. Half my hair was dry. The other half was still dripping wet. I looked like a deranged llama in the mirror. In front of that very mirror, Adna proceeded to shake her head several times. She then yanked the blow dryer from my lap and resumed drying my hair.

"Unbelievable!" she said.

"What's unbelievable?"

"That you see nothing wrong with my arms."

Meanwhile, Adna went on to tell me how her boyfriend, who worked in the ship's kitchen, had to steal leftover passenger food for her whenever the chef wasn't looking. In a few days I would meet this chef and would be able to vouch that his eyes weren't always on the stove, and that his tastes went beyond the ordinary salty and sweet. For her part, Adna volunteered that since starting this job she had lost *at least* ten pounds.

"My arms are too skinny," she said. "I'm surprised you can't see it."

I wanted to tell her the reason I couldn't see it was that I lived in the United States, where all the people in magazine covers were anorexics. But while anorexia might be enviable in certain circles, say, runways in New York or Milan, it certainly wasn't the most appetizing thing to say to malnourished Adna. The better to help me visualize her predicament, Adna offered details. That's how I learned that in the mess room below deck 4 there was a misnomer of a buffet where bowls of lumpy rice were served to the ship's crew twenty-four hours a day.

"I've been eating rice every single day for six months," she said. "If I see rice one more time, I promise I will vomit!"

"For six months?" I said, trying to get the vomit visual out of my head.

"Why do you think the kitchen jobs go so fast?" she said.

"I never visit kitchens," I said. "I can't cook."

By then, I was about to get on my knees. I was about to beg Adna to finish, or to let me go. If necessary, I would dry my hair with a Chinese fan.

"You know . . ." she said, "if you're not going to eat the chocolates they leave on your pillow every night, bring them to me. I prefer the chocolates to a tip."

"I don't like chocolate," I said. "I'll bring them to you as soon as we're done here."

Having been raised by my mother with Pavlov by her side, I recognized an incentive when I saw one. Perhaps the promise of chocolate would get Adna to hurry up.

"Who doesn't like chocolate?" she said, cornering me with a pair of black eyes smeared with blue eye shadow all around.

By the end of the blow dry I realized that in much the same way that Venezuelans watch too many telenovelas and this tends to lace our speech with a little cheap drama, so do people from war zones have their manner peppered with a pinch of violence. Dumping a hot hair dryer on someone's lap was nothing compared to being held at gunpoint with an AK-47.

Later that evening, I brought Adna all the chocolates my mother and I had stacked in a little corner by the vanity mirror in our cabin. Both of us loved chocolates. But we had vowed not to gain any weight during this majestic adventure.

¿Qué?

After my Bosnian blow dry, my mother and I went for cocktails at Neptune's lounge. That's where we met Pepito. We had taken our seats by a set of small windows, and though by then it was too dark to see the ocean, we had a tantalizing view of what looked like a moving sky sprinkled with shooting stars. It was, of course, the ship that was moving. But the illusion that comets and galaxies were flying after us was far more compelling.

My mother and I were talking about Azucena and the kids, about what they might be doing at this hour in Caracas, when out of the blue, or more exactly, out of her side, a little round head sneaked through, extended a hand, and asked my mother to dance.

Pepito was the shortest person I had ever met who wasn't officially a midget. He had round, eager eyes and an inviting manner. But even the smart tuxedo he was wearing did very little to elevate his Lilliputian frame. There were to be many unexpected encounters in the high seas, but meeting Pepito turned out to be one of the most memorable, if anything because it isn't every day that anyone catches my mother off guard. And also because of who Pepito turned out to be. Oh, Pepito, Pepito, *pobrecito* Pepito. There were so many things I wished to tell this well-intentioned stranger who stood by my mother's side, patiently awaiting her reply. First, I wanted to tell him that being an old-school South American woman, my mother would rather drink Liquid Plumber than dance with a stranger while in a state of marriage. I also might have told Pepito that in much the same way that some height-challenged individuals fall prey to the Napoleonic complex, people as tall as my mother oftentimes grow up looking down on the people of Lilliput. For all her aloof ways, though, my mother has never had it in her to offend anyone. Building self-esteem, helping people break up with their snakes, that's what she's all about. So rather than saying, "No, thank you," she smiled in Pepito's direction and shook her head, just a teeny, teeny bit, almost imperceptibly. Only because I'm her daughter, and because I know how huge her small gestures can be, did I know that she wanted to slap him for both, the sneaky intrusion and the advance. But for someone who didn't know her, she seemed coy, flustered even, by this man's attention, which is to say, Pepito was encouraged.

"Maybe the next one?" he said, his round eyes beaming with hope.

At this, my mother gave him her best amnesiac stare.

After Pepito left, we made a toast and watched the people dancing on the floor. That's when I saw him. Sitting by himself at a table not too far from ours was the man I had seen during safety training; his right arm was casually draped behind the chair. Meanwhile, with his left thumb and forefinger, he was carefully rotating his wineglass on the table at an angle. It was a precarious movement. But he looked like someone who had done it a hundred times; the glass neither fell nor slipped out of his hands. There was an earned confidence to this that I found quietly erotic. I smiled briefly and he nodded, raising his glass in my direction.

After dancing a few sets with several women, Pepito returned and asked my mother to dance once again. Unwilling to decline him a second time, my mother said, "*Con permiso*," a decorous way to say "fuck off" in Spanish, and got up. Where she was going I had no idea. Despite the linguistic barrier, though, Pepito wasn't easily dissuaded.

"With your permission," he said to me, "I will join you."

At any other time in my life I would have said, "Pepito, our dance cards are full until the next lunar eclipse." But after spending a year in solitary confinement, the wind was definitely out of my sails. I had no energy to offer even the slightest opposition. So I said, "Be my guest."

Unfortunately, this was all Pepito needed to sit down and start describing his life in vivid detail. I wasn't the least bit interested, so I only heard two things: that he was from Manila and that he was an escort.

"You mean as in a gigolo?"

Pepito laughed good-naturedly at this backhanded compliment. Surely he had a mirror in his room, even if it was tiny like ours. So I supposed that being taken for a gigolo was a huge upgrade.

"You are so charming," he said. "No, I'm not a gigolo. But I do have friends who are. It pays extremely well. But no, not me. I work for the company," he said proudly. "During this voyage it is my job to ask lonely ladies to dance."

"Ha!" I blurted. Uh-oh. I had been locked up too long; I'd forgotten not to blurt public. "Hmm, I didn't mean to laugh," I said, trying to recover from the little insult he had bestowed on my mother. "How best to put it?" I said. "My mother isn't lonely. She's happily married. To my father."

"I was talking about you," he said, the smile never leaving his face.

"Oh? . . . What about me?"

"Would you like to dance?"

Oh, I get it. Let's add pepper to the wound. Do I look like refried beans to you? A leftover? Valentina, Valentina, relax. Maybe he's being nice. Maybe what he lacks in height, he was given in compassion. No. Maybe he has a dance fetish—a man who must dance at any cost. He'll even dance with someone twice his height and risk looking like a lollipop on the dance floor. But what if he's a sniff dog? What if it is his job to smell loneliness and dancing is just a polite excuse to approach the most hopeless cases? Well, Pepito, I'm not a fucking charity case!

"Well?" said Pepito, extending a hand.

"Well what?"

As it so often happened, I exhausted myself from overthought. I wore myself out to the point of having to say, "Sure," just so I could take a break from the voices in my head. Maybe that's why my mother so loved her schizophrenics. She had raised one.

In the end, Pepito turned out to be a very good dancer, even if the height discrepancy made it a little cumbersome on the dance floor. At one point, during a turn, I noticed the sexy philosopher looking at us. At first he was frowning. Then he raised his eyebrows. I shrugged. He nodded. We had a whole conversation in sign language. Could he tell I'd been driven to this by sheer thought exhaustion?

At any rate, by the time my mother returned from whatever stowaway closet she'd gone to hide, I was ready to tell her what I had learned about Pepito—that he was an escort and that it was his job to spot widows and sad ladies and ask them to dance.

"It's a true vacation from real life, Mamá," I wanted to tell her. "You've been spotted and stamped as a gullible *tonta* who can't tell an escort from a real man." I also wanted to tell her that from then on, to avoid unwelcome company, I would try turning my face to stone the way she often did. Going forward I also planned on giving up the chatter. Thus far in my life, talking over the discomfort had been my approach: talk, talk, talk, and the faster the better. Don't ever give people a chance to muse on you, or allow them to get even a half inch closer. That way, you don't have to wake up one morning and find out that the person who'd been resting on the pillow next to yours all night decided to leave for good without the courtesy of leaving so much as a grocery list behind. Clearly, my approach needed a little fine-tuning.

"So how did you get rid of him?" my mother wanted to know.

"You'll never believe what he does for a living, Mamá."

"Whatever it is, please don't tell me."

"He's a gigolo."

"Well, good luck with that," she said, sipping her martini.

FRIENDS OF BILL. FRIENDS OF DOROTHY. AND FRIENDS OF JESUS.

So who was Bill? And who was Dorothy? I knew who Jesus was. I just didn't know that he was traveling with us. At first I thought Pepito had it made. But the best job on the boat, bar none, went to the priest. He was also a rabbi. He was also an imam. Despite his three jobs, though, the man was rarely busy. He was always by the pool, sharing his blue drinks with a boatload of

LGBT unbelievers. As far as I could see, my mother and a handful of Jesus devotees were the only ones who went to Mass. Friends of Jesus met on Sunday in the same theater where movies were shown on sea days. I must confess that it was a little delicious, watching the few devout taking communion in front of the very screen where Angelina Jolie had been giving blow jobs earlier in the week.

As for the Muslims, everyone knows how reclusive those folks can be, especially the women, always hiding behind those black veils. So the priest cum imam was able to leave his Koran CliffsNotes by his nightstand.

Just when you thought this boat carried as many crew members as passengers, you began to spot many familiar crew member faces. *Wait, wasn't that you holding Mass at eleven? What are you doing wearing that silly beach hat now?* It was as though Jimmy Buffett had traded his guitar for a cassock and changed his tune from "Let's get drunk and screw" to "Jesus loves you." If this boat was going anywhere, though, it was to the bottom of the ocean, where every single last one of the LGBT sinners on board was going to sink and be eaten by sharks as part of God's punishment for their miscreant ways.

Friends of Dorothy turned out to be a daily meeting for lesbians on board. I had no clue what they talked about. How to get your dildo past the pricks at TSA, perhaps? Friends of Bill was the same thing, but for alcoholics. Why, dear Jesus, why, oh why, would you go on a trip where drinks are free 24/7 if you're an alcoholic? Weren't there less tormenting vacation options out there? Was this some sort of self-flagellation fix?

What was a little more intriguing than an inebriated pool bum playing "Jesus has come," "Jesus will come," and "Friend of Muhammad" at the same time, was the implication that people named Bill could not kick the bottle, and that women baptized Dorothy were penis-averse from the start. So when my mother asked me what the nice lady she had met at Mass had meant when she urged her to pray for Dorothy's friends, I did what the Lord expected of me and told her the truth.

"Lesbians, Mamá. That's what the nice lady meant."

"*Por Dios*, Valentina. I didn't know they allowed lesbians in here."

"Don't sweat it, Mamá. That just goes to show you that God, who forgives all, gave all the lesbians on this boat a free pass."

"*Hija, Dios te va a castigar.*"

"God? Punish me? What do you think Jesus was doing when he was all alone in the desert for forty days?"

For once, my mother and I agreed to agree: it was all a little hard to believe.

GUMBY tHE JUGGLER

Considering he had already performed the same juggling act two hours earlier I'm going to call the juggler brave.

The only thing that happened at seven that didn't happen at the later show is that at seven the seas were not yet rough. Rough seas aren't ideal for many performers. Besides the discomfort of the turbulence underfoot for both, the audience and the performers, there are the details of the act to consider—a pianist's sheet music flying away, for instance; a singer's microphone skidding around the stage. But for a juggler, whose job it is *not* to miss the multiplicity of objects dancing up in the air, standing on shaky ground is, effectively, the end of his act. As it turned out, troubled waters were only part of the young juggler's problems.

His name was Ring-O, a stage name he had chosen—he explained at the beginning of his act—to commemorate the day when he managed to juggle a set of balls while keeping a hula hoop balanced on the tip of his nose. Ring-O had the playful disposition of a boy who had shared his toys with siblings, cousins, and friends growing up. He was bouncy and lighthearted, and despite the queasy circumstances, there wasn't a tense bone in his body.

So pliable was he, his limbs appeared to be made of rubber. Ring-O was lanky and awkward in a way that made you smile right away. Had it not been for his sincere desire to delight his audience, I'm sure people would have walked out of his act as soon as they realized the problem. It didn't take a stagehand to figure it out. All it took was setting foot inside the Odyssey Theater and looking at the ceilings to realize this wasn't going to work.

The Odyssey Theater was located somewhere toward the middle of the ship. Either by accident, or by design, it was situated halfway from anywhere to everywhere. I wouldn't swear to the accuracy of this perception, though, seeing as I've never been one to get oriented anywhere. After a couple of days I still couldn't tell aft from bow. In any case, this sizable auditorium was where all-important events happened.

This is where celebrity chefs set baked Alaska on fire with great fanfare to great applause. This is where movies were shown on sea days. This was the place where crew members from various lounges materialized at showtimes wearing different outfits than they had two hours before, transformed.

As for Ring-O, he was a straight shooter from the start. The moment he boarded the ship—he explained to his now-rapt audience—he did what all entertainers do. He went to his room to drop off his luggage and immediately set out to check out the venue where he would be performing his act. *¡Ay Dios Mío!* doesn't begin to cover it when Ring-O came to the sinking realization that his head almost touched the very low ceilings on the stage. If there's something that flying balls require it is room to fly.

"So what I'm going to do tonight, ladies and gentlemen," he went on, "is a small variation on my regular act."

By then, the fury of the angry seas was such that we were grateful for any distraction. No matter how stultified Ring-O's act might be, his balls would be going up in the air, instead of down into the ocean, which was my fear about the ship. Ships are unlike airplanes in many ways. One way in which they are different is that a ship's captain never grabs the microphone to say, "Ladies and gentlemen, I'm looking for calmer air. Please buckle your seat belts." I suspect this is because it's futile, because turning around a massive block of floating steel is like trying to tickle a whale with a toothpick. That's just a theory, though. I really don't know why ship captains lack empathy. All I can say is that the turbulence was all the more frightening because of the captain's silence; not a peep issued from the bridge as furious waves slapped the ship around and slapped it some more.

We're going to drown, Max. We're going Titanic. Death by shark. This is what I feared all along. Can you hear me, Max?

And then there was fire!

My panicked ululations turned to puff when Ring-O brought out a hula hoop in flames and dropped to his knees. That was the variation in his act. That's how he ultimately managed to overcome the low ceilings, by performing the entire act on his knees. Unable, or wisely unwilling to touch the fire with his bare hands, he began to chase the hula hoop on his knees while juggling a set of sharp knives through it; never keeping his eyes off them, never dropping a single one. And to prove the knives were, indeed, sharp, at the end of his act a stagehand brought out a balloon that went "pop!" on contact with the tip.

The cliché that you had to see it to believe it was buoyant in the seven seas. By the end of his act, none of us doubted that Ring-O had planned a different kind of splash. Still, we gave him a standing ovation for his courage and charm. When he took a bow, his body seemed to fold in half. It boggled the mind, how flexible he was. Gumby came to mind.

WHEN LARRY GOT HAIRY

As we exited the auditorium we ran into Larry and Alastair by the door.

"Talk about juggling his balls," Alastair said.

"Did you ladies enjoy yourselves?" asked the ever-appropriate Larry.

The black silk shirt with a priest's collar made him seem a little starched. Alastair's sartorial preferences leaned toward wrinkled linen with a touch of the casually disheveled.

The matter of the gift watch seemed to have been entirely forgotten, as if the offer had been made in another lifetime to another woman whose name wasn't Valentina. My mother would later remark that everything that happened on the cruise was of vital importance *at* the time; making a new friend, wearing a native outfit from a remote corner of the world, sampling an exotic fruit, were all forgotten by the allure of the next port of call. Meanwhile, we continued to be shoved forward a few baby steps at a time by the mass exodus of cramped humanity behind us, until the four of us were left standing in the brightly lit atrium. Alastair, as was to become a trademark, was holding a drink in his hand.

"Take a sip, dearest," he said, handing it to me.

"What's this?" I asked.

"Bailey's," he said. "Sinful."

My lips had barely touched the rim when Mother's mouth creased into a grimace of undistilled disgust. For his part, Larry observed the exodus of people with an evenness that put to mind a water sprinkler; left, center, right, and then again. Doubtless he was accustomed to Alastair's impromptu gregariousness and frequent stops and had a wellspring of patience, perhaps honed at mind-numbing board meetings. It's also possible he was bored to tears and just happened to have one of those benevolent-seeming faces.

While I held his drink, Alastair produced a phone and proceeded to show me a series of pictures, a brief sequence of a balding head becoming slowly populated with hair.

"A video game about hair?" I ventured a guess.

"Silly, dearest," he said, snagging his drink. "Guess who?"

"What do you mean?"

"Guess whose head this is?"

"He loves embarrassing me," Larry said, peering into the small screen.

"This is your head?" I asked, taking in Larry's mass of soft hair. "Are you wearing a . . .? Never mind," I said, eyeing my mother, who was staring into a wall, her odd way of praying for the banality to stop.

"Hair Now. Hair Tomorrow," I said. "I've seen the infomercials!"

"No. No. No. No," said Alastair.

It turned out Alastair did hair transplants for a living. That's how he and Larry had met.

He was very proud of his work and longed to be admired for it. When I called him a hairdresser, he was hurt beyond words. Doing transplants was painstaking, meticulous work, he explained. "More art than science."

Whatever the challenges, I had a hard time admiring anyone in the business of growing hair. If I didn't shave my legs twice a day I risked having to braid them. I was a slave to the razor. I had also tried electrolysis, various hair-removing creams, and had occasionally enjoyed my hair being yanked out of its pores with hot wax.

"We're throwing a little party in our suite in a few days," said Alastair. "Look for the invite."

"That sounds . . . wonderful," I said, catching my mother's eye. "Good night, guys."

"Does that mean we're not seeing you at the Sky Lounge later tonight?" said Alastair.

If looks could talk, my mother's look would have been the question: "With a pair of homosexuals?"

"I think we're in for the night," I said, heading toward the elevator.

REVENGE OF tHE SEA PUPPEtS

As soon as we opened the door to our little sea prison we were greeted by the stressful list of competing choices that awaited us nightly at the foot of our bed. So much to do. So few hours in the day! That night, the array of brochures included a guided tour of some ruin or other at the next port, a brief description of the next port of call, along with an assortment of shore activities. As if that were not enough, there was also the regular calendar of events to consider. Oh no! What if sea bingo was going on at the same time as that watch-shopping expedition ashore?

There were also more chocolates placed on our pillows, a small card reminding us of the time change, and a sea puppet fashioned with towels by Ina. The choice puppet that night was supposed to resemble a baby octopus. His beady eyes were achieved with two black shirt buttons affixed to its plump little head with glue, possibly toothpaste—ours.

As we were to learn from those familiar with cruising trivia, this puppet-making was required training for all room attendants. Apparently, for this particular cruise line, these amorphous towel creatures made the guest satisfaction ratings go up. But because the majestic seas are flooding with irony, this nightly load of extra towels in the shape of sea puppets usually sat next to a small card that read: "Please help us save our oceans. Recycle your towels whenever possible."

I ended up saving our small puppet collection by setting them against the wall, if anything, to give the overworked Ina an extra ten minutes on her evening shift and also to save a cupful of detergent here and there. But on the day that Ina graduated from hand towels to bath towels and we found a giant stuffed walrus sitting on our bed wearing *my* sunglasses, I took every single one of the towel creatures and dumped them on the hallway to put an end to the nightmare. That night, after carefully moving the octopus to the wall to join his towel brethren, I realized I wasn't sleepy in the least.

"Where's the library?" I asked my mother.

"Right next to the casino."

"How balanced of them. I'm going to get some magazines. I'll be right back."

As it turned out, *Glamour* and *Marie Claire* were not in the cards for me that night.

RUSSIAN ROULETTE AND ROMANTIC MONOMANIA

Aboveboard, at least, the situation looked like this: The Dutch ran the ship. The Americans owned the entertainment. And the Russians ran the casino, which was located, as my mother had said, next to the sandbox she had generously called the library. It was at the casino that I spotted Ethan and Marco. Or rather, I was on my way to the so-called library when Ethan (whom I had secretly dubbed "the sexy philosopher") got up from the roulette table, came up to me, and asked if I cared to join them. I looked behind me and said, "Who, me?"

"Yes, you. I'm Ethan, by the way."

"I'm Valentina. And I don't know any games."

For some reason this made him smile. It wasn't quite a smile, but rather an amused screwing of the lips from side to side that made his perfect lips look even sexier. I thought he might be about to say something bogus, like "Please, don't let me keep you."

"That's not a problem," he said. "We can teach you."

"We?"

"Yes. Come meet Marco. He's an inveterate gambler."

"I don't know what that means," I said. "But it sounds like a bad habit."

At this point I should probably mention that I'm not the sort of widow who, on her way to get a copy of *Marie Claire*, gets talked into heading for the casino to test my luck with a foreign couple with a penchant for roulette. I'll admit that I'm somewhat impetuous, but always of my own accord. Only once did I let myself get derailed off my tracks by another person. I married him. I left my job. He opted for early retirement and left me in a spooky state of limbo. So who can say why I followed the strategically faded, body-hugging jeans in front of me and proceeded to sit at the roulette table with his partner. Maybe it was the way Ethan was sizing me up, through those shrewd philosopher's eyes, as if daring me to say no. Because if there's something I can't resist, it's a dare. It turned out I missed the intention behind that look entirely. That's probably because the whole time we'd been gliding through majestic waters I was drowning in my little dilemma, in too deep to come up for air and get an accurate read on what was really going on around me.

I grabbed a seat on the stool next to Marco, though he hardly noticed. He wasn't going to ingratiate himself to anyone, or to stop what he was doing to introduce himself. His gaze was fixed on the rolling roulette wheel while the woman standing directly across from him efficiently moved little towers of chips around the green felt table. Her name was Olga, and she was the croupier. Just like the rest of us Olga had a pair of eyes. But the way she observed anything that moved—whether person, object, or microscopic atmospheric lint—made it seem she had eyes everywhere, like a sea scallop. Olga would have noticed a mosquito pausing for breath after a long flight on the glass casino door. She had white-blond hair that was cut razor-sharp on one side and draped to the chin on the other. This odd fashion statement was the only uneven thing about her.

Ethan's partner was Marco Mangini. There was something affected about him, starting with the name. Or rather, *all* of Marco was affected. Whether still or in motion, the man was perpetually aware of making a statement. The boxy glasses with the thick black rims made him look like a movie director from Hollywood, except that both Ethan and Marco were from Australia.

My mother was probably sound asleep by then, but I could almost hear her sleep-talking, "Valentina, why don't you ever meet men who are actually available?" Or, to translate for the euphemistically challenged: "Why can't my daughter bring home a man who uses his penis for the purpose for which it was invented so I can be a proper grandmother?"

Ever since I can remember my mother has suffered from a bad case of romantic monomania; the theory that all of the world's inhabitants can be happy only in a state of coupledom, more specifically as heterosexual couples who would then go on to "be fruitful, and multiply upon the earth," through the majesty of biblical arithmetic mandated by God in the Old Testament my mother knew by chapter and verse. This was Serena Serrano's view of a psychologically healthy universe. On such a basis, she came up with complex analyses of people she encountered who were not engaged in a heterosexual relationship. This one was emotionally stunted due a scarring relationship with a mother who purposefully withheld love in her formative years. That one was dysfunctional due to a workaholic father, who in turn caused her to question men in positions of authority while longing for a sexual relationship with them at the same time.

My mother took her analyses as gospel, often disliking people such as Larry and Alastair, for instance, strictly on the basis of the narratives she had constructed to explain their mating choices to herself. Her theory of healthy coupledom was not unlike the religion to which she fervently adhered. If you believed in the original premise that there is a God, then the saints and angels fell neatly into place. Why, you could even hear them singing sometimes! To question the theory of a peasant woman named Mary giving birth without the benefit of a birth canal was inconceivable at that point.

My own theory of the Universe, albeit not as complex or holy, allowed for a broader view of things. There was much more to being a human being than existing in a perpetual state of compromise with another person. This is why in the first year of our marriage Max and I had lived in separate houses. The way I saw it, being in a relationship could share mind space with other, more interesting preoccupations, for instance: height and personality disorders, the recently rich Chinese, fifty shades of kale, the appeal of Candy Crush, or, say, people opting for early departure. After Max's unexpected curveball hit me on the side of the head, I suffered a lobotomy of sorts. Afterward, I became partial to pouring wine in large quantities and succumbed to heavy doses of *People en Español*. Why deny it? Candid photos of other women's cellulite were much more soothing than opening bills to find mounting credit card debt staring me in the face.

"Here's the quick and dirty," Ethan said, cutting my mental detour short. As for Marco, while his mate tried to teach me to gamble, he looked on wordlessly through those unnerving boxy frames of his. Was Marco the jealous type? I wondered.

"There are 37 slots on the European roulette," Ethan explained. "You may play odd, even, black, or red, in various combinations. You may also play *manque*, as you see written on the table, which means you may bet on numbers 1 to 19. Or *passe*, bets on numbers 19 to 36. There are many more nuances," he said. "But these are enough to get you started. Here are some chips."

What was it with everyone on this boat offloading their possessions?—Larry offering me his watch; an escort asking me to dance; now Ethan pushing a stack of chips in my direction. Was it so obvious I was down on my luck? I looked at my dress. The leafy pattern was sunny enough. And the dress was also brand-new. I looked at my feet. The pedicure still held. Maybe it was my nails. It hadn't always been the case, but recently I had started biting my nails. They weren't gnawed to the cuticle or anything that spelled "cannibal on board." But perhaps they betrayed a little stress? In a mini-bout of self-consciousness I brought my hands to my lap, trying to hide them.

"I can't take your money," I said.

"Don't think of it as my money," said Ethan. "Think of it this way. We have nowhere to go and the chips are buying us some fun to pass the time at sea. How's that?"

Throughout Ethan's tempting rationalization of gambling, we were being guarded by Olga, who didn't seem to own a smile. Or, for that matter, any other gesture that might distract her from the task of making sure the floating casino didn't lose track of a single euro.

"Okay," I said. "Put one chip on the number 8. But just one."

"That's my lucky number," said Ethan. "I was born in August."

Olga rolled the roulette. Marco might have rolled his eyes. The play went by in a flash. I watched with great disappointment as the little rubber marker landed on number 23.

"I lost all your money," I said. "I'm really sorry."

Marco shook his head. Doubtless, he was thinking something unflattering.

"You're just warming up," said Ethan, encouragingly. "Try again."

"You try it," I said. "I don't like losing."

"No one likes losing," Marco said, by way of enlightenment.

Max used to call people like Marco a pill. I never knew what that meant exactly. Still, I wanted to say, "Marco, you are a pill." But suddenly the expression struck me as borrowed. Since when had I started borrowing thoughts from Max? Was this why my mother had diagnosed me as "clinically"? Before meeting Max, I would have called Marco "*un narciso*," or some such. Whatever the case, the insult would have come to me in Spanish. But somewhere along the way, during the years of our marriage, a large chunk of myself must have gone missing. Now I was trapped inside my head thinking Max's wife's thoughts. Why was I was gambling in a floating casino with two Aussies and a Russian mole? I wanted out of this place. I also wanted out of my head. But the chain of thoughts kept yanking me back inside. Is that how it happened, Max? Did you want out of your head but the thoughts kept yanking you back?

"Way to go, mate," said Marco.

While I'd been lost in my yarn Ethan had amassed a few little towers of green and black chips. For the roulette uninitiated, each green chip is worth twenty-five dollars and each black chip is worth one hundred dollars.

That night Ethan was wearing what turned out to be his signature look of faded jeans and a white shirt rolled to the elbows. As he leaned into the table I noticed how strong his forearms were. He either spent a lot of time at the gym or hanging from a rock somewhere. As for Marco, he was the opposite of Ethan. He was of average height, but made himself taller through a studied combination of ignoring others, striking poses, and imposing a silence that made him seem more interesting than he was. For now Ethan was on a roll. Stacks of chips continued to get shoved and pushed around. He won and won again. Olga's hands were busy, though never as busy as her eyes. At one point Marco leaned in, chin resting on his right hand, no doubt another tried-and-tested pose.

After a while Ethan handed me a stack of chips from his winnings.

"Your turn," he said, grabbing my hand and placing a small tower on my palm. Was I imagining things, or was this an excuse to hold my hand?

I blinked a few uncomfortable blinks, shifting from my hand to Ethan's eyes. He nodded encouragingly. I shrugged my shoulders. We had another one of those silent conversations.

"Put all the chips on number 2," I said to Olga.

"Wait, wait," said Ethan. "There's only 1 in 37 chances of it hitting the number 2."

All of a sudden, I had Marco's attention. He got up from the stool and looked on as Ethan tried to talk me into at least splitting my bet. For now, Olga's hands were on hold, but her eyes remained trained as ever. I looked up and noticed tiny beads of sweat that made her pale skin look like an alien's. What a stressful job, I thought, and mentally crossed it off from my potential list of career moves. Admittedly, mine was a slightly nontraditional approach to job searching. Still, it wasn't completely useless research to observe other people at work and take quick reads on their happiness meters.

"Are you sure about that?" Ethan asked.

"I'm sure."

Number 2 was Derek Jeter's number. Derek Jeter was Max's favorite baseball player. I had a good feeling about my bet. Was I being foolish? Wasn't this how people ended up vacuuming car mats at the car wash?

"What do you say?" Ethan tried again. "Split them?"

I shook my head.

"Are you withdrawing you bet?" Olga asked, impatiently.

"Put it all on 2," I said.

Once again, Olga rolled the roulette. It was easy to get mesmerized staring at the wheel of red and black blending into one color as it rolled along. It was also very exciting. In a little while the wheel began to slow down; it went slower, then a little slower, while all of us held our collective breath. The small marker made a little thump as it tried to stop at number 5, then 4. We were so close. Finally, as the tiny marker paused for good on the number 2, all of us exhaled. Ethan's eyes were wide with disbelief. Marco got up and left, leaving his sweaty drink behind.

"The lady wins," said Olga, doing the math.

"I won!" I said, impulsively reaching for the chips that Olga pushed in front of me.

Maybe there was something to gambling after all. This green table was a much friendlier version of an ATM machine. As I went to reach for my winnings, Ethan looked at me with a full-on smile. He had square teeth that seemed cut to order and his dark, philosopher's eyes beamed with glee under the lights.

"Congratulations," he said.

"It's your money," I said, trying to rein in my excitement.

"Not that it's any of my business," he said, changing the subject, "but why were you dancing with one of the escorts the other night?"

"Why not?"

"Well . . . they're here for lonely widows and such; women no one would necessarily ask to dance. But you, on the other hand . . ."

"You don't know anything about me," I said, cutting him short.

If the sharpness cut through him, his face didn't show it. Ethan reminded me of those people pledged to a cause; people who wore buttons that read: *Lose Weight Now, Ask Me How*, or *Let's Make Cancer History*. At one point in his childhood Ethan must have been given a button that read, *Remain Charming Above All*.

I wanted to run. Standing in front of this stranger, idiotically trying to conceal my chewed-up fingernails and my status, I wanted so badly to escape being Valentina. I also wanted to stay, if anything, so I wouldn't have to spend the rest of the night alone. But I felt too exposed; as if my face were a screen and the story of my life were scrolling through it on repeat.

"I have to go," I said, walking as fast as the fat carpet allowed. By the door, I stumbled on an invisible door stopper that was camouflaged by the busy carpet pattern.

"Valentina, wait," Ethan said, going after me.

"What is it?"

"You forgot your chips."

"They're *your* chips," I said.

"You won them fair and square," he said. "I'll save them for next time."

By then I was halfway down the atrium stairs. I knew there would not be a next time. I wasn't a gambler. I didn't even look up, or say good night.

Halfway through the corridor on the next deck I took off my sandals and kept walking as fast as I could. By the time I reached our cabin I had to lean against the door to catch my breath. Where did I put my key? I must have left it inside the room in my rush to get to the library. I had no idea what time it was, but more than likely my mother was asleep.

I sat on the floor, sandals by my side.

"Can you believe how crazy that was, Max? Two is still our lucky number."

La Viuda Alegre Meets Rusty Kuntz

It was early yet in our majestic passage, so we had not gotten around to learning all the insider tricks. We didn't yet know, for instance, that arriving even five minutes later than the scheduled calendar time for dinner meant that you had to eat dinner with strangers. For some people, this was the point of going on a cruise; to meet and mingle with other adventure seekers they had never seen before. But my mother was not "some people." She was shy, discerning, and always suspicious of untested blood types; a root canal would have been preferable to making small talk with people she didn't know and the potential risks involved.

According to the calendar of events, dinner was to be served in the main dining room between 7 and 9 p.m. To us, this meant that any time in between would be fine. But showing up twenty minutes after seven as we did, we had to join the line outside the dining room, where people who longed to dine with strangers chatted animatedly about what to do *after* dinner. One thing was certain, no matter how many events were scheduled each day, people always wanted more. Our predicament was laid before us. As soon as we put in what he thought was a simple request—a table for two—the maître d standing by the podium with a little map of the dining room shook his head vehemently and said, "Impossible." Still, he cocked his head and looked around for two empty seats, perhaps to see if his bare eyes were better than the sitting chart he kept consulting over and over while taking furtive glances toward the long line that continued to grow behind us. In the end, unable to delay what he already knew could not be delayed he apologized for not being able to accommodate us and ended up sitting us at a large round table where everyone had already started on their salads.

It was after meeting Rusty and his singular dinner companions that evening that my perspective about certain events in my life began to shift a little. Rusty's table was like a big party that had already started and would go on beyond this night. There was much laughter and loud conversation, so we said our awkward hellos, excused ourselves for interrupting, and quietly sat down.

"Welcome, young ladies!" said the one man among a half-dozen cheering women.

"My name is Rusty Kuntz," he went on, and proceeded to introduce us to the women around him, most of them in their sixties, a few in their early seventies, perhaps. Rusty, himself, was pushing seventy-five, though you wouldn't have known it because he was fighting it with all his might. Trim, tanned, and fit, Rusty was in better shape than my mother or I.

Already acquainted with Friends of Bill and Friends of Dorothy, on meeting Rusty and his cheering admirers, I had to ask myself, *Whose FRIENDS are these?*

"I'm Zoe," one of the women said.

Like everyone else around the table, Zoe was full of enthusiasm. Her neatly coiffed silver hair had the faintest trace of lilac and she wore a diamond-encrusted brooch in the shape of a rose on the lapel of her sequin dress, presumably because the sequin wasn't quite dazzling enough. At one point during the evening, Zoe volunteered that she was from Connecticut.

"We have this little thing we do with new members," Zoe said.

Immediately, my radar lit up. *Members? I don't remember signing anything.* And then, her expression toned down a notch, she said, "How long has it been for you, ladies?"

Get to the point, why don't you, Zoe?

Upon hearing Zoe's question, I wished I could channel my mother. Seeing as she was in the business of listening to schizophrenics, my mother rarely felt compelled to answer anyone's questions. The only question I remember her answering that night was "I'll have it medium-well."

For my part, I took a sip of water and decided to redirect, a conversational trick I once picked up at a management seminar when I used to roam among the employed. The long and short of redirecting boiled down to answering a question with another question.

"So," I said, "did everyone here join in Athens?"

Among cruising aficionados, this question never failed to get even the most reclusive of creatures to talk. As we were to learn, many people on board had been traveling for months. Many were on a world voyage, and the Majestic Mediterranean leg was just the beginning of the Age of Aquarius for them. In the end, the village elders were a tough crowd to fool.

After hearing my question, Rusty frowned, an exaggerated gesture that made both gray eyebrows come together.

"Young lady," he said, "that's the oldest trick in the book. Did you really think we'd let you away with that? Zoe wants to know how long it's been." And then, by way of encouragement, he added, "It's been two years for me. But some of my lady friends here have been at it a little longer, haven't you?"

Oh, I get it! We're seated with Friends of Tiger Woods!

With Rusty as their ringleader, the women nodded as if on cue. Some eyes went demurely downcast. This crowd was getting stranger and stranger by the minute. I supposed that if I stopped to think about it, I, too, missed having sex. But to go public with these intimacies . . . These people were competing with my mother's patient, *señora* Ruiz and her snake. Perhaps the estimable therapist among these undersexed elders might offer some alternatives, give them some relief.

"Excuse me," I said, calling on our waiter, "do you have any rum?"

"You're scaring them, Rusty," a thin voice chimed in. "Why don't you ladies tell us what your names are. I'm Fannie, by the way."

Fannie's coy introduction was a small step in the right direction. Still, my mother remained on mute mode; her eyes placid, her hands resting on her lap. As usual, it fell to me to introduce the two of us.

"I'm Valentina," I said. "And this is my mother, Serena."

"Is that a slight accent, I detect? Where are you ladies from?"

"Venezuela," I said.

"Well, Miss Venezuela," Rusty said. "Answer the question. Are both of you widows, and how long has it been?"

Wha . . . ? I didn't see that one coming.

"That's more than one question," I said, scrambling for what to say next.

Telling the truth was off the table. I'd just as soon swallow a raw egg than tell Rusty I was a widow. I was positive he would tie me to my chair until he wrung out every last detail about how I came to that fate. And besides, my situation was slightly on the sordid side; I could barely make sense of it myself. My mother's life was a lot easier to explain. All she had to say was "Married, two kids." My story included a few detours—what with a couple of husbands, and one of them gone under such inauspicious circumstances. If these people had anything, though, it was gumption. Gertrude, the lady sitting next to me, poked me in the ribs and whispered, "Rusty gets around. But so that you know, Fannie's got her eye on him."

"Oh, don't worry," I whispered back. "You can put Fannie's mind at ease for me."

I could not wait for our food to arrive. At the very least, I figured that chewing would be a little cumbersome, if not time-consuming, for some of these folks. I wouldn't even mind if they removed their dentures and set them on the table to give their gums a little rest— anything to keep them from the bizarre interrogation they were bent on pursuing. But I was out of luck. Our table was so large that the damn food was going to arrive after the next digging of Pompeii. Now all eyes were on me. Bat eyes in a dark cave came to mind.

That single moment of quiet anticipation was probably the only time during the evening when the merry widows were not hooting or cheering. I'm sure there was some weirdly perverse lesson I was supposed to learn here. But in mid-interrogation, I had no clue what it was.

"Actually," I said, "we were seated here by mistake."

"That's my rotten luck!" Rusty said.

"More for us," one of the ladies hooted.

"Not that we mind sharing him, mind you," Zoe put in.

The whole scene reminded me of *La Viuda Alegre*, a very famous operetta by Franz Lehár that was much in favor at our house, especially during the years of our adolescence. Except that at our house, the *Merry Widow* wasn't invoked for artistic reasons. Her name was Hanna Glawari, and she was from Pontevedra, a town in the southwestern Galician coast. Half the population of Venezuela is from Spain, and many are from Galicia. So the *Merry Widow* operetta was extremely well-known, and not just in our house. It was extraordinarily successful around the world, frequently recorded, adapted, and revived. For all that, Azucena and I had never seen it onstage. But my parents had. *La Viuda Alegre* and her outfits turned out to be the bane of my existence during my teen years. Apparently, the only color the bon vivant widow ever wears for the duration of the operetta is red. It was my misfortune that red had always been my favorite color. As a teenager, I owned buckets of red lipstick. I married Max wearing a ruffled red skirt fashioned after a flamenco dancer's. To my mother, though, red had one and only one meaning: whore. My memories of adolescence would always be tainted with the question, "Do you think you're *la viuda alegre*, Valentina? Go change."

At last, after much debate about best ports visited and best ports yet to be seen, our food arrived. By then, after my mini rum bender, the widows around the table went from prying and annoying to charming and amusing. It took me a little while, but as the evening wore on, I started to gather that the hoaxes and the loopy humor were part of a brave act about outwitting the inevitable. Had Jules Verne been into comedy, he might have penned a different story: "Around the World with Rusty Kuntz."

Right before our meal, Gertrude, who seemed to be the shy soul among them, said, "Let us toast our dearly departed." And this, too, seemed to be part of some quirkily cathartic ritual.

"To Harry."

"To Woody."

"To Rocky."

"To Dick."

Hmmm. Could this be the reason Rusty felt so encouraged among these ladies?

After gaily toasting their dead spouses and wishing they were happy elsewhere, the conversation turned to something called bucket lists.

"What's in your bucket list, *señora*?" Rusty asked, catching my mother off guard.

Unexpectedly addressed, my mother dabbed her lips with her napkin and looked at me, as if I were simultaneously her translator and attorney of record.

"I'm sorry," I said, looking at Rusty, "but we don't know what that is."

It was Zoe who explained that a bucket list was a list of things you wanted to do before you died. Most of the people around the table had seen the world, and then some. So their bucket lists were already full, or done, or getting more difficult to bucketize, I guess. Still, the world is a very big place and they hadn't seen *all* of it.

"I've always wanted to go to the Amazon," Fannie said, dreamily.

Oh, she's lost it, I thought. It's always the people who live far from the Amazon who can give voice to such a stupid wish. *Let's see, which part attracts you, Fannie? Let me guess, it's the Yanomamo Indians. Or is it their endocannibalistic rituals? Should I tell the innocent Fannie that the Yanomamo eat ONLY their own? But then only after death, and then away from their village, so as not to offend? And then, only after they pulverize the ashes. But the ashes must be mixed in with plantain juice—to sweeten their relatives' aftertaste. Is that it, Fannie? No. It's probably swimming with the* pirañas *in the Orinoco Delta that attracts you to the Amazon. Maybe it's the malaria. Or is it dengue fever you want?*

"Have you, really?" I said. "Sometimes it can get a little muggy down there. Tell me, Fannie, where else have you been?"

Could someone please hurry with dessert?????

It was now Rusty's turn to tell us about his bucket list.

"I want to hide with a few of these ladies under a tarp," he said, cracking up.

"And how are you going to manage that, Uncle Time?" said Zoe.

"I got all the time in the world, Zoe. Just don't forget your bib."

How to thank the maître d for seating us among such spirited people?

The evening turned out to be very inspiring, after all. I could stand to learn a thing or two from these merry widows. For one, while on this majestic adventure I ought to get started on my own bucket list. I had always wanted to go to Egypt. It was an unexpressed wish of mine to ride on a camel in Cairo. No. Make that Cairo during the riots. That way, my camel wouldn't notice the flies the size of roaches feasting on its rotting teeth. And thanks to the gunfire, I wouldn't notice the brown snot dripping from the camel's enormous nostrils. But there were other places, too. Egypt wasn't my only option. For now, though, the time had come to leave such stirring company.

"Good night, everyone," I said. "Thank you *so much* for hosting us."

This was my mother's cue to get up; I hoped she figured it out. A brief shower of farewells rained on us:

"The *pleasure* was all ours," Rusty said.

"Come join us any time," said Zoe.

"Are you ladies going to the auction?" Fannie asked, her eyes smitten with the idea.

Just go. Go. Go. Go. Do not answer any more questions, Valentina, I told myself. But I did wonder, albeit in passing, what kind of auction Fannie was talking about. Rusted pool chairs, forgotten sunglasses? In any event, the goodbye was one of those prolonged affairs that lasted almost as long as the meal itself. I just needed a tiny, tiny opening between all the waving and well-wishing to start running.

"Try not to miss the captain's party!" Gertrude said.

"We won't," I said, urging my mother by the elbow.

We walked quietly, if a bit hurriedly, toward the nearest elevator; lest we be yanked back for further interrogation. As for my mother, I could see from the arch of her brow that she had questions of her own. As befits a therapist, she was simply waiting for more private quarters for her little inquisition. Because, no sooner had the elevator doors closed in front of us than she asked, "What was that all about?"

"*Ay*, Mamá! I don't know. Some things just get lost in translation."

"Like what, Valentina?"

"Well . . . do you remember that maid of Azucena's whose name was Cuca?"

"How can I forget?"

"Well, that was Rusty's last name."

"Por el amor de Dios, hija."

"That's where you're wrong, Mamá. God wants nothing to do with these people. These are no Friends of Jesus."

EPISODIC UNEMPLOYMENT

It was late. But after so much sensorial stimulation it was hard to get to sleep, so I went outside to one of the decks looking for fresher air. The shifting reddish moon rendered the black water crystalline, an illusion that made the ocean look rock solid and fluid at the same time. It was easy to get lost in the strange beauty of the night and for a few rare minutes of rapture my mind went blank. If this was the kind of bliss that so many people claimed could be attained through meditation, maybe I ought to give meditation a try.

After a while, though, once I started to replay scenes from the dinner with the hyperactive widows, the realization that I could not afford a life of leisure like theirs became very real for me. What exactly was I doing here among the idle in the middle of the ocean? So much for the rapture of the deep. Instead of majestically floating nowhere, what I needed to be doing was looking for a job. But where to start after all these years?

Once, I had a job as a bilingual operator for a credit card company. During the expedited training we received, the trainer explained that we were to be inbound and outbound operators simultaneously. The training took about thirty minutes, at most. The credit card company was really shorthanded, which is another way of saying that the people doing the hiring didn't have time to check anyone's references. This fact alone should have made me a little suspicious. But who has time to worry about felons as coworkers when you're desperate for a job? The people in HR were busy, busy, busy. So busy, in fact, that they handed you a phone set while you were completing the job application. From the company's point of view it was cheaper and more efficient to lose dozens of plastic phone sets if things didn't work out than the alternative. The one command from top management seemed to be "Get bodies on the floor. We don't care whose bodies."

In the end there was a body on the floor. But it wasn't alive.

Meanwhile, phone operators didn't last long. After three or four weeks of taking abuse over the phone most of them quit. This job placed enormous demands on your nervous system. Having to conceal your wish to become a serial killer can take a lot out of a person. But as so often happens when you're an immigrant, you can't get too, too picky. You can't say, for instance, that only one break every six hours might interfere with your bladder function. You don't want to be pegged as difficult from the start. The rare breaks were hardly the issue, though. The floor manager was so stressed-out dealing with the daily waves of new hires and unexpected departures that she hardly had time to check on the ex-cons who remained on their chairs. I was sitting very close to one. But I didn't know it yet.

Inbound meant that calls came into the call center. It was a simple, if stressful, concept: a phone rings, you answer it. But it wasn't as simple as it seemed when you considered we had to meet hourly call quotas. Our job was to get callers off the phone as fast as was civilly possible. The reasoning being, that the longer we stayed on the phone with one caller, the fewer approved credit card applications there would be by the end of the day. As for the bilingual operators, answering in Spanish meant there could be anything, and I do mean anything, on the other line.

"*Mi nombre es* Valentina, *en qué le puedo servir?*"

At this, the person on the other line might say, "*Por favor, señorita*, do you know where the nearest Fred Loya is?"

Who's Fred Loya?

And the caller, secure in the knowledge that she had pressed "2" for the Spanish prompt, would launch into a monologue—in Spanish—that included pining about life in Mexico, El Salvador, Nicaragua, Bolivia . . . wondering why she needed to have insurance when she barely made enough money to buy a taco from *Señor Taco* truck, and other similar laments. In an effort to meet my quota and to avoid getting fired, I usually tried to interrupt the caller politely to explain that this was the credit card company. If I succeeded at this—which didn't happen very often—the caller might say, "*Señorita*, if you would be so kind, do you know when *Betty La Fea* is coming on? Is channel 64 *el canal* Telemundo *aquí*?" In Spanish *aquí* means here, but the caller might have been calling from anywhere in the United States. Explaining the concept of "outsourced call center" would have gotten me a bewildered: *¿Qué?*

For those who aren't bilingual *¿Qué?* = What the fuck?

Outbound meant something else altogether. Since we were the ones dialing out, this meant we could dial as fast as our fingers could point the computer mouse to the preprogrammed list of phone numbers on our screens. Our outbound call quota was even stricter than the inbound. In turn this meant that between incoming laments in Spanish, we had to call people named Thor, who wasn't so thrilled to listen to what a steal of a deal it was to have a preapproved credit card offer with an 18 percent APR.

More often than not, the phone went Bam! But only after a handful of choice profanities. By the end of a week of outbound calls, you needed a hearing aid. Such was the outbound abuse that anyone with a half an accent would pine for the Spanish callers. Now I looked forward to the inbound calls. After a while, taking a page from my mother, I even started to engage them. "*Señora*," I would say, "you are calling from the land of opportunity. Have you, by chance, read a book called *Thriving Not Surviving*? Once you commit to thriving, there's no going back to El Salvador." Sometimes, I would try the encouraging assimilation route, "Have you tried catching reruns of *One Life to Live*? I don't know what *Betty La Fea* is about, but seeing as you have only one life, try sprucing up your English. The rest of the time, you can spend in a beer coma, or wishing for whiter teeth. If your income level ever gets par with mainstream America, by all means try the Crest strips and shout, *¡Viva la vida!*, without shame."

For all their quirkiness, the requests for obscure insurance companies and Mexican soap operas I had never heard about weren't enough to make me quit. I quit on the day that the guy who sat at the end of the row from mine pulled out a gun and killed the girl sitting next to him. But only after this fair warning: "No one gets a free ride, you bitch! I don't give a shit about your motherfucking boyfriend."

Uh-oh. I think I'll go on my break now.

Who knew that yapping to her boyfriend for the duration of her shift, instead of talking APR, was going to cost Jenny her life? It's so hard to predict what will set somebody off. Still, seeing as the gang member by the window appeared to be between gangs, it occurred to me that the job of phone operator wasn't such a great fit, for either of us. On my last day there, I noticed someone from maintenance changing the locks to the call center.

It's hard to say why that job of long-ago became a fixture on that spongy night. Perhaps it had something to do with Rusty and his merry widows. These people were at the end of their lives. Some of the passengers—the young honeymooners, for instance—were at the beginning. And some of us were somewhere in the middle. Being in the middle meant what it meant. I wasn't on honeymoon. And I wasn't retired. I had to get a job!

Tucked away in a tiny corner of the daily events calendar were the words *Internet access*. Perhaps I should spend the next few days combing through Craigslist while people sipped blue drinks by the pool. But at two dollars for every minute you spent dazed in front of the screen, this was a very expensive idea. More troubling still was the fact that while helping Max raise his kids, I had been out of circulation for a while. Getting a job was going to be a challenge in ways I probably could not begin to imagine. Should I move? What to do about the house? Should I sell Max's watches to a museum? Should I pretend to be a man and become a limo driver in Las Vegas? Driving was a no-brainer. And as a bonus, I'd be good company for my rides. Come to think of it, I didn't have to impersonate a man to drive a limo. I had totally forgotten that Vegas being part of North America, I could grow a set of balls if I wanted to, and remind the HR person at the limo company that if I didn't get hired as a limo driver I could sue the company for discrimination. And to underscore my right to be a woman in the driver's seat, I could belch loudly while I wrote down my references. Already I envisioned my first day on the job. Black bellman's cap to hide my hair. Loose-fitting black uniform to hide the boobs. Sensible shoes to better keep my foot on the pedal. And then, after overcoming the hiring hurtles, on greeting my charge at the airport, and after saying, "This way, sir," the guy holding the briefcase would look at me and say, "Are you sure you know how to turn this thing around?"

 Brilliant as my plan was, at the height of night and fog, the idea of mounting a full-on job hunt felt a little doomed. Don't get me wrong. I love a challenge as much as the next *chica*. I also love meeting new people. I especially thrive among HR types. But it's holding on to the job that's a problem for me—what with the accent that keeps you down, and the serial killers who beat you to it.

The thing to do, for now, was to work on my bucket list. Dreaming cost nothing. And unlike trying to access the Internet thousands of miles from the nearest civilization, the little pad on the nightstand in my cabin was free. Now where to find a pen?

MY BUCKEt LISt

1 Make a piñata with Helen's face.

2 Have dinner at Red Lobster, order the extra crab legs to go, and leave without paying.

3 Approach the "Ten Items, Or Less," lane at the grocery store carrying a ladder and a bucket of red paint. Climb up the ladder, cross over the word "Less," and paint "Fewer" in bright red.

4 Make a piñata with Helen's face.

5 Go to dinner at a steak house and sit next to the anorexic model at the bar eating the kale salad. Order a side of melted butter with my gluten-rich bread.

6 Make a piñata with Helen's face.

7 Approach the newly refurbished, "Ten Items, Or Fewer," lane carrying 100 items. Take photos of the passive-aggressive stares and post them on Facebook.

8 Get a Facebook page and find out what people mean when they say they like you.

9 Make a piñata with Helen's face.

10 Have sex with a snake (the way my mother's patient used to). Afterward, when the snake is all cozy and coiled in postcoital bliss, ask him: "You didn't forget to wear a condom, did you?"

11 Ban Kale.

12 Figure out how to get Max to come back.

RUNNING UP THE BILL

The invitation was brought to our cabin by someone from the purser's office.

At first, I was afraid to open it. During the past year, any envelope addressed to me only meant one thing: there was a bill inside. Would this be a bill for dry-cleaning, or for high-priced Internet access at a sea? Had my mother overdone it at the spa while I was curled up with *Marie Claire* at the library? One thing was starting to become clear: whatever you did over troubled waters cost ten times as much as its counterpart on land. Curiously, the bills were brought up to your cabin by a very busy runner at the purser's office mere minutes after whatever service you indulged. My guess was that processing checkout for eight hundred people on the last day might not be all that practical. Still, this running of the bills was inhospitable; as if you'd throw yourself over board and risk the sharks to avoid paying for a bad blow-dry.

The envelope was made of thick, expensive linen. Where were all these reams of paper coming from? Was there a Kinko's outpost on board? Our names were printed on the front of the envelope as follows:

Mesdames Serrano and Goldman

The first thing that came to mind was, "Why French?" Azucena would know. Perhaps in the same way that English is the international language of business, French might be the gold standard for invitations at sea? I had no clue.

The inside of the invitation read:

MESSRS LARRY BEDFORD AND
ALASTAIR DOUGLAS
REQUEST THE HONOR OF YOUR COMPANY
THIS TWENTIETH OF SEPTEMBER
AT 6 O'CLOCK IN THE EVENING
IN THEIR SUITE
Please RSVP at the purser's office

So this was the "invite" Alastair had mentioned on leaving the Odyssey Theater. How did people find out about these things? How did Alastair know, for instance, that you could throw a party in your sea cabin and get someone to print invitations when we were miles away from a printing press? I had a working theory about the rich. It needed a little fine-tuning, but it involved knowing secrets not available to the rest of us. During the years I spent developing this theory I had learned, for example, that if you paid cash for a car, you could get it for at least half the listed price. It helped if you took out your wallet and counted hundreds in front of the dealer. I had also learned that if you were a famous basketball player you could bypass an entire line of people who already had New Year's reservations at a club by giving your autograph to the bouncer. This happened to me one New Year. When I went to protest to the club manager, he stared me down with disdain and said, "Can you throw a hoop the way he can?" I suppose I needed to practice my dribbling.

Now that I was holding this elegant invitation in my hand, I had learned that somewhere in this boat there were stacks of gorgeously expensive paper in case someone had the urge to throw a party. And I wasn't done learning, either. After going to the party, I would learn that if you had enough money you could get someone somewhere to fly in stone crabs from Florida all the way to the Mediterranean and that you could demand they *not* be frozen, but be shipped on ice instead.

But before getting access to yet more mysteries of the rich, I had to RSVP.

So I took the invitation to the front desk; not because of any eagerness to visit someone else's shoe box at sea, but because I was now very curious to see how this whole process worked. Once I got to the front desk, the concierge on shift asked to see the invitation, produced a secret clipboard that was kept under lock and key, and made a tiny checkmark on whatever was affixed to the clipboard.

"Is there anything else, Madame?"

"No. Hmm . . . Yes, how big a party is it? And what should we wear?"

Once again she consulted the clipboard and also the events calendar. No one around here ever moved a muscle without consulting the events calendar first.

"Six guests in all, Madame. Attire is formal on that day."

Formal, or informal, there was nothing I could do to convince my mother to come to Larry and Alastair's party. The world has always revealed itself to my mother in changing shades of black and black. You were either a Friend of Jesus, or you were the enemy.

BOW, OR BOW?

Larry and Alastair's cabin was located on a different deck, where a handful of suites bore names burnished on gold plates, rather than numbers stuck to the door with crazy glue. I read the names as I walked past: Captain Cook, Captain Drake, Captain Nelson, Captain FitzRoy.

Theirs was the last suite at the end of the secluded corridor, which meant the first suite on the ship, which meant that when you went out on their deck you could practically stand on the ship's bow and take a dive into the ocean. Before knocking, I read the gold plate on the door: Garibaldi's Suite. Was Captain Garibaldi so famous that they didn't bother with the title? Or had this seafaring mariner failed the safety drill and was destined to go down in history as a sailor, rather than a captain? My first guess was probably closer to the mark. Sailors don't get suites named after them. Sailors are the ones inside, the ones who make girls sing, the ones you can't lure to come, until light starts to issue from the porthole.

When Larry came to the door my eyes had to adjust to the grand surroundings. So this is how the other third lived? People might like to think that the world is fifty-fifty. I seriously doubt that half the world could afford a place like this. Larry looked striking in his tuxedo. I was wearing a simple spaghetti-strap dress in black and had borrowed one of my mother's bracelets as my one and only accessory. I was the first one to arrive, so Larry offered me some Champagne and a tour of the place. And speaking of bubbly, I had never been offered so much Champagne in my life. It seemed that going on a cruise was just an excuse to drink something fizzy at all hours of the day and on as many venues as possible. When I heard the word *tour*, I thought Larry might be exaggerating. But no. Don't get me wrong. It's not as if you risked getting lost in the Garibaldi suite, but still. There was an expansive sitting room where a pair of binoculars sat abandoned on a capacious wine-colored leather couch. There was also a small wine cellar. The long and polished bar was everything but mini. And unlike the plastic posters in our cabin, the fixtures on the walls were actual navigational charts, probably antiques. One of them was Magellan's. Even amid this respectable attempt at luxury, the critical eye of a perfectionist's daughter had to ask: What are Magellan's charts doing inside Garibaldi's suite? Had Garibaldi sunk his ship and his charts been lost for all time? Or did Magellan tip the bottle and forget his charts in his mate's room? It was also possible that Garibaldi hadn't discovered a thing, the way Magellan had. That was a job for Google when I got back on firm land.

Throughout my life this neurotic fixation with discrepancies ensured one thing: I could never enjoy anything. I entered a perfectly appointed room and noticed the one burned lightbulb, the one missing tile on the floor. Had I driven Max out of his mind? Had perfection been the only standard at our house? And, realizing that it was an unattainable ideal, had Max decided to give up trying altogether? As I was starting to find out, one the most disconcerting things about suicide was how often random thoughts like these ambushed you at the oddest times. Larry was busy with the Champagne. I hoped he didn't notice how much there I wasn't.

In a little while he approached holding two glasses and invited me outside.

The ship was moving but the seas were so calm it didn't seem an irrational thought to jump into the ocean and go for a quick swim. We appeared to be gliding on a giant piece of glass.

"How's your mother liking the cruise?" Larry asked.

He was too polite to say, "Why didn't your mother come?"

"She has a migraine," I lied. "I'm sure she's very sorry to have missed this. Thank you for thinking of us."

Hard as I had tried I failed to convince the estimable Serena Serrano that homosexuality wasn't a hobby. Who was I, a mere mortal, and one "clinically depressed" at that, to rescue a working psychotherapist swimming in the roiling waters of prejudice?

In any case, Larry and I leaned against the railing, taking in the gentle breeze and the vastness of the sea. Suddenly I liked cruising. But only if you could do it this way.

"Where's Alastair?" I asked.

"Oh, he's down there somewhere, arguing about the crab legs. These things matter so much to him."

"What crab legs?"

"He wanted stone crabs flown in from Florida. But it seems they ran into a snag. So we're having crab legs from Alaska, which Alastair doesn't like."

"Would it help to tell Alastair I don't know the difference?" I said.

Larry shook his head and smiled, as one speaking about one's spoiled child.

"I just want him to be happy," he said, wistfully. "These things don't matter to me."

We stood out there for a while sipping Champagne, watching water swoosh this way and that. If time had stopped just then that would have been fine with me. Perhaps the secret to happiness wasn't to keep moving, as I had always thought, but to stay still as a tulip when you recognized a moment worth holding in your hand. By turns we were quiet. By turns we talked. Larry was so easy to be around. I wondered what had happened between him and his ex-wife. Maybe he wasn't always like this. Maybe I was sipping bubbly with the Larry who came *after* she was done trying to fix whatever was wrong with him. It was also from Larry that I learned a little more about what it might be like being Alastair and why Larry was so eager to indulge his every whim.

When he was fourteen years old, Alastair's family embarked on a road trip to visit his mother's sister in Minneapolis. There was a bad snowstorm that day. Alastair remembered his parents arguing about it after watching the storm in the news. In the end, his mother prevailed. She was eager to see her sister, whom she had not seen in a while. The snowstorm was as bad as predicted. Both parents and Alastair's sister, Hannah, died after the car skidded out of control and crashed. The fact that Alastair was the only one alive could only be explained by one of those odd turns of chance. As bad luck would have it, Alastair ended up having to live with his aunt, his only relative. But they couldn't manage to get along.

"You'd think they'd hang on to each other after what happened," Larry said. "But life doesn't always work out the way we want."

"Dearest," said Alastair, surprising us, "isn't it too dark out here?"

Let's Eat, Grandpa

George Worthing was dressed in a pinstripe suit of the finest fabric. A perfectly starched shirt peeked out of its sleeves, its French cuffs pinched together by silver cufflinks in the shape of old coins. The attire that night was formal and all of us were dressed for events that would take place later in the evening. A tuxedo-clad waiter walked discreetly about the suite offering Champagne refills. Another one carried a tray containing a silver bowl full of caviar. And here they were, at last, the crab legs that had turned Alastair into crabby pants.

"How did you manage the crab legs?" George asked Larry, grabbing one from the tray.

Someone else might have said, "Because I'm filthy rich."

But Larry wasn't that kind of person. Larry enjoyed offering his expensive watches to strangers. In his amiable southern drawl, he simply said, "We managed."

After exchanging a few more pleasantries, Larry excused himself and went to talk to the other guests. I was left standing next to George.

"Lovely gathering, isn't it?" George said.

No. It's horrible, I wanted to say. *I've had it with the crab legs and caviar!*

Instead, I opted for nodding pleasantly. Talkative though I am, small talk isn't my thing. So I had to remind myself that a pause, much like a well-placed comma in a sentence, had great implications for how we might be perceived. It isn't the same to say, "Let's eat, Grandpa," as to say, "Let's eat Grandpa."

"What do you do?" asked George, in an effort, I suppose, to fill the pocket of silence.

To be sure, there was much to remember about this majestic adventure but what will always stand out in my mind is the feeling that I was always being prequalified for a loan. Why was everyone so interested in everyone's occupation? What lack of imagination! Why not ask someone, for instance, "Do you think giraffes suffer from back pain?" or "Do you think the captain gets seasick on land?" Adding to the stress of being asked the one question with the miserable answer, was the conversation I'd had not twenty minutes earlier with my mother. In her humble opinion, the blue contacts I was wearing that night made me look like a phony. It was okay to cut and dye your hair, but wearing blue contacts over your brown eyes was going too far for her.

"You look like a shocked zombie," she said, when I was done with my makeup.

"That's just what I need on my way to a party—some positive reinforcement."

All this to say that I felt like a fraud in front of George, who turned out to be—of all things—an art historian; an expert in authentication! I sipped the Champagne, trying to think of an answer that would not expose me as the counterfeit I was. Should I tell George I was recently widowed? But who needed the pity? The way I saw it, widowhood was something of a disgrace. But I wasn't an ordinary widow; I was the kind of widow who had hoped at one point after the ordeal that the insurance policy might cover part of the loss—the money part. Unfortunately, the life insurance policy Max had taken out had a suicide clause no one had bothered to read at the time, because . . . well, because the only people who consider suicide statistically significant are actuaries.

I also didn't want to tell the stately George that as result of my life falling through a sieve, I had nothing except a collection of expensive watches I wore from time to time, a wishy-washy stepdaughter, and a couple of step-twins who had fled the scene of the crime. By the time I came to stand in front of George in the middle of the Majestic Mediterranean, my once-thriving career in New York seemed as wholly imagined as *Alice in Wonderland*. So I did what I always did in social emergencies. I redirected.

"I didn't catch your name," I lied.

"I'm George Worthing," he said. And he said it so formally that I half-expected him to give me the little number after his name, the Roman numeral befitting kings and their nearest relatives—as in George Worthing the IV.

"And George, what do *you* do?"

"I'm an art historian."

"Professor?"

"Used to be. Now I'm an auctioneer of Old Master paintings at Sotheby's in London."

"Sounds fascinating."

I knew I had him then; that I would not, under any circumstance, allow the conversation to shift back to me. George Worthing was mine now. No more nosy questions about where I was from, or what I *didn't* do for a living. All told, it was hard to picture the mild-mannered George raising and banging a gavel as he proclaimed the Vermeer SOLD to the gentleman in the back. Unfortunately, in the few seconds it took to jump inside my private train of auctioneer imagery, bang came the gavel with the next question.

"Where are you from?"

This conversation has been moved to the trash, I wanted to say.

"South America," I said, keeping it vague.

"*¿Habla Español*, then?"

"*Sí.*"

"*Yo también hablo Español,*" said George.

This happened to me all the time. People told me they spoke Spanish, only for me to discover after two sentences that they had learned it in a fifteen-second Taco Bell commercial. This was the equivalent of me saying that I spoke French because I once got a perfume called *La vie est belle* as a Christmas present. No matter. I decided to humor the ambitious Englishman before me. So I kept answering George in Spanish.

"*¿Por qué habla usted Español?*"

"*Porque viví en España cuando era joven.*"

"So George had lived in Spain when he was younger. Hmmm."

"I want to show Barcelona to Karine," he said.

At the mention of this otherworldly name, the small, prudent eyes behind the glasses became animated.

"How did the two of you meet?" I asked.

"Oh, that was the finest day of my life," George mused aloud.

He then went on to tell me that he and Karine had gotten engaged in London and now were here to celebrate. He had such a crush on her. He followed her around the suite with guarding eyes, as if she were a moving piece of art that might be stolen from him at any moment.

"Now it's my turn to apologize for not catching your name," George said. *"¿Como se llama?"*

"Me llamo Valentina," I said.

"Es un placer, Valentina," he said. "Now, if you'll excuse me, I must look for Karine."

Not "I'm going to look for Karine" but "I *must* look for Karine," as if it were a matter of life and death until he saw her again. In a few days I would remember every word of our exchange.

After playing hide-the-truth with George, I was little worn-out. So I went back outside to recover. But there's no going undercover on a ship. In no time, one of the waiters came out on the deck holding a tray and offered me a bite-size pancake topped with a tiny mound of what looked to me like insects' eyes hiding under cream. And just as the waiter took his leave, Larry showed up.

"Do you like blinis?" he asked.

I tried to swallow as fast as I could. But this was difficult. Very urgently, I wanted to deposit the slimy concoction someplace outside my mouth, but I didn't want to eschew Larry's generosity. So down my throat the blini went.

By the time I went back inside to say my goodbyes, I saw Karine and George talking effusively to another couple from England. The woman's name was May Wood. I would see her again. For now, May Wood seemed to be lost in Karine's face, which was easy to do. Karine had large, intense eyes and a wad of black hair she wore tied back to the middle of her back. That was the first and also the last time I saw her.

tHEY SHOULD HAVE WARNED US

At least twice during this majestic voyage the events calendar featured a port that wasn't on the itinerary. Uh-oh. What did this mean? This meant what it meant: this port was less than majestic. How you knew that we were about to dock near a Batfish aquarium was because Michael Coin—or another Mensa graduate from his entertainment staff—had something like this to say about the port in the events calendar: Volos. Founded A.D.1300. Used to be called Iolcos in ancient Greece.

This fishily brief description, instead of: "Azure, unspoiled harbors that are a haven in this magical and unforgettable odyssey where you can visit the six-towered castle featuring sparkling waters and moats on three sides."

At these minor ports, the adjectives and superlatives were gone, gone, gone, the way of Dionysius after a weekend bender. And speaking of famous Greek gods, the gods in these second-rate harbors were virtual unknowns. No Dionysius in Volos, but a local bum called Demos who had crowned himself unchallenged.

Another clue as to our destination's pedigree was that a giant photo of that evening's entertainer was usually placed above the suspect harbor, the better to divert attention from the filthy waters. It fell on the entertainer's broad shoulders to help passengers recover from the experience; to make up for the fact that there wasn't a single Diet Coke, or a decent cheeseburger within walking distance of the pier. Cruising connoisseurs like Alastair knew not to go ashore in these oily refueling docks. The only people who went ashore were crew members who had to get laid at any cost and the spa staff, people like Adna, who had not had a day off in six months because she had to do nails, hair, and massages for the demanding evenings on board.

Unfortunately for me, I didn't have any of this intelligence. So I went ashore in Volos.

Thank God I don't look like a tourist. Thank God that due to a lot of native disturbances in my own neck of the woods circa 1492 I could pass for Greek, Italian, or Spanish any day of the week on any foreign land. This infiltration of sorts, albeit unintended, has always allowed me to feign ignorance, and also to listen in on unsuspecting tourists who think I don't understand a word they're saying. And this is something I enjoy from time to time, being incognito. Because if there's something I don't hear often enough it is "Valentina, you are very mysterious."

The couple sitting at the table adjacent to mine while I took Max out to lunch in Volos was as innocent of our shared predicament as I was. They made the mistake of going ashore in a *minor* port, and as a result, were in for a *major* surprise. And, as any globe-trotter will tell you, the point of traveling is *not* to be surprised. In any case, once I was comfortably seated at the shoreside café, I took Max out of my purse and set him on the place setting next to mine with the intention of sharing a light lunch with him, the way we used to do on weekends when he was in town.

Despite everything I've just said, the day was radiant. I'd bet the Greek language doesn't have an expression for "clouds in the sky." So I enjoyed the cloudless sky until a paragon of dockside masculinity—read: serious ink on scary biceps—came up to me and wordlessly handed me a menu printed in Greek. To make up for the squiggles on the words, though, the menu featured photos of the food; a visual "Greek Food for

Dummies," if you will. Meanwhile, tension was brewing at the table next to mine.

"What do you mean they don't speak English?" the man said.

"They should have warned us," echoed his companion.

"And what's with the brick cobblestone? You really feel it in your lower back."

"They should have warned us."

"And why do they charge for water? We're surrounded by water, for Christ's sake! That's close to four dollars for a bottle of water. I'll be right back."

Enough is enough, isn't it? The man had had enough, so he got up. It was fairly obvious he was going to complain; he had "that look" on his face. I was enthralled by the possibility of free entertainment. And the pictures on the menu looked delicious, too. I might take a risk and point with my finger to something that looked suspiciously like a local fish. It was flat, very flat, as a matter of fact. The little herbs on the photo looked like parsley. Probably something like "Corfu *al Ajillo*," or something along those lines—a local delicacy, no doubt. Max loved fish, especially if it was flat and unfishy. So that's what I planned to order if the waiter survived the assault for charging innocent travelers for dock water passed off as Greek Perrier. Given that English was Greek to the Greek waiter, I had to wonder how their little skirmish was going in the back.

As it turned out, I was wrong on every single count. That's the problem with lack of imagination: some things simply do not cross your mind. As the man made his way back to the table I had a chance to taken in his T-shirt. A brown moose with very long antlers was pictured across the front. Below the moose, the following words were printed in bold, block letters: NICE RACK.

Above the moose, the man's satisfied face beamed in every direction.

"That'll show 'em," he said, setting the bottle on the table.

"What you do, John?"

"What any sensible man would do, Laura. I refilled it in the john. From now on, I'll either not order water, or I'm going to have them bring me my food into the bathroom."

"You know, John, this place is starting to remind me of Pompeii. I mean, nothing against Mount Vesuvius, but the place had even fewer restaurants than this."

"I hear you. The business to go into here is either bottled water, or window shutters. What's with all the shutters on every damn window, anyway? Is this a Greek thing, or an all-Europe thing?"

"I don't know, John. Maybe it's to keep out the lava."

"What lava? Sometimes you can be so ignorant, Laura. The lava was back in Pompeii."

Eventually, my food arrived. The Corfu turned out to be delicious. I described every bite to Max. It was tempting to describe the conversation next door, as well. But to what end? On top of everything else he had going on, I didn't want to bore Max with something as redundant as "Can you believe that?" For one, there was nothing unbelievable about faucet water. And besides, if there was something I had learned in the past year it was to stop pestering him with the obvious. The only thing I wanted that day in Volos was for Max to have a good time.

tHE "NO SMOKING" DRILL

When death was likely, but optional, there were signs in bright, yellow letters that read: DANGER, DO NOT ENTER. When death was certain, it was the captain, not the cruise director, who got on the speaker. And, as we were soon to learn during this majestic saga, when death was accidental, no one breathed a word.

Ladies and gentlemen, this is your captain speaking. Please be advised that smoking while we are refueling is strictly forbidden on all decks. I trust you're enjoying the sunshine in Volos.

Let's see . . . What to make of this little watered-down warning? *Did he hit his head on a diving board?* Maybe I heard him wrong. Maybe the captain knew everyone was in Volos and was speaking to our luggage? Or, was he aware that Volos was a throw-up port and was speaking with a full deck, but through his inebriated PR representative?

As for cigars, cigarettes, and cigarillos, apparently people who take to the seven seas do so only on one condition: they must smoke. Forget the sharks, fatal dives, or going *Titanic*. Smoking was now a clear and present danger. What if someone who was *enjoying the sunshine in Volos* returned two seconds *after* the captain's announcement, decided to light a cigarette, and dropped the match by the fuel tank? After that announcement, there was not to be a moment of peace. I could not get the thought out of my head: We are going to blow up!

Nothing more to report from sunny Volos.

UNVERIFIABLE

The wind was blowing up a storm on the back deck, where I had gone to escape the crowds with a memoir by Ellen DeGeneres. The book was very funny and I was seriously entertained, laughing unself-consciously on the vacant deck no one ever deigned to visit because there was neither pool nor bar—two terrible oversights, to be sure. But as the seagoing mantra goes, one person's dry deck is another person's paradise. I was giddy with the certainty that "no bar" meant I wouldn't see another soul.

Growing up, my parents had forbidden television, dubbing it "noxious and brain-numbing." This meant that whatever Azucena and I learned about popular culture we had to piece together from telltale photos in *Hola* magazine, friends who liked to gossip, and, as I grew older and moved away, from books like the one I had found in the boat's library about this very funny woman named Ellen. Curiously enough, once you grow up with whatever you consider normal, everyone else begins to look like they are the crazy ones, prompting you to offer misplaced condolences to strangers, such as "You grew up watching television? I feel soo sorry for you!"

At one point during my secluded reading adventure the wind went from very agitated to seriously evil. My hair was blowing witch-style. My water bottle rolled down the deck, followed by the sunscreen. And pretty soon just about everything that wasn't inside my bag had rolled out of my sight.

"Would you like another water bottle, Miss?"

Damn! I thought. *Who else knows about this deck?*

As I peeled off my sunglasses, the better to eye the unwelcome intruder, I was overcome by a deep desire to French-kiss whoever had aimed the word "Miss" in the direction of my thirty-eight-year-old self. Thanks to my mother and father having married compatible DNA, I looked closer to thirty. For all that, the wrinkles of the real years were practically tattooed in my heart. I felt about 107. I cupped my eyes with my hands the better to size up the pool boy (he was twenty, at most) who had offered me the water. He was standing a foot away, waiting for my answer. Ringlets of brown hair adorned his round, pink face. He had a sweet, if sad smile, which I attributed to the dullness of his job.

"Hmmm. No. I'm fine. But thank you."

"If you'd pardon the intrusion, Miss. Where's home?"

"I'm from the most dangerous country in the world," I said, evenly.

In retrospect, this sounded a tad theatrical. But with the daily dose of horror stories issuing from Venezuela—thieves chopping people's wrists to steal their watches; a guy aiming a bayonet at his neighbor's poodle, charging the wrong political affiliation (not the poodle's); a customs official shredding the shoes of a CNN reporter—I felt that my characterization was, at least, defensible.

"Where is that?" he asked.

His round, innocent eyes were now studious and alert. It's hard to say why this odd thought visited me at the moment; that the ship's standard uniform (navy blue shorts, neon-bright white shirt, and topsiders), which made all crew members appear to be in in tip-top nautical shape, looked sad and washed up on him. *You should be in school*, I wanted to tell him. For his part, I think he was expecting me to name a war zone; to say Kosovo, Serbia, Kabul, or something along those lines.

When I said, "I'm from Venezuela," he smiled his sad smile, and a little relief passed through his features.

"Where I'm from," he said, "a woman gets raped every seven minutes."

Never mind the word *rape*. I was surprised that he had the statistic so ready at the tip of his tongue. Seven minutes is a very, very specific amount of time.

"And where is that?" I asked.

"I'm from Johannesburg," he said. "Have you ever heard of it, Miss?"

What with Nelson Mandela and apartheid alone . . . I put on my sunglasses and nodded that yes, I had heard of South Africa. I told him I had also heard of Johannesburg. And, trying to lighten the conversation, or in a ridiculously feeble attempt to empathize, I told him I had heard that Johannesburg, too, suffered these violent thunderstorms that brought with them the same kind of oppressive heat with which I had grown up in Venezuela.

"That's true, Miss," he said, as he continued to fold a mountain of pool towels.

Something shifted inside me as I observed this young person, so far away from home, looking forward to an afternoon of folding blue towels under the braising Mediterranean sun. Suddenly I felt a twinge of shame for having complained about my job at the mail order catalog company to Max at one time. I remembered whining about how repetitive it was, how *so very boring, how degrading* it was to stuff envelope after envelope, hour upon hour with the same cheap catalogs when I had a master's degree. There were worse occupations in the world than having your coworkers be envelopes and the job hazard an occasional paper cut.

There were also worse jobs than folding towels while being lulled by the swooshing sounds issuing from the blue ocean. But after our brief exchange, I couldn't shake the feeling that while this boy barely fresh out of adolescence was stacking pool towels, his eyes were seeing something else. I couldn't get back to my reading for wondering if his sister, or someone close to him, had been viciously raped in Johannesburg.

When did you first learn to mistrust life? I was tempted to ask him. *Is folding towels your response to a place where nothing keeps its promise and everything falls apart?*

It is, of course, absurd to take an event in someone else's life and claim it as your own. But that's exactly what happened after Max took his own life. When the police officer called to ask if he was speaking to Mrs. Goldman, I suspected he was about to tell me something irrevocable. And from that moment forward, what Max had done and my role as an unwilling participant branded me as a certain kind of person—that woman whose husband committed suicide. I can't say I was buried on that day. No. I can, however, say that on that day I passed to a different world, a world known only to me, a place where any contact with another human being was doomed to become a loaded encounter that would lead, inevitably, to the one thing I feared most: being found out. For a while, the world beyond my front door became a world full of naïve strangers who did not know what I knew. Depending on who the person was, I was tempted to warn them, in case they, too, fell for the sham that you could actually be happy. I wanted them to grasp the danger they were in by placing their trust in another person, by pinning their hopes on something as unverifiable, as ridiculous as love.

It took a while to recognize the feeling, to be able to admit to myself how angry I was at Max for his betrayal. I felt cheated and deceived. It also took a while to come to terms with the fact that in addition to losing Max, I had lost another valuable, and that there was no way to get it back. There are certain things, which aren't really things—like innocence, for instance—that can never be reclaimed. There isn't a grade for the calculus of certain kinds of losses.

HoME IS WHERE H _____ L _____

One reason to have a home is to keep out certain people. But what if the people who are already inside are the ones you want to keep out? From the beginning, our home was too crowded—what with the Jehovah's Witnesses and their bikes, the Girl Scouts and their cookies, the changing UPS crews, plus the evil girlfriends and their shifty sleepovers, Max and I had a full house. And that's not counting phone calls from telemarketers, usually around dinnertime. If it wasn't a surprise family visit, or yet another holiday gathering, there seemed to be, always, some unexpected crisis or distraction that left Max and me very little time to be married to one another. Were we the only married couple who would have gladly fled our own house to become refugees elsewhere?

For a couple of years, for instance, a conversation with Emily might go something like this:

>*What's the matter, Emily?*
>*Nothing.*
>*Then why are you upset?*
>*Who says I'm upset?*
>*You said something happened in school.*
>*Maybe.*
>*Maybe?*
>*Maybe I imagined it.*
>*What did you imagine, Emily?*
>*Nothing.*

Oh, I get it. We're living with Hangman!

From time to time I wondered if all these roller-coasters and demands had weakened our love somehow. A lot of people think that love is fragile, I believe, because that's what romantic people want us to believe. But love isn't fragile. Love is like my grandmother's cast iron skillet. Nana used to say it took a lot for iron to rust, which is why her favorite pan was made of sturdy cast iron. You could scratch it, you could bang it; the stubborn thing never broke. Love is a lot like cast iron in that regard. You could scratch your head about it, you could hit your head with it; you could even bang the other person's head with it in a flight of inspiration. But in the end, it was someone's head that was going to split, not love. Love remained, stubborn and strong; it hunted you down all the way to places swimming with sharks and fins, long after you'd sworn it off.

During our marriage, most of the scratches to our love had to do with Helen. For years and years, our briefer and briefer marital spats devolved into uncreative tiffs that went something like this:

Helen's alimony
Child support
Helen's alimony
Child support
Helen's alimony
Child support
Helen's alimony
Can we please talk about someone else?

And when she wasn't at our house in spirit, Helen paid visits to our flower urns.

Some nights, after days that looped around like *Groundhog Day* around the same subject, I tried to cradle Max's head in my arm so we could fall asleep.

"I can't sleep that way," he'd say, moving away.

On nights like these, when my sole wish was to levitate toward the ceiling by way of escape, I wondered if Max was afraid of getting too close. Because when you get too close, you stand to lose everything. In the end, the joke was on me. I was the one left with the shaking hands and no place to put them. I had never expected anything *less* in my life. During the weeks and months that followed, impersonating someone sane proved a challenge. How flimsily constructed can a creature be? But not love. Despite everything, I still loved Max.

tHE CoSt OF A LEAK IN SANtoRINI

Santorini was in the air.

Those who had been there before swore that it was paradise. "You have to take the donkey to the top," they urged, a touch of the fanatic in their voice. If vertigo wasn't your idea of adventure, equally unsolicited advice came from those who claimed that the funicular was *the only way* to reach the top of the cliff. If what makes romance romantic is expectation, the anticipation of Santorini had everyone smitten, sight unseen.

Santorini is what is called a caldera. Simply put, this means that a long, long time ago, a volcano started boiling underneath the ground, and when it was finally hot enough in seventeen-something or other, it blew up. The whitewashed slab of lava that rose to the surface, literally out of the ashes, became what is known today as Santorini.

Over the years, the optimists who decided to settle down on top of a volcano started dotting the limestone precipice with boxy structures made of the same color as the lava rock; a whitish sort of stucco. But no one likes hearing this, especially not people arriving on a cruise ship. No one ever refers to Santorini as a dangerous cliff; people insist on calling it an island, when in reality, it is what was left—the ruins. Santorini was the name given to it by the Roman Empire, but the official name in Greek is Thera. So here we were in Thera, at the very heart of civilization, with nothing between us but six hues of blue everywhere you looked; a skip and a jump from the oldest known examples of the Greek alphabet, and what did people want to do? They wanted to shop.

On most days you hardly noticed the ship was carrying so many people. Arriving at a place as stunning as Santorini, though, you were suddenly assaulted by loads of humanity packed in halls, stairs, and elevators. Every deck displayed an identical sign: Today, the gangway is on Deck 4. People did their best to line up. But as is often the case with good intentions, their best got bested by wants of the primate order: elbows jabbed, toes were stepped on; pricks were not uncommon. The debate about whether to take the funicular to the top of the mountain, versus the donkey, had everyone on edge. "You won't believe your eyes," a woman said behind me. I wondered if any place could live up to that kind of worship.

The ship was too large to dock, so we anchored in the middle of the sea and tendered ashore. Once we got out of the wobbly little boats, it was a race to see who could spend the most money in the shortest amount of time.

My mother and I have never been donkey people. So we patiently awaited the arrival of the busy funicular. Choosing the least of two transportation evils didn't mean that we were safe by any means. Once we got out of the dangling wagon, we still had to negotiate every single uncertain step through dangerously rocky paths in what started to feel like a doomed expedition. Some sections were so steep that we had to hold hands and lean back to avoid tumbling forward. On our way to the summit we caught sight of the fabled donkeys being led up the hill by an old man beating them with a stick. The tourists riding the smelly animals had nervous smiles on their faces.

Eventually we came to the top of the precipice; panting, but still alive.

The view below and beyond was nothing short of spectacular. I was reluctant to blink, lest I miss a millisecond of awe. The only thing Santorini asked of you was that you stare at it and take a bow.

Doubtless accustomed to the sight of sweaty tourists about to pass out, the Greek god standing outside one the white stucco boxes we had seen from below ushered us inside with the promise of cooler air and "perhaps some ouzo?" Whatever ouzo was, I wanted him to feed it to me, preferably mouth-to-mouth.

Like every hotel and taverna on the island, the restaurant afforded an uninterrupted view of the stunning landscape, an infinite expanse of water touched by a golden halo of sunlight. For all that, having lunch atop a precipice took some getting used to. Once we were seated, I set my sunglasses on the table and stared out to sea. The simplicity of the place was beyond fetching, and for a hallucinatory instant the thought of moving to Santorini crossed my mind. What would life on top of a cliff entail? Watching water change colors at various times during the day would be a peaceful pastime, to be sure. But would that get boring after a while? There were also the moody winds to consider. Would I be the stranger among them, the woman who stayed behind after all the tourists went back home? Would my fellow cliffers nod good morning, wave good night, and return to spinning their worry beads between meals? Or would they notice me and say, "There's that stranger, sitting on the old bench again"?

If the views beckoned you to come, it was the silence, or rather, the absence of noise, that made you want to stay. It was a soothing thought: saying goodbye to flinching; to living on high alert. But the most welcome thought of all was the possibility of finally shedding the otherness; never again having to answer the tired question: Where are you from? with its inescapable implication that you were an outsider. In time, though, once I learned the Greek alphabet, I'd be able to make out that the locals asked the exact same questions here. No place on earth was safe; nowhere to hide from the feeling that I was the odd one out. It was a relief, though, even if it was momentary, to be swallowed by the sheer vastness of it. There I was, bewitched by the idea of escaping my borrowed life elsewhere, and what were the first two items on the menu? Hamburgers and hot dogs. My mother wondered aloud why even in this remote corner of the world they catered to North Americans.

"Be grateful this isn't an Outback Steakhouse," I said, "Or some other imitation of an imitation."

In the end, we ordered the lamb gyros, which were brought to us with two baby glasses filled with lukewarm water. When you stopped to consider the risks, it was hard to imagine anyone bringing an ice-maker all the way up here. A single misstep and you'd risk becoming part of a local legend—that guy who tumbled into the Aegean with his ice-maker. Our cliffhanger of a meal concluded with complimentary glasses of ouzo, which turned out to be jet fuel in a glass.

While standing in line at the restroom after lunch, I overheard the following exchange.

"What do you mean it costs a euro to take a leak? Are you insane? This is a public toilet."

The bathroom attendant didn't say a word. He just stared the belligerent tourist. It wasn't a dumbfounded stare, either. It was a smug stare that probably meant, "You're in my country. Pee in your pants for all I care."

"This is bullshit," the man said, and walked right out.

DÍA DE LOS MUERTOS

The guy from Montreal thought he was still in the 1920s and that our ship was the *Titanic*. He was deeply tanned, I thought, for someone of the blond variety, and wore expensive shoes without socks. By night he wore an ascot and smoked cigars. Some veteran cruisers got into that sort of thing, adopting objects and imagery from bygone times.

On the day we were supposed to leave Santorini, all the decks were packed; people were crammed against the railings, cameras at the ready to snap last shots of one of the most photographed spots on earth. In a "Did you know?" sort of voice, the woman on the stool next to mine volunteered that only the Eiffel Tower was more photographed than Santorini. What to make of such a claim? If I'd learned anything by then it was that the seven seas were practically overflowing with sweeping statements.

The air that day was salty but light. The lazy low tide made an inviting, lulling sound. And the white foam that brushed the shore was a dream in slow motion. But something was amiss in the cramped volcanic precipice.

"How come we're not leaving?" someone asked.

"What's the holdup?" someone else pitched in.

Perched on the bar stool I had an almost unobstructed view of the boxy white squares on the hill. At that hour, all the white stucco structures were beginning to absorb the emerging hues of the sunset, as if a painter were trying on different colors until the fiery orange prevailed. My mother cut a great, indifferent figure, sitting nearby reading a book behind her big movie star sunglasses. She and the captain must be the only two people not interested in catching a last glimpse. Been there. Done that. Got the postcard. This must be what she was thinking. As for the captain, it turned out he had other, more pressing matters at hand than maneuvering his ship back into deeper waters.

"The name's Jean-François," said the man sitting next to me.

"Whose name is Jean-François?" I asked.

At this, he produced a suave smile, as if my ignorance of his person were a put-on. He turned out to be a French Canadian running away from whatever iceberg he came from, taking a break from eating seal sushi for lunch. He professed to love the warmth the way some people say they believe in Christ.

Anything that moved in front of us, or rather in front of him, ended up reflected in the small circles of his aviator glasses. At the moment, there were a few impatient figures reflected on the greenish tint of Jean-François's specs.

"Can I get you a drink?" he said. "We might be here for a while."

"How come?"

"One of the passengers is missing."

And this is something that would continue to surprise me, the insider nature of cruising. Not only did everyone but me knew where to eat in Mykonos, what the best stall was at the Grand Bazaar, or that the Rocco Forte Hotel was *the* place to stay in Abu Dhabi. But they also had certain insider knowledge that could only be categorized as gossip. Until I met Jean-François I thought Alastair was an isolated case because he had a gossip-seeking gene and simply adored drama. But no. There were more than a few rumormongers on board.

"What do you mean one of the passengers is missing?"

Just like that, the woman seating next to me joined the conversation. For good measure, she clucked and added, "I thought ships didn't wait for anyone. Don't you hate these latecomers? What makes them think they're so special? I'm Lynn, by the way."

"Hi, Lynn," I said.

"Santos, get them some Champagne," said Jean-François, addressing the bartender.

In short order, two glasses of Champagne glided toward us. The obliging Santos slid one in front of me; the other one he placed in front of Lynn.

"I'll pass," said Lynn. "I'll decide what I want to drink."

For his part, Jean-François waved her away as one does a bug too small to squash. The slight, yet potent gesture was all I needed to know that Azucena could grow to love this man. One of my sister's pastimes is dismissing people. She also has a weakness for superior brands. At once, I started looking for brands on his person. The moment I spotted the Cartier watch, I considered asking for his phone number and getting his credentials. It isn't every day that a man passes two tests in such a short period of time. An undergraduate degree from an Ivy League school was a must for the discerning Azucena. A terminal degree preferred. A PhD would be best, might even tempt her to take off her shirt. It rarely worked out, though, my playing matchmaker for Azucena. That's because when I thought I was on to something, when I thought Cartier was de rigueur, my sister surprised me with something heftier, like "Everyone knows Baume & Mercier is what old money wears." And I suppose hers was bona fide knowledge, given she was the editor of the glitziest magazine in Caracas, and all that jazz.

"So?" Jean-François said, turning to me.

Here we go, I thought, *the choo-choo train of nosy questions has arrived.*

"Where are you from?" was always first. Usually, this was followed by "What do you do?" And finally, what some people really, really wanted to know was "Who are you with?" a delicate and mysterious way of asking: When can we fuck?

Perhaps the lulling waves and sumptuous sunsets awoke a curiosity that was otherwise dormant on land. The assumption of coupledom was particularly irksome. At one point I considered inventing a new status; something akin to a coveted fashion trend, along the lines of: I'm biased. As in, "Are you single, jilted, or biased?" Biased had potential. Like Alastair, biased could go either way. It could mean, for instance, that I was biased *toward* divorce, and *against* marriage. It could also mean I had a bias *against* widowhood. Or that I was biased *against* humanity, in general.

I was lost in my little status jamboree when Jean-François launched the first question.

"Where are you from?"

"Venezuela," I said, my mind racing ahead like a bungee jumper trying to avoid hitting my head on the rocks.

"You live there now? Your English is too good."

"Hmm. No. I live in the States."

"I thought so," he said. "And what do you do?"

I riffled for a quick answer to my current state of unemployment. Then I remembered my neighbor Marilee's brother, Jeremy. He was a drummer who had moved to Canada to play for a band. When I had asked him the same question while he was visiting Marilee, Jeremy had said with great ease, "I'm between gigs."

So that's what I said to Jean-François, "I'm between gigs," a lie as obvious as anything.

"Are you, really?" he said.

More than likely I was being humored. I tried to gauge his eyes for any sign of duplicity, but this was impossible through the tiny, round mirrors; all I could see was part of my face, distorted, glinting in the sun. At my earliest convenience—as Azucena liked to say—I must turn this conversation around. I must avoid revealing my current status: "unemployed widow; not the rich kind." And the more degrading, accompanying details, the fact that I'd been kidnapped to the now Majestic Aegean by a woman to whom I was related by blood and who had pronounced me unfit to go on sitting on my comfortable chair by labeling me "clinically depressed."

What to say to the snoopy Jean-François?

Single at thirty-eight would smell fishy. Twice divorced, reeked of difficult bitch with a potential personality disorder. Still, it was preferable to widow carrying ashes in an Advil bottle. Now, if you added unemployed widow with sullen stepchildren, any conscious creature of the male species would make a run for his orange vest. Would I care if Jean-François nosedived into the caldera? I would not give a beach pebble. But I happened to like my privileged view from the bar stool. So I said, "How about you? What do *you* do?"

"Oh, this and that," he said, casually taking a sip from his drink.

WTF? Why didn't I think of that?

From that sunset forward I would practice saying this inane phrase in front of the mirror, "Oh, this and that." What the fuck was that supposed to mean? More importantly, though, why was I complicating my existence with the truth, why was I trying to explain my life to strangers when there were so many lame phrases at the ready? But then again, what was the big deal with sharing some trivia about your life with an accidental tourist? I might have told Jean-François that at one point in my life I had worn wool socks meant for men to stave off the cold in a place called New York City. He couldn't have cared less, I'm sure. To me, though, these trifles were worse than intimacies; they exposed me to the bare bones. They begged the question again and again: What's wrong with women socks?

Looking at the illusion of an infinite horizon it was easy to think that those of us on this enormous ship were it. We were *the* chosen ones, the last people on earth, chosen by Herculean gods in Mount Olympus to rule the earth. It was a heartening thought, until I pictured all of us scavenging for lava rocks from the volcanic explosion that had blown up Santorini. A few people on the ship—the ones who asked for a third omelet at the Veranda on most mornings—might survive and go on to rule over generations of humans and Mercurians to come. But the rest of us would wither and die shortly after we ran out of bottled water.

It was dark by the time we left the fetching caldera behind. Many people were beside themselves, giving voice to their discontent, throwing careless words to the four winds. We were now late for Mykonos! What if Mykonos decided to move somewhere else in the next five hours? We might not survive.

The body of the missing passenger had been found.

BROKEN DOWN

Something Max might have said and been justified in saying is this: I married a judge. Max was one of those credulous souls who actually believed that people meant well. Poor Max. This groundless faith in his fellow humans made him unable to judge. We could not have been more opposite. Every ripe avocado has its soft spot; mine is judging. I judge easily, often, and much. To me, passing judgment on the world isn't a bad character trait, but rather, a virtue. The moment I open my eyes in the morning, I try to move through my day and keep them that way—wide open, never flinching. I've always had a particularly keen eye for other people's shortcomings. When confronted with any irregularity, I'm the one ready to say, "Why is that man peeing on the lettuce?" But my observation isn't yet complete. I'm always compelled to add, "What a pig! Who pees on lettuce?" Max, on the other hand—missing the judgment gene as he was—might have said, "Someone who has to pee."

Deep inside, if I were completely honest with myself, I envied Max his blindness. Because isn't the inability to discern penis from pig, a kind of blindness? Sometimes, albeit on very rare occasions, I used to wish I were blind. But only because judging can be such a chore. When you're a judge—one who takes herself seriously, at any rate—you owe it to yourself and others to keep score. You have to develop charts with numbers and then compare one failing against another. This way, you can speak with authority when you say, "David is dumber than Dumbo!" To which Max would say, "Dumbo was an elephant. Elephants are very smart."

Besides the occasional setting me straight on all things animal kingdom, Max had other virtues as well. Unlike his brother, Ira, who placed both his faith and his money on qualified professionals, Max liked to fix things himself. A typical Saturday at our house might involve, but not be limited to, the following updates:

"I just fixed the lightbulb in the garage. It was burned."

"Cool."

"There's a leak by the washing machine. I'll go check it out."

"Cool."

"Fridge needs a new water filter."

"Sounds good."

"The ironing board is missing a screw."

"Not *just* the ironing board," I'd say, in the level of a whisper.

"Have you checked out your car tires, Valentina? I think one of them might be flat."

"I never check my car tires, Max."

"The garage door might be about to . . ."

"How can you stand it????? Can't you see? Can't you see, Max, that all these things are breaking down on purpose? Just stop. Stop giving them so much attention. You're making them act up."

In looking back, there was something sweetly naïve to all this fixing. Max actually believed he'd be able to outstrip the inevitable rotting of things. At one point, though, he must have concluded that all effort is ultimately futile; that not a single one among us can outrun the ultimate breakdown.

tRIcK QUEStIoN

When Max showed me the email from Helen, I had to hang on to the back of his chair to balance my response.

"How did she get your email, Max?"

"No idea. Probably from Emily."

Many of the things we can't fathom are bound to have happened before; they just happened to someone who isn't a friend of ours; to people we don't know. Car wrecks in which a person loses all her memories and goes amnesiac all of a sudden are not entirely out of the realm of possibility. That must be what happened to Helen. The alternative was some kind of an operation. Did they do lobotomies anymore? There were also the *Born Again Christians*. But didn't you have to be Christian in the first place to do it *again*? All this to say, that ten years is quite a chunk of time to demand not to be spoken to, except through lawyers, and then send the *cuchi* E-vite that Helen sent. (*Cuchi* is Spanish for UN.FUCKING.BELIEVABLE).

I was positive Max's computer had been hacked.

Dear Max:

I was thinking that for Emily's graduation we should do our best to put our differences behind us and all go to dinner. What do you say?

It would be good to see you. Please give my regards to Valentina.

Helen

Wha . . . ? Had Helen been secretly doing her downward dog and was waiting for Emily's graduation to spring her yoga teachings on us?

Only in Hollywood do people change. And that's because of the easy access to plastic surgeons. *¡Por favor!*

It was Max, oh he who could not judge, who said, "I think we should do it for Emily."

"Should we? Now it's *we*, who have to do this for Emily, to go to dinner with Ashtray Interrupted? I don't think so."

When I was an adolescent I watched Nana's sister go insane. Her name was Jacinta. One time, I accompanied Nana on one of her visits to Jacinta at the asylum. *El asilo,* as it is called in Spanish, wasn't an amusement park, even if from my pubescent perspective there was plenty of wildlife. People who lived at the asylum seemed to drift in and out of wakeful nightmares and to crawl out of hidden places whenever visitors arrived.

Can't hang myself yet. Gotta slit your throat first, Doc.

My eggs? You ask how I like my huevos? I like them hard!

Ven. Ven aca, bonita. I won't hurt you. Haven't you been living with your stalker?

These and countless offbeat remarks ran together at the asylum. Jacinta had a different approach. She didn't say a word. Instead, as soon as someone knocked on her door, she proceeded to take all her clothes off and started running around, flapping her arms in the air until people dressed in white came at her with a needle that made her stop, dead in her tracks. It was really mystifying; why the staff insisted on wearing white at a place like this. Unfailingly, there were always lots of messes; smears, spilled fluids, and many things I have forgotten or that simply were filed someplace inaccessible in my memory bank. Whatever was in Jacinta's needle, though, I wanted to Google it and see if Amazon might ship it free of charge by the time of

Emily's graduation. I didn't say whom I planned to tranquilize. Did I?

Finally, the not-anticipated day arrived.

Was the car wreck simply awful, Helen? Does your head now feel as though it's full of roasted coffee beans? I wanted to ask, by way of greeting.

"Good day to graduate, isn't it?" I said, instead.

We met the teachers. We talked to the other parents. We congratulated Emily. Helen complimented my hair. At one point during dinner, getting a bit choked up, Helen said that Emily and the twins were the best thing that had happened to her and Max. *Really? I thought you had called them the biggest mistake a while back? Was that your evil twin, then, who burned Zach's hand with your cigarette? Have you tried patenting burning as the most effective way to stop a kid from playing video games?*

Don't get me wrong, I'm all for corporal punishment. I was, after all, practically raised by nuns who whacked our hands with rulers as a way to instill a little discipline in us. But using your son's hand as an ashtray seemed a little excessive; up there with nailing a guy to a cross for misrepresenting himself.

Whatever potion Helen was on that night, I wished she'd pass me some with the bread basket. I, too, wanted for someone to erase my memories of the past ten years. And pronto!

Quite frankly, I preferred Helen before the lobotomy. Sitting around the table with this version of Jack Nicholson at the end of *Cuckoo's Nest* was very disappointing on two fronts. For one, Helen had lost her edge. And, because of that, we couldn't hate her anymore. What to do with her now? After the years she spent writing love letters to her attorneys and taping them to our front door as reminders, should we offer to pay for dinner this evening? Maybe the thing to do was to tap a reigning Olympian on the shoulder and say, "Hey, are you planning to hang on to your medal? If not, I know someone who wants one."

No. The thing to do was to figure out a way to piss off Helen royally during dinner, say, by coughing phlegm on her water. Or to start digging in her purse and steal her meds, so she'd return to her former, deranged self. The sooner the better. Because now that Helen had healed, we were jobless. We couldn't go on hating her without cause. Forgiving her might have crossed someone's mind. But if judging was my guiding light, forgiveness was the off-switch. My approach to forgiveness was quite simple:

"Please form two lines. Sins against yourself please go see my mother—or any therapist of your choice, prequalified by your insurance carrier. Sins against others, please go see Christ."

I hadn't come to this earth to be anyone's redemption pal. Neither had Max. Or so I thought. At one point, it crossed my mind that on the day that was to be his last, Max went to Helen's house, not to kill her, but to forgive her for all the despicable things that she had done. Me? I took it as a matter of pride that I'd carry my grudges well into the next life. *If* there was a next life.

What about forgiving Max, though? The way I saw it, Max could stand in either line. There was no doubt he had hurt himself. And the circle of grief around him was getting a little crowded—his parents, his brother, his children, the whole wide beauty of an extended family, and on and on.

Erasing him from my memory for hanging me out to dry among desert shrubs was a better idea. And yet, despite the many majestic distractions, the radiant sunsets, the pods of dolphins, the active volcanoes, forgetting Max was proving a little difficult. But forgiving him? That was a trick question. Had to be.

VOLCANIC COLLAPSE

I needed to accept the idea of a new and different future, a future free of ashes or doomed thoughts. More importantly, I needed to believe that starting over was a worthwhile pursuit. Ultimately, that's what happened after I went to pay George a visit; I was able to envision a new life, though that wasn't the reason I went to see him.

By now everyone knew that George's fiancée, the former ballerina by the name of Karine, had fallen to her death from a donkey in Santorini. In a few short days, Karine's peculiar manner of dying had reached the proportions of legend. And though the accident was much discussed among passengers, no formal announcement was made by the captain, or by anyone else. As for George, the main person affected by the tragedy, Alastair had told me that he had called, knocked, and left notes on his cabin's door, all to no avail. So I wasn't expecting George to answer. It was even possible that he had disembarked. Under international maritime law, a dead body has to be repatriated to the country of origin.

The reason I went to see him was that I remembered the many so-called friends who did vanishing acts after what happened with Max. Back then I thought of them as cowardly. In retrospect, I was able to recognize that not everyone was gifted with the facility of speech bestowed on me by a God who wished to torment my parents and future listeners. Even the briefest of condolences gave many people a bad case of word tripping. Formerly normal friends had approached me, sweaty and tongue-tied, before finally spitting out, "I love your furniture," in a bizarre effort to relate to an unrelatable situation.

A distant cousin of Max's from New York hovered around me for a while before going in for the kill. "I know how you feel," she said. "I know you are frightened because you are alone. So alone. But you are not *alone.*" At which point I wanted to tell her, "I *am* frightened. But it's because I'm *not* alone right now. I'm frightened you may never leave my house."

The one thing I hoped for George as I prepared to knock on his door was something I knew he had already done. It is uncommon to be aware of doing something for the last time—the last time you will look at a sunset; the last time you will hear someone's voice, for instance. It was safe to assume that as he climbed up the volcanic remnants of Thera, George could not have known he was looking at his fiancée for the last time. But I knew from speaking with him at the party that he had been paying attention.

I, on the other hand, had been too engrossed in my own mental detours on the day that would become his last to pay attention to Max. Yes, I noticed he put an extra spoon of sugar in his coffee. In retrospect, I should have asked. But I was too busy with my own concerns to give it another thought beyond "that's odd." In the guilt-sodden months that followed, versions of the unasked question would continue to play on repeat. *Why didn't you ask about the damn sugar when you had the chance?* In turn, the nagging private inquisitions were followed by a never-ending string of maybes that chased me all the way to the Majestic Aegean. *Maybe Max was begging you to notice. Maybe you could have saved his life, if you had only asked about the sugar. Had you asked a simple question, perhaps you wouldn't be standing before a closed door in the middle of the Greek Isles.*

Most of what might be said in a situation such as this risked sounding insignificant. But by now I was convinced that saying something to George was better than staying away. When David Warren, who had been Max's business partner for years, became, for all purposes, a missing person, I was still too struck by the loss to sort out his absence. The disenchantment arrived late, much later, once I snapped out of the trance.

As for George, unlike the day I had met him at Larry and Alastair's party, when he looked every bit the cultivated art historian, today he was wearing a robe carelessly cinched around his slim body. Without his glasses, his eyes looked smaller than I remembered. The only reason he answered the door was that he was expecting someone else.

"I was expecting someone else . . . from the purser's office," he said. "Arrangements for disembarking and so on."

"George, I came by to say how truly sorry I am."

"It's kind of you. I'm sorry I can't offer you some tea."

"I don't like tea," I said.

Before coming here I had vowed not to treat George any differently than I would have at any other time. I didn't want to treat him delicately. I didn't want to be caught dead saying anything *cursi*, such as "Your view is nicer than ours." Or "I'd love some tea!"

"It's a pity," said George.

I wasn't sure if he meant about Karine's death, or about the fact that I didn't like tea.

Say you're sorry and be gone, I told myself. Staying even a minute longer and I'd risk making some bizarre remark about the furniture, the way Max's friend had done to me. It was at the tip of my tongue to tell George I knew exactly how he felt. In truth, I could not know how he felt. We shared a certain kind of loss; the unexpected kind. But that was the extent of it. I couldn't know what it was like to go on living without Karine in London, any more than George could fathom what it meant to be a bilingual widow from Caracas in cactus-ridden Arizona. And besides, George had nothing to forgive Karine. She hadn't plunged to her death on purpose.

I might try the distract-the-pain routine, which some people had tried with me. Tell George, for instance, Try marijuana, I hear it helps. Or hobbies. Have you any hobbies, George? I've heard hang gliding can take your mind off things. Maybe you can learn to be a pilot. Or take up golf. My husband says golf is relaxing. But I've always found it really boring.

It was the bit about golf that gave my stomach a squeeze. Up until then, I had not thought that carrying Max's ashes with me was an act of madness. Quite the opposite: the thought of leaving the ashes behind *was*. But you can't always be "on the verge" of madness. At some point, after being delusional for a while, you will start to feel at home with the delusion. I had no idea how madness worked. But my mother did.

Feelings never seem to know their place. Why would the middle of the ocean be the place to become frightened that my mother had found me unhinged enough to get on a plane and haul me thousands of miles out of the way? Standing before George, who had half-plunged into the abyss in just a few days, I glimpsed, albeit accidentally, a kind of insight—that for me to keep from tipping over the edge something had to change.

"How am I going to explain this to her family?" George mused.

The question was obviously rhetorical. George wasn't there. More than likely he could not even see me. He may never remember getting a visit in the middle of nowhere by someone named Valentina. As for me, if I was to move forward, if I was to envision myself afloat and not adrift, I couldn't keep swimming with my boots on. At some point, the self-defeating questions: *What about me, Max? Wasn't I reason enough for you to carry on?* would have to stop.

In looking back, I have come to see that brief encounter as the moment when letting go of Max went from impossible to conceivable. In George's dilated stare I glimpsed how long a climb he had ahead before he could crawl out of the abyss.

"Is there anything I may do for you, George? Anyone you want me to call, perhaps? I can do that when we get to our next port."

"It's kind of you," he said.

"Well, George," I said, taking my leave. "My mother and I are in cabin number 205. Please call on us if you need anything at all."

"I'm very sorry," he said, "But I didn't catch your name."

"*Me llamo* Valentina," I said, nudging him about our first conversation.

"Ah, yes, Valentina . . . It's kind of you to call."

PART III

tHREE SHEEtS IN tHE WIND

A GENUINE FAKE

What to do while at sea on the way to Mykonos?

Sit by the pool and suck on blue drinks through neon straws.

Get a massage from untrained hands at the spa and risk a lifetime of scoliosis.

Hit your head against the low ceilings at the floating gym.

Eat.

Sleep.

Gamble.

Throw up.

Eat some more.

"I have an idea," said Alastair. "Let's go check out the art auction."

The art auction? Finally, a little bit of culture around here. It was with great expectations, then, that Alastair and I headed down to Poseidon's Art Gallery for a little bubbly to rub elbows with Goya, Chagall, and Rembrandt lovers. I couldn't wait. My feet practically walked to the gallery without me. As was his wont, Alastair saved the surprises for last, the better to capture his victims on video, or perhaps a photo that would garner likes and shares on Facebook.

On the way there, he told me that he had attended many of these seafaring auctions in the past. The auctions themselves couldn't have interested him *less*. For Alastair, the pleasure lay in watching gullible strangers tread in the shallow waters of bidding on counterfeits tendered as catches.

From masters of the Renaissance to contemporary luminaries, read the sign at one of the entrances.

"Hi, I'm Carla," said the auction coordinator. "Would you care for some Champagne?"

Alastair accepted the glass of bubbly and in just one sip pronounced it undrinkable.

"I hate it when they pass Cava as Champagne," he said, leaving his glass on a shifty ledge. Likely it would stumble and break.

After a brief tour of the gallery and a few casual waves and nods to people we recognized, Alastair and I took our seats toward the back. Through his choice of seats, I found in Alastair a kindred traveler who grasped the critical nature of a sound exit strategy. I've never understood people who arrive at a theater, a classroom, an auditorium, or any public venue for that matter, and head toward the front row. Don't these innocents realize the unwisdom of being trapped inside a room full of strangers and being unable to run should the urge arise all of a sudden? Alastair recognized as well as I did that, Where is the exit? was as important a question as, Why are we here?

We were here to entertain ourselves. But Carla, the auction coordinator who wore way too much lipstick for her cartoonish features, didn't know this yet. So she came over to where we sat and handed us a couple of paddles with numbers on them.

"There will be two bidding rounds," she said, brightly. "One hour each."

"Wha? I can't be here for two hours," I said to Alastair.

"Don't worry, dearest. We're here to learn . . . for the next time around."

Now he winked. And then, flirting with the bubblicious Carla, he said, "We're auditing the class! May we keep these as souvenirs?"

Uh-oh. This mind-bending question wasn't in Carla's training manual. Judging by her panicked stare it was evident that Carla was seriously stumped by the paddle question. Already I could tell that Alastair had something devious in mind. If there was such a thing as throwing an auction, I suspected him of secretly plotting it at that very moment. Whatever his plan, I longed to be as unscrupulous as Alastair. All my life, I had played by the book. And where had that gotten me? It had gotten me to an auction of fakes at sea.

"I'll go ask Kyle," Carla said. "More Champagne?"

"We'll pass," said Alastair.

On dry land, no doubt, Carla's slip-up would have cost her the job. By rules governing the auction, only those registered to bid were allowed to wield these paddles. But that was the thing about Alastair. He now had an alibi. Should anything go amiss, he could honestly claim that he had asked Carla, "and she said it was okay."

"Why are you keeping these?" I asked.

"You'll see," said Alastair.

This was my first auction, which is to say, I hadn't a clue. All I needed was a little insider information from the seasoned Alastair to learn that people who planned to bid had been prescreened in advance. Their credit cards had been run and checked for limits, lest someone drink too much bubbly and raise their paddles in excess of what they could afford. The auctioneer had a list of these people at the podium.

Everywhere I turned my head there seemed to be a secret society of some sort. What did it take, I wondered, to be in the know of anything, to be an insider for a change? How come everyone walking around the gallery seemed to know one another and also their way around? They also knew the auctioneer, who was, at this very moment, talking to Fannie, the sweet widow who had wanted to go to the Amazon.

The "talk with the auctioneer" part of the event was highly encouraged. Thanks to this encouragement, most attendees were on a first-name basis with Kyle Brewster, whose implausibly bright teeth and swirls of bleached blond curls announced a phony for a nautical mile. As for Fannie, she was either a serious art connoisseur or was pulled toward Kyle by the sheer magnetism of the guy. This wasn't so hard to fathom. Between passing waves of "Wow, I like the new hair, Mrs. Carlson," and "Glad to see you again, Mr. and Mrs. Meyer," Kyle had everyone eating out of his rostrum in very short order. Innocents like Fannie, and starfuckers in particular, loved to be seen "talking to the auctioneer."

To his credit, Kyle had done his homework. Alastair, the God of All Insiders, explained that today's auction had been preceded by enrichment lectures, art viewing parties, wine-and-cheese tours of the gallery, and hands-on arts classes, presumably so that future bidders experienced, in the flesh, how frustrating it can be to hold a brush in your hand, stick it inside a bucket of paint, and proceed to create a painting that reminds people of something a hyena threw up.

Poseidon's Gallery was very inviting, though. The plush royal blue carpet that covered the meandering space was as good as walking on foam. Poseidon himself would have been proud to be so remembered, revered, and represented. For my part, I wanted to throw myself on the carpet, get a pillow, and go to sleep humming "Rhapsody in Blue." Gershwin wasn't the only one painted into a corner around here, though. Very reluctantly, Fannie let go of Kyle and ceded her place in line to a couple of newcomers.

"Isn't this wonderfully exciting?" she said, walking up us.

"Alastair," I said, "meet my friend, Fannie."

"How do you do, Mrs. . . . ?" Alastair said.

But if there was ever a buoyant mind in this gallery, it was Fannie's. Such was her excitement that she was unable to recognize any talk unrelated to her purpose here.

"Oooh, I have my eye on a Rembrandt," she cooed.

"Wouldn't you know it?" said Alastair, fanning himself with the paddle.

"Good luck to you, dears," Fannie said, before walking away.

The works about to be auctioned were, as Alastair pronounced them, "the genuine fakes," Rembrandts that could not be returned once you Googled the fact that Rembrandt could not be here because he was still hanging at the Rembrandt House Museum in Amsterdam.

"If you're that stupid," said Alastair, "you deserve to be scammed."

The audience packed, as the saying went, a house that could have been sold at twice the size. Mostly, I remember the fierce desire by those in attendance to be regarded as sophisticated collectors of fine art. And this was, perhaps, where Kyle Brewster excelled. Kyle showed extraordinary talent in his ability to read this hidden desire while also coming across as someone beyond the people in this room. He was very much the young auctioneer who intended to surpass this moment. But all that would come later, when he would tell another rapt audience, say, in Montreal, London, or New York, a few years down the road, "I started as an auctioneer at sea," just to get them laughing; to put them at ease by putting himself down just enough for everyone to loosen their ties and prepare to part with more substantial fortunes.

For now, though, people continued to trickle in, their faces painted with glee. Here it was, the opportunity of a lifetime to own art and to beat someone to it. There was cachet in that, wasn't there? In beating someone. And Kyle knew this. He understood only too well this innate desire that humans have to compete for fewer and fewer resources, to snatch and run off with anything dubbed "one of a kind."

"Here's a bidding tip," Alastair said, leaning into me. "If it's a mug and they sell it at the ship's boutique, chances are it isn't an original Chagall."

In all fairness to amateurs at sea, though, it was hard not to get infected by the prospect of "owning real art." (Is there any other kind?) For his part, Kyle Brewster continued to work the room and to hand out compliments until the very beginning of the auction.

PIRATES ON BOARD

"This is an excellent entrée into the world of art collecting," Kyle began.

Those were spellbinding words. Now I was glued to my seat. Whenever you want to impress, or to scam someone, just say the word *entrée*. French does that to people. Kyle went on to impress upon his rapt audience that this was to be a real-time, or continuous auction, by which he meant there would be activity throughout, thereby increasing the expectation: *Will I, or will I not, get the Rembrandt for five thousand dollars?*

A made-over race car driver came to mind as Kyle continued to explain the rules governing this particular game. Blond ringlets in disarray fell on features addicted to risk. As Alastair had predicted, Carla had forgotten to ask Kyle whether we were allowed to have our paddles. So we still had them. I knew that this spelled trouble, even if I could not yet say what kind.

"After the auction," Kyle went on, "*all successful bidders* will receive their COAs."

Was it me, or was this a subliminal message? Please raise your hand if you want to be unsuccessful. I don't know about you, but I would give up my chair to avoid being called an unsuccessful bidder, especially in front of all these people. But I digress. COA stood for Certificate of Authenticity. Except, few people at Poseidon's Gallery knew what this meant, precisely. By way of an aside, there are only two people in the world who have the last word on the authenticity of a Picasso. Those two were probably tied up in the Costa Brava, so they weren't traveling with us. It would be a safe bet to assume the same was true of Goya and Rembrandt, which is to say that the Certificates of Authenticity to be handed after the auction were probably printed on paper from Hobby Lobby.

And there was another catch. Because we were at sea, bidders were not able to get a serious appraisal on a given work, even if the works were, as Kyle claimed, "all originals and limited editions of the artists we're proud to represent."

Right before the bidding wars were to begin, Kyle went in for the kill.

"You buy art because it makes you happy. You buy art because it brightens your day. What you will take away with you today will be a reminder of the places where you've been and the bonds you have forged during this voyage. Ultimately," he said, pausing for effect, "there is *no price* you can put on that kind of happiness. Let the bidding begin."

The auction started with modern classics, Peter Max and Romero Britto, whose wild paintings were the stuff of nuns' nightmares. The couple of Chagall prints featured in the program went fast. For his part, Kyle kept raising and dropping the gavel on the rostrum to indicate that a particular bid had come to a close. Whenever he pronounced a painting SOLD, you sensed the electricity might set the gallery on fire.

By way of testing the savvy Kyle, Alastair raised his paddle midway through the Chagall auction.

"Smooth sailing, dearest," he smiled. "Play all you want."

At the mention of the name "Rembrandt" the auction reached a turning point. A hush fell over the room as Kyle described *The Card Player* in all the glory befitting a true original; except, of course, it wasn't.

"Notice the exquisite detail in the card player's hands," he said. "Pay special attention to the downcast eyes. Rembrandt was a true master of the shadow."

And with that little tidbit of artistic platitude, the bidding started in earnest.

"One thousand from the gentleman in the back," Kyle said.

For the first time, Fannie raised her paddle.

"Fifteen hundred from the lady in the front. Do I hear two thousand?"

"Yes."

"Thank you for your bid. Do I hear thirty-five hundred?"

We were off to the races. My hand was a shaking a little when I raised my paddle at forty-five hundred."

"Forty-five hundred from the lady in blue," said Kyle.

Now all eyes were on me. Why deny it? I felt as though I was the last contestant on *Who Wants to Be a Millionaire?* Who could ignore all this attention?

"Let's not get carried away, dearest," Alastair whispered in my ear.

To everyone in the room, he must have looked like my legal advisor. But now that I was on a mission, no one could stop me.

"Do I hear five thousand?"

Both Fannie and I raised our paddles at the same time. All of a sudden, the collective buzz turned into a collective gasp. Five thousand was the hammer price for the Rembrandt. Fannie's eyes were pleading with me. As for Kyle, he was salivating like a bloodhound.

"Ladies, is there a bid for six thousand?"

What to do? I looked in Fannie's direction and was met by a pair of sad gecko eyes. I was about to raise my paddle again when Alastair placed his hand firmly on my forearm.

"Are you mad?"

I shook my head.

Fannie was as determined to have the painting as anything. Still, I sensed we were approaching the limit of her bank account. Had this been real money, I might have blacked out. But somehow, because I didn't have a dime to my name, the whole thing felt like I was playing with Monopoly money. What if I needed a get-out-of-jail card?

Vamos, I said, raising my hand for one last round.

My bid was followed by echoes of "Wow," "Who is she?" and "She must be rich."

Shortly thereafter Kyle declared the auction closed. But as he was about to say: The Rembrandt sold to Ms. . . . , he realized he didn't have my name on his roster. The noticeable tightening of his jaw, followed by his abrupt departure, struck a different kind of note at the end of the auction. A stunned silence fell on the room when Kyle excused himself, but it was quickly replaced by the unmistakable whispers of gossip and intrigue. While he was gone, someone from his staff came out from behind the curtains and proceeded to hand out Certificates of Authenticity and to obtain shipping details from successful suckers. By the time Kyle came back out his eyes were glistening with rage.

"Excuse me," he said, his tone no longer affable. "May I have a word with you?"

"Oh, hello," I said. "You were great up there! Do you just *love* being an auctioneer?"

Apparently, his use for small talk had reached its expiration date.

"We don't seem to have your name on record," he said curtly.

"Are you sure?" I said. "I'm a passenger here."

"Throwing an auction is illegal," he said, raising his voice a notch.

"I'm so very sorry," I said, "but this is my first time. I guess you made it all sound so exciting . . . I just . . . got carried away."

"Did you?" he said, evenly.

Brute! I wanted to say. *Taking advantage of innocent widows.*

"Maybe you want to check in with Carla," Alastair put in. "She gave us the go-ahead."

"Carla?" he said. "I don't believe this. Carla!!"

Who knew? Who knew that the pirates on board wore such nice clothes? Or that they spoke knowledgeably and persuasively about art, and that while their smiling assistants poured the bubbly, they proceeded to rob people blind. No doubt Kyle Brewster had surpassed Jack Sparrow in *Pirates of the Caribbean*. But the real casualty of it all was Fannie. She was standing by herself in a corner by the entrance of the gallery; her head hung like a beat-up doll, so I went up to her to explain.

"You should have said something, dear," she said, on the verge of tears. "I really wanted that Rembrandt. He was Jim's favorite painter of all time."

"Fannie," I said. "I was just trying to save you some money. There are no Rembrandts around he—"

"Oh, Zoe," Fannie wailed to her friend, "the most dreadful thing just happened."

"What is it, Fannie?"

"She outbid me."

"I haven't the faintest of what you're talking about," said Zoe.

"The girl. The girl who came to sit with us the other night . . . She got the Rembrandt."

"Fannie, darling," said Zoe, turning to look at me. "I'm very sorry I got tied up. We'll get you a Rembrandt," she said, guiding her friend out. "There are more Rembrandts where that came from."

"That's what you get," said Alastair.

"What is that supposed to mean? I was doing her a favor."

"I hate to break it to you, dearest, but some people don't want to be saved. As far as she's concerned you're the biggest dream thief she's ever met. You need to stop playing Jesus to the lepers in your head."

By the entrance of the gallery the ship's two photographers were on hand, the better to snap photos of the recently mugged holding new art acquisitions that could be tweeted to friends with the following caption: "Can u b-lieve? Got Chagall 4 only $5K."

As for the so-called Rembrandt, given that I had not been prequalified, my bid didn't count. But unlike beauty pageants, where the second runner-up gets the crown if the winner turns out to be bulimic, there are no runner-ups in an auction. After having to void my transaction, Kyle was at sea without a flare. I'm pretty sure it crossed his mind to whack me with his gavel.

The whole episode was cringe-worthy.

LOVE'S ULTIMATE PURCHASE

After the bidding wars Alastair and I headed to the photo gallery, where candid shots of all passengers were pinned to a very, very long wall.

"You must contain yourself, dearest," Alastair said, by way of warning.

"Don't worry," I said. "I learned my lesson."

"You'll see many pictures of yourself on that wall. I promise you'll want to buy every single last one of them."

"Me? But I've hardly left my cabin. How could there be photos of me?"

"Trust me on this," he said. "You'll want to buy them so no one else can see how far your thighs can spread on a pool chair."

"You're making this up, Alastair."

"Have I lied to you yet?"

Sure as the next sunrise, there was a gaggle of passengers lined up along the picture wall. More than a few were giggling. Given what Alastair had just told me, it was safe to assume they weren't giggling at pictures of themselves. Some of them were pulling photos off the wall at a fairly rapid clip. The floating paparazzi who had taken these candid shots also doubled as cashiers. With half of the damage done, they were now ready to swipe passengers' credit cards in exchange for stacks of embarrassing photos—a kind of seaside blackmail.

Standing under the exit sign close to the end of the wall, I spotted Ethan, his eyes intent on a photo.

"I could *do* him," said Alastair, following my gaze.

"He's taken."

"Everyone can be seduced, dearest. The trick is to figure out what makes a person tick."

"Not everyone," I said. "The only thing I could be seduced into doing would be to eat a second chocolate croissant. And it wouldn't even count as a seduction because I already want it. But anyway, he's with that other guy."

"You mean Marco?"

"How do you know his name? Did you try seducing Marco?"

"Not my type."

"So how do you know his name?"

"Let's just say I *know*."

While we pondered seduction schemes Ethan walked up to us.

"What have we here?" said Alastair, leaning into him.

After a quick peek at the photo, Alastair pressed his lips together. It was obvious he was trying not to give anything away. Now I was curious.

"May I see it?"

Oh. My. God. Hair on fire didn't begin to describe it. It was a picture of me wearing the orange vest during the safety demonstration; a mass of unruly hair blowing across my face. I looked like someone who'd just seen a shark.

"That's me!" I said.

"So it is," said Ethan, smiling.

"What are you doing with it?"

"He's planning to bribe you," said Alastair.

"You can't have my photo," I said. "That's robbery."

"I just remembered . . ." said Alastair. "I forgot something in my suite."

Lying was like breathing to Alastair. The branded sunglasses casually resting on top of his head made him look like the seasoned traveler he was. He wasn't headed to his suite.

"Give it back," I said to Ethan.

"This one's mine," he said. "If you want a copy, they can print you another one right over there."

Having read the intention in my eyes, Ethan took a step back. Still, when I sprang forward to snatch it from his grip, the photo got ripped. Ethan clucked a few times.

"Now, *that's* assault," he said, playfully. "Don't go anywhere. I'm going to ask for another print."

"Where's Marco?" I asked, going after him.

"Do you always change the subject when people are trying to pay you a compliment, Valentina?"

"Is that why you're on this cruise?" I said. "To steal photos of strange women? Are you some sort of pervert?"

"The answer is no to both. I am *not* a pervert. And I don't steal photos of *beautiful* women. I was buying the photo to surprise you with it over dinner. As for why I'm on this cruise . . . after Marco's fiancée broke up with him, the only person who could stand to be around him was his old mate. It's my first time on a cruise, as a matter of fact."

"Mmm . . . I'm not buying what you're selling," I said.

The insinuating cut of his lips was even sexier when Ethan smiled. Ethan's voice was slightly animated, but not too much; there was an intensity underneath it that became even more pronounced when he lowered it to say, "Which part aren't you buying?"

"I'm not a mind reader," I said. "So I can't tell you which part. Something just smells . . . fishy."

Ethan was squinting now, the same way he'd been doing at safety training, as if trying to figure something out.

"I still have your chips," he said, changing the subject. "Maybe we can spend them at the next port? I hear Mykonos is a stunner."

Just then, Michael Coin's voice began piping through the speakers.

"Ladies and gentlemen, we regret to inform you that due to port authority concerns at our next port of call, we are being redirected to Istanbul."

What? How could this be? How could we miss Mykonos, where Greek gods and goddesses awaited us with turtle gyros by the beach? I felt sorry for the front desk staff. Waves of future discounts were headed in their direction, no doubt.

"I'll bet it's the strike," Ethan said.

"What strike?"

"Greece is always on strike," he said, as if he were Australia's ambassador to Greece.

My father would have liked Ethan. Anyone able to digest world news before his first sip of coffee had my father's vote. It was all the more impressive when you considered that we were adrift like fish in a Jacques

Cousteau film, and Ethan still had managed to be in the know.

"Maybe our captain thinks he's Columbus," I said.

"How's that?"

"On his way to the Indies, Columbus kept two sets of logs. Basically, he was lying to his crew to head off a mutiny. Maybe the captain knew all along that we weren't going to Mykonos."

"That's an interesting theory . . ."

"Don't *you* think it's a little suspicious? I mean, breaking it to us when there's nothing we can do . . . Anyway, who was your Christopher Columbus, the one whose statue is in every plaza, even though he gave everyone gonorrhea?"

"Hmmm, I think I liked it better when we were talking about spending your chips in Mykonos."

"But we're not going to Mykonos. It seems that due to a strike, we've missed our connection."

At this, Ethan frowned. But it wasn't a confused, dumbfounded frown—more the look of a great athlete who'd missed a couple of points and was trying to change his strategy mid-match. It was plain as tap water that I was dodging his invitations, even if I had no idea why. This much I knew: before getting tangled up in someone else's fishnet I needed to swim alone for a while. I also had to free myself from a few locked-down beliefs; the notion, for instance, that in a world designed for couples, being single was some kind of incurable disease.

And there was something else that spooked me. It seemed Ethan already had everything he could want. He had money to gamble. He had time to spare when his friend asked him to pack his bags and go cruising. He had a twin brother, and together they were heirs to a wine fortune. As far as I could tell, the one thing missing from Ethan's life was a woman. The problem with him was that he didn't seem interested in renting. Not even in lease-to-own. Whether he was aware of it or not, Ethan broadcast it for several nautical miles that he was ready to make love's ultimate purchase.

And me? I already had. And I wanted my money back.

"You should try the auction sometime," I said—a clumsy attempt at changing the subject.

"All fakes," he said. "I've got my eye on a real beauty."

On the way out, I whacked my knee on a low chair that was squarely on my path. Completely turned around; that's how I felt in the vicinity of Ethan.

A PINCH OF AUTHORITY

The racket at the front desk was worth a stop; the growing gathering left no doubt that someone was about to be preserved for easier transport.

This was the long and short of it. A woman had signed up for the cooking class with Chef Paolo and now, after getting the menu for what they were going to be making in the class, she wanted a full refund. The attendant at the front desk was trying to explain in a mysterious foreign accent that "Yez, mam," they could issue her a "reefund" for the class but not for the entire "cruz" as the woman was demanding. The girl's tone was so unconvincing that it did little, except cause the woman's indignation to escalate.

"I demand to see the captain," she said.

More than a few eyebrows were raised. People on their way to other places stopped dead on their tracks to see how this little fire in the kitchen was going to be put out. A more opportunistic passerby, on hearing the commotion, said to her friend, "I meant to sign up for that class. Maybe I can now." Apparently, the cooking class had been sold out since the day we set foot on the port of Piraeus. And if this skirmish went a certain way, there just might be room for one more in Chef Paolo's kitchen.

Her vacation had been ruined, the woman went on. Her injured tone and flared nostrils evinced that a great act of barbarism had been committed against her. Now that she had an audience, she was fortified and encouraged. How was she supposed to go back to Ohio and explain to her girlfriends, who were all foodies, by the by, that she had not been able to take the cooking class because she was allergic to grape leaves? Couldn't Chef Paolo change the menu from Dolmades to something else? At her mention of grape leaves I had a flash of Catholic school back in Caracas where the nuns offered us points for class participation. Now I felt the urge to participate; to raise my hand and say, "And I'm allergic to cactus!" How many points could I get for naming another leaf, a different species, or a brand-new allergy altogether?

By then, the ship's purser, a woman by the name of Lorraine, had emerged from behind the front desk the way sea creatures appear in horror films. Carrying her broad-shouldered self in full uniform, Lorraine intimidated. Had Lorraine commanded a regiment somewhere, the gold bars on the shoulders of her stiff, white uniform would have placed her somewhere in the rank of first lieutenant. Lorraine had a dispassionate stare that said, "I've pitched urchins overboard before." Before long, in the calm tone owned by those who have real authority, Lorraine proceeded to explain the options to the woman from Ohio, "Madame, we can give you a full refund for the class. You may learn to make stuffed grape leaves and impress your friends back in Ohio. Or you may disembark at our next port of call. It's up to you. Which one will it be?"

There was a sudden hush in the lobby. As people exchanged uncomfortable glances the woman walked away without another word. On the upside, there was now a vacancy in the class for aspiring chefs and opportunists.

"This is your chance," said Alastair, elbowing me in the ribs.

"My chance to what?"

"To get in the class!"

We were surrounded by people. So I did my best with a head shake and hoped no one thought I was having a seizure. But Alastair wouldn't have it.

"Come on, dearest! Larry and I signed up back in Athens. We'll drink by the bottle. It'll be a load of fun."

How to explain to Alastair that in the home of my childhood my mother used the fridge to store her perfumes and cold cream? Azucena and I grew up thinking that Estée Lauder made milk, which they did—body milk. And besides, the thought of being trapped in a floating kitchen with inebriated people wielding knives didn't sound all that appetizing.

"I'll think about it," I said.

Obviously, I wasn't going to think about it. The thing to tell Alastair was that "cooking" and "root canal" were synonymous to me. Except I'd been blessed with a mutant empathetic gene that practically dictated to me the words: Let them down easy. Sometimes I added the word *maybe*, in a last-ditch effort to soften a blow. That was how "No fucking way" often became "Maybe, I'll think about it." But I hadn't counted on foodies being such militant people.

"Have you no clue about how lucky you are?" Alastair asked. "Making Dolmas in Greece is the opportunity of a lifetime."

"Except, we aren't in Greece, are we, Alastair? We're floating in the middle of nowhere, and yet you're making it sound as though we're going to barbecue at the Parthenon with Apollo. That's not exactly the same thing."

"Oh, I get it. The splitting-hairs excuse. But since you bring up Apollo, have you checked out the chef?"

"He's probably illiterate."

FEAR OF CARVING

Erica Jong said women had fear of flying. By way of encouragement, my mother would have argued, "Erica, why limit your fears?" An otherwise sensible woman, my mother has always been fluent in the language of dread. Growing up, the things to fear multiplied whenever Azucena and I left the premises—my name for our house. For many years, crossing the street had the highest value on my mother's fear scale. Whenever we were about to cross a street, my mother would say, *Niñas, qué peligro*, and choked our tiny wrists as a maniac might a victim's neck. For good measure, she would add, "Most children don't see their fifth birthdays." And by way of clarification she would offer, "Parental lassitude," shaking her head in disapproval.

Sometimes her fears gave off sparks.

It was an unsuspecting maid from Colombia, a woman by the name of Neva, who brought yet another one of my mother's fears to light. By putting her wet hand inside a socket, Neva offered a full, if unwitting, demonstration about how electrical sockets were not supposed to work. From my point of view, had Neva listened to one of my mother's lectures about sparks, she might have been able to keep her own hair from getting charred. My mother wasn't so sure, though. In her opinion, there was no avoiding the accident. That's because my mother has always maintained that people of limited means cannot grasp certain basic concepts. She believed with all her heart that the concept of electrical sockets was a notion beyond Neva's grasp. As for Azucena and I, given that my mother didn't consider either of us "people of limited means," this meant only one thing. From the socket day forward, electricity was destined to become the favorite subject at our house, and my sister and I my mother's favorite audience. With all the talk about outlets and plugs, she ensured there would be no carefree living for us; then, or ever. There would be no careless plugging of hair dryers right out of the shower, no careless shaking of sparklers at Christmas, no mindless multitasking whenever sparks might be involved.

"A house is a minefield waiting to explode," my mother was fond of saying.

As for Neva, we had to grant this poor native of Colombia "best show" of my mother's worst nightmare. Neva had been washing clothes outside when she decided to come into the house to plug in the iron. Tuesdays were ironing days at our house. Because she was barefoot and her feet, as well as her hands, were wet, there was no unplugging her. I was the one who found her, screaming banshee-style as her hair continued to get charred and give off sparks. As miracles go, despite the terrifying jolts passing through her body, Neva still managed to yank the iron cord somehow. But maybe that, too, was an accident. For all the talk about "people of limited means," I didn't know what to do about it, either. I was nine years old at the time and the most I could grasp in that moment of shock was that there was a woman on fire in front of me, her body contorting maniacally.

Unfortunately, it didn't end there. Neva's misfortune all but guaranteed that future lectures would merely *start* with electricity, and that other potential threats and subjects would grow from there. Knives would cut. Oil would burn. Gas would terminate you.

As for school, it was my mother's unerring belief when she said goodbye to us in the morning that we really weren't going to school, but rather, to a mad scientist's day camp. Who knew what could happen? As a result, lest we fail school altogether, Azucena and I had some serious borrowing to do. We had to go around the schoolyard like beggars, asking other girls if we could go to their houses to work on dangerous projects. Gluing magazine cuttings to a piece of black cardboard for a project called "Collage" had to be done at my friend Cristina's house, lest we accidentally sniff the Pega Ega—our version of Elmer's Glue—and had to be rushed to the hospital for sudden spotting of the lungs. If it wasn't the looming grimace that betrayed she was looking at bad art, it was my mother's panicked stares that gave us a tad of performance anxiety.

Naturally, after turning in my collage and getting 20 points—the equivalent of an A—I was eager to show it to my mother. Most normal parents might have said, "It's beautiful, *hija*. I'll hang it next to the Picasso in the living room." Not my mother. After carefully examining the thing, front *and* back, she looked at me and said, "Where is the glue? Where did you get the glue, Valentina?" As I was to learn, not only could glue be sniffed, it could also stick! Now we had to be careful with the furniture. You could never be careful enough with school supplies. But nothing posed as much danger as wood carving. Why, oh, why, did she let me sign up for it?

In looking back, the wood-carving class will go down in my personal childhood chronicles as the biggest artistic misstep of all. That wood-carving class was the first time in my young life when I actually heard a little voice that whispered, "You have a calling. You're an artist."

On the first day of class our teacher gave demonstrations on different types of woods; their name, their pliability, and many other details that make wood, well, wood. At the end of the class he asked us to think about what we might wish to carve; a frog, a flower, a foot, whatever. He then gave us a list of materials. Sadly for me, the moment I saw the first item on the list I knew I would not be returning to class.

"X-ACTO knife" stood out like a loaded weapon.

Right below it, the teacher had listed the different kinds of blades you could attach to it, their level of sharpness, their grade, and so on. I knew it in my bones that the words *knife* and *blade* would not sit well with my mother. So rather than handing her the list when I got home, I just told her we needed to go to the art supply store to get "a few things."

"Things like what, *mi amor*?"

"Supplies, Mamá. Our teacher just called them supplies. You have so much to worry about with your patients. Let me worry about my own art supplies."

"You're always so considerate, Valentina," my mother said with a smile.

The bliss was short-lived. The moment I asked the store clerk if he had X-ACTO knives, my whole future as a mixed-media carver later to be shown at MoMA in New York city vanished before my eyes.

"Valentina, may I take a look at the supplies list?"

To this day I remain mystified. I don't know what she was thinking we would use to carve on wood. All I remember is that she was practically paralyzed when she saw the word *knife* on the list.

"You don't have to do it exactly as the teacher says," she encouraged. "Be creative."

Since when? Didn't we have to do *exactly* as the nuns said, lest we be whacked with a ruler and risk a severed pinky?

So I went into our P.O.W. closet—a claustrophobic rectangle where creativity was encouraged of Azucena and me—and proceeded to draw on the wood plank with some crayons my mother ended up buying me at the supply store. I think I drew a bird, or something. But still, who would have the nerve to return to a wood-carving class and tell the teacher, "This is my wood drawing. What do you think? A little more blue, perhaps?"

Years after the X-ACTO incident, after I had moved abroad, I went to see a therapist about the voices inside my head. Surprisingly, it took more than one session for this man to unravel my childhood and get the whole picture. Sometime during our last session, he trained his eyes pensively in my direction and said, "I understand now, about those conversations you keep having with yourself. Good luck to you, Valentina."

How to tell Alastair that knives were out of the question? How to say, for instance, "I once took a wood-carving class. But we carved with spoons."

LOOKING FOR CAVITIES

By the time that Mimi Fors and her husband began wooing me in their direction, Mimi already knew that my mother was a psychotherapist, that we were from Venezuela, and that I didn't like fish. It was frightening, the speed at which information traveled at sea. More troubling still was the fact that my inconsequential life was of any interest to anyone. Having been chained to the same chair for quite a while, I had very little of any interest to share, other than what I read in *Hola* magazine about debauched monarchs from Monaco and Spain. But, as so often happens to me when I'm busy asking and answering my own questions, I missed the point of this apparently gracious invitation entirely.

My antenna should have gone up from the first "we."

Mimi was petite and agile as a chipmunk. She had restless hands she could not keep still and was in the habit of nodding and smiling when people were talking to her, as if it was her job to encourage everyone she came across. When she told me that she was a dentist, I tried very hard to believe her. The hands were lithe enough, true. But how could this jittery creature keep a drill still inside someone's mouth while fixing a cavity? The thought of that rotating peg drilling into my gums made me squirm in my chair a little.

Mimi was married to Thomas, whom she observed eerily throughout dinner. When Thomas wasn't busy straightening objects (including other people's knives and forks), his eyes were fixed on people's mouths, an unnerving habit, I presumed, germane to his profession. Were neon bright teeth a prerequisite to his friendship? It sure seemed that way, which is why, on the evening I joined the Fors for dinner in the main dining room I made it a point to keep my mouth small for the duration of the meal. I spoke small, I chewed small. Mostly, I nodded, afraid that if I broke into a smile Thomas might run into the nearest supply closet and make me gargle with bleach.

These impromptu dinner invitations were a fairly common occurrence in the high seas. Someone might see you standing alone by the entrance of the dining room and say, "Would you care to join me for dinner?" Apparently, the days of assigned seating on cruise ships had died with Magellan. Choosing their dinner companions was how today's seafaring adventurers expanded their horizons. Usually, I had dinner with my mother, who was a wonderful deterrent to any kind of mingling. She and Azucena have been blessed with the kind of stares that make even the most gregarious of creatures begin to walk stealthily past in the opposite direction. I'm the one stuck with the stupid ingratiating smile, permanently fucked by my desire to give eye contact, which is how I ended up being taken for someone of a completely different persuasion.

By the time I took my seat at the Forses' table, there were two other people already there. Nicole was a lanky woman with supernatural boobs visibly on display that evening through a very, very low-cut aquamarine blouse. It would later surface that she was strung out on cocaine for the majority of the voyage, apparently the only remedy for her sea-borne claustrophobia. Nicole was there accompanying her friend Robyn because whoever was supposed to have come with Robyn had canceled at the last minute. This seemed to happen a lot, these last-minute cancellations. I, myself, would have gladly sent one of my neighbors in my place, had my mother not been so persuasive with the word *clinically*.

"Thomas simply adores exotic women," Mimi said, between bites of lettuce. "That's why he married me," she said. "I'm from Hawaii."

"Does he? Are you?"

The effort of keeping my mouth small was a bit of a strain. I was unusually tongue-tied.

Now that Mimi had put it out there that she was from Hawaii I searched her face for exotic features. So yes, in a little while—when she managed to keep her face still for maybe three, four seconds, to take a sip of water—I detected something in the cheekbones; the kind of cheekbones that have been cut with a tomahawk. So yes, there was something exotic to her face when it wasn't in movement. And the long black braid she wore over one shoulder made her vaguely resemble Pocahontas, a third cousin, perhaps?

During dinner Robyn told us about her work in New York. She worked for an art gallery in Brooklyn, she said, and started praising some mixed-media artist or other, someone I had never heard about. By then my natural cynicism was practically running on steroids. From the captain on down almost everything everyone said I considered suspect. Seagoing vacationers seemed to be on some sort of holiday from their back-home selves; not lying, exactly, but taking huge liberties with the truth, as if the fact that we were in the vicinity of whales made it all right to make their lives seem bigger than they were. At one point Robyn mentioned having lived in Europe and sighed in a way that made you think she had birthed a lovely child in some European meadow.

Throughout, Mimi nodded at Robyn encouragingly while Thomas's eyes shifted in the direction of Nicole's buoyant cleavage. In his defense, it took great restraint not to be taken in by such generosity. By the time the ice cream arrived, Nicole had excused herself at least a half dozen times. After each return, she smiled anxiously around the table while brushing the tips of her fingers against the tip of her nose. Thomas took the frequent homecomings to help her with her chair.

"Valentina," Mimi said, pausing.

The full measure of her undivided attention gave me a little jolt. This was obviously a rare occurrence, this pause of hers. The rare instance when Mimi was not nodding was outright strange. And then, she got it all out in one breath.

"Thomas and I were wondering if you'd care to join us for a party later tonight?"

"A party? What kind of party?"

"*All of you* are welcome," she said meaningfully. And still, I didn't get her meaning.

"I'm supposed to join my mother at Neptune's lounge," I said. "Is it okay if she comes along?"

At that point, Robyn did a half turn in my direction, almost involuntarily. "You're mom's a swinger?" she said. "Wow."

I must confess that until then I hadn't considered Robyn exotic. I could see it now, though. Everything is always a sparkler in retrospect. Nicole's red hair was cropped so short it resembled a helmet painted on her head. I supposed it might have passed for exotic somewhere in Planet Zombie. And maybe there was something to the green eyes set a bit too far apart on her face. I could definitely picture Robyn as the sadist in a vampire film. Was that exotic? Maybe. Maybe not. Who was I to say? I wasn't a swinging dentist from Hawaii looking for cavities to explore.

tHE MARRIAGE BUG

After several days at sea people started to get cranky.

We were now midway through our detour on our way to Istanbul. Besides cranky some passengers were beginning to get a little emotional as well. Istanbul was either someone's dream come true—oh, the magic carpets at the Grand Bazaar—or someone's worst nightmare—we'll be tortured in that Turkish jail in *Midnight Express.*

While my mother was at the spa and Larry was busy putting out some crisis or other back in San Francisco from the comfort of his suite, Alastair and I headed to one of the pool decks; he, to catch up on email and I to finish my Ellen DeGeneres memoir. Hard as Alastair and I tried, though, it became practically impossible to stay focused on our intended leisure activities. There was no ignoring the couple arguing next to us.

"I can't believe you're not getting out in Istanbul, Chuck. What am I supposed to do?"

Chuck was resting—or trying to rest—on one of the lounge chairs. From where I was, I could see a pair of huge tennis shoes in bright, lime green hanging over the edge of the chair. He was longer than the chair by at least a foot. I wondered if his ankles hurt.

"Well . . ." Chuck said, treading carefully, "maybe you can go on a tour."

"Why do I have to go a tour when you could come with me?"

"Tracy," he said, in the anxiously solicitous voice of a man for whom staying alive depends on certain conditions, "I just don't . . . trust those Arabs."

"Chuck, you can be so ignorant sometimes. Turkish people are not Arabs."

"Then why are their women covered up with togas? Explain that."

I couldn't see Tracy's face, but I could see the mass of blond curls bouncing as she shook her head. If she wasn't already there, she was approaching exasperation.

Just then, Alastair set his phone on the side table and made a little moving gesture with his fingers on his left palm. I had not a clue what he meant by this, so I mouthed a silent, "W-H-A-T?"

"Should we W-A-L-K?" he mouthed back, his fingers walking again on his left palm.

I didn't care one way or the other, so I shrugged.

"I can't believe you just said that. God! I can't stand this."

"Can't stand what?" Chuck asked, sincerely dumbfounded.

"Don't play dumb, Chuck. You know perfectly well what I'm talking about. I know exactly what you're doing. You're sitting there calmly, looking reasonable just to make me out to be some kind of hysterical woman, which, by the way, I'm *not*. You know *I'm not that kind of woman*, Chuck. So why are you doing this to me?"

Ever so slowly, the mass that was Chuck sat up and leaned carefully into her. His bright orange shirt looked brighter still under the glaring sun.

"Can you tell me precisely *how* I'm making you out to be hysterical? The only thing I remember saying is that you could go on a tour."

"So why did you come? Why did you come on this cruise? It's like you just . . . ugh . . ."

"As far as I recall, you said it would be fun to go on a cruise. No one said anything about hanging out with a bunch of Arabs."

"I just told you: they're *not* Arabs. Ugh . . . Why are you being so dense? Are you trying to get me to jump overboard?"

"Tracy, I swear, I'm not. It's just . . . that . . . look at me. I'm six feet tall and I have a red beard. Whom do you think they're going to shoot first when things start getting out of control?"

At this, Tracy inhaled and exhaled deeply through her nose. She was trying, and failing, to control herself.

"Fine. Fine! I don't care. I don't care if you come or not."

"Tracy . . ." Chuck said, not unreasonably. "If you don't care if I come, why did you ask me to come in the first place?"

"Maybe if you didn't wear fluorescent clothes you wouldn't be such a target."

"So now you're admitting it!" Chuck said.

"Admitting what?"

"That I might be a target."

"Ugh . . . I should have stayed home and watch the Food Network. You are *such* a turd!"

As Tracy stomped away, Alastair shot me a sidelong eye-roll. I was suddenly grateful to be here with Alastair reading a book and not "in a relationship." I used to tell Max that marriage was overrated. Max had always insisted that it wasn't marriage; that when you found the right person these marital fender benders simply would not occur. After Max's wordless departure, I had my doubts about handing out any philosophy credits.

For a short while after Tracy left, Chuck buried his beard in both hands, as if asking himself, What did I do wrong? After a while, he, too, got up and walked away. Despite the fact that he was a huge guy, his pitiful stride made him look defeated.

"Poor guy," I said. But I don't think Alastair heard me. He was busy playing with his phone.

Had I driven Max out of his mind with my not infrequent verbal detours about having to live in Arizona?

But we just sprayed for bugs, Max. That spider was the size of my fist. And by the way, I'm over raising Rosemary's Babies in the desert. It's probably why it's so hot in here; because Satan lives just down the street. And I'm so over all these shrubs! How can you stand it?

"Oh, Max . . . I should have kept my mouth shut. It wasn't that important."

"Who are you talking to?" Alastair asked.

" *Was* I talking . . . ?"

"Just promise me one thing, dearest."

"What?"

"Promise never to become a nag."

"What's a nag? Is that some sort of bug?"

"You could say that. Think of a nag as a marriage cootie."

"As in VD?"

"As in VD," said Alastair.

DATE AND SWITCH

"So, tell me, Alastair, is that why you gave up on women?"

"Who said anything about giving up, dearest? I'm just taking a short break. But yes, nagging is almost a serious an offense as not having a sense of humor."

"I'm being serious, Alastair."

"Shall I spell it out for you, then?"

"I'm all ears."

At this, Alastair set his drink down and his eyes switched to full-on mischief mode. I wasn't sure what I was going to get by way of an explanation.

"Picture this," he began, with great theatrical flourish. "It's a lovely Sunday morning in San Francisco. I'm at my place having coffee in the kitchen nook by the window, and what is that I hear? Little steps walking in my direction. Where am I? Ah, yes, I'm at my house. Sooner rather than later I see my girlfriend standing in front of me. Let's call her Polly. On that lovely morning, Polly's wearing a matching flannel top and bottoms with tons of little blue rabbits—the kind of dizzying pattern you see on the Cartoon Network. Polly surveys the room in a flash, and after assuring herself that I am, in fact, happy, she looks benevolently at me and says, 'How long have you been up, Alastair?' The seemingly innocent question comes with a sweet smile, which, silly me, I confuse with 'I'm glad to see you after seven hours of sleep.' And then Polly goes, 'Remember you promised me to go antique shopping today?' Do you know what happens after that, dearest?"

"Let me take a wild guess. You sprint forward toward the counter and stab Polly in the heart with the butter knife."

"I'm afraid it's a lot more tragic than that, dearest. Before falling facedown on my cereal and dying of an intracerebral hemorrhage, I take one last breath and call 911. I die screaming to an operator from an overseas call center: 'Zombies. There are zombies in my house!' And the operator says: 'Mr. Doogliz? Am I speaking with Mr. Doogliz?'"

"I get it. But not all women are like Polly. Some women I've met in the States are just the opposite, in fact. They like to wear men's clothes, instead of rabbity pajamas."

"What a coincidence," said Alastair. "I've met those, too. Those women won't get upset if you don't like their pumpkin spice cookies. They want to fry your balls for breakfast, instead. Wheel me to the nursing home, already."

"So you've framed yourself inside a box. Is that it? How about the real reason you don't like women?"

Alastair started to respond, trying to concoct another outlandish illustration for my benefit, but then he thought better of it. His sensitive side, though it rarely surfaced, made Alastair look incredibly fragile. He pretended to fiddle with his phone. But that stage smile he always wore was about to shatter.

"I'm going to get another drink. You want one?"

"Ask the bartender if she can make a mojito," I said.

After a while, Alastair returned with two drinks in hand, and handed me a tall glass that looked like a lab experiment.

"She might have overdone the mint," Alastair said. "No mojitos in Romania is my guess. Now where were we?"

"You were about to tell me why you're done with women . . . for now."

"Ah, yes. That."

"It's not that interesting a story," he said. "But since you insist. I know you already know part of it. I overheard you and Larry the other night."

I was about to deny it, to defend Larry. But I was afraid Alastair might change his mind. So I let it go.

"On the night my dad told my mom *not* to go on the road because of a dangerous snowstorm, my mom nagged and nagged, kept busting his balls, until my dad simply gave up from sheer exhaustion. After a while, he started loading the car. You could tell he didn't want to do it. So I gave him a hand. My sister Hannah went up to her room. She was very sleepy. Hannah didn't want to go on the trip at all. After dad and I finished loading, I went to get Hannah. Finally we got in the car. It was really, really dark, and the snow was blowing so hard you could barely see two feet in front of you. But my mother kept saying that we'd make good time, and all those things that pesky people say to keep proving their point even after they've won the argument. The snowstorm was much worse than we had seen on TV. And the next thing you know, Hannah is on my lap. When I came to, I thought she was asleep. I liked Hannah. I miss my little sister, sometimes . . ."

"So you blame your mother."

"Blame her?" he said, his voice returning to its more familiar, sarcastic register. "You're obviously OD in pop psychology, dearest. Life's a tad more complicated than that."

"Don't forget I'm the daughter of two Freud fanatics," I said. "Or that I was brought here under false pretenses."

"Yes. I wonder what Mamá bear would have to say about our little Hallmark commercial."

"She'd probably lecture you on Sodom and Gomorrah," I said.

"Now that's my kind of party," said Alastair. "Turning into a salt sculpture after a great orgy isn't a bad way to go. Not. At. All."

MY THEORY OF EVOLUTION

No! Don't leave me, Alastair! You can't go just yet. I see Ethan walking my way. Alastair. Alastair. Please come baaack.

By the time I spotted Ethan it was too late to call Alastair back; he was almost to the pool exit. After he left, I had planned to move somewhere in the shade. So Ethan caught me between intentions—a woman undecided between two chairs, holding an Ellen DeGeneres book in one hand and a blue pool towel in the other.

With a little help from sea breeze and sea salt, Ethan's hair had acquired some waves, which, had he been a woman, would have required real money at a salon to get them to look so natural. My hair, on the other hand, was precariously pinned to the top of my head. I half-expected Ethan to ask, "Have you made up my room yet?" But no. What he had in mind was closer to "How come you're not in my room yet?"

"Good book?" he said, glancing sideways at the cover.

Was that a trick question? Was Ethan trying to figure out if I leaned in Ellen's direction? Did people from Australia even know who Ellen DeGeneres was?

"She's very funny," I said.

The wind was blowing really hard, so I reached for the railing to avoid falling on top of Ethan and scarring his perfectly bare chest with the edge of Ellen DeGeneres's memoir. During the near stumble, one of the straps of my dress fell off my shoulder, so I had to let go of the towel to put it back. Ethan was wearing sunglasses, which meant I couldn't see his eyes. But I will say that the subtle moves of his head reminded me of a laser in a James Bond film—it scanned everything within a short radius; not in a leering kind of way, but in a laser kind of way. And who wants to be scanned by a laser? Lasers can spot pimples. Lasers can tell if you need to wax your upper lip, or if your eyebrows need plucking. What I wanted now, more than anything, was to take a salt-free shower and to dry my hair.

These were the times when I became truly angry with Max. Why did he have to leave? If he were to come back, all my problems would disappear and I wouldn't have to be standing here trying to avoid shallow conversation in a rising tide with some guy from a former thug colony. All the more depressing was the color of the sky. It was blue, blue, crystal blue, a radiant day if there ever was one; a day pregnant with hope, alive with possibility, and why was I stuck here with the wrong guy?

I've always had an eye for guys graying at the temples, which, contrary to popular cliché, has nothing to do with wanting to marry a paternal figure and all that fizz. If Alastair's hetero-paralysis stemmed from an unfounded fear of rabbity pajamas, my fear of men like Ethan went all the way back to Darwin and the origin of species. Whenever I saw a man like Ethan—a walking testosterone bomb at the height of his reproductive prowess—I was overcome by visions of legions of children, except, these weren't the same kinds of visions that affected women, who on looking at pictures of babies, transmogrified into milk spigots. My visions of children involved feelings a bit more primal still. They were closer to hallucinations.

"What are you looking at, little person?" I would ask.

Standing in front of the toilet would be my child, at four years of age, or around the time when they've begun to fathom the endless possibilities with which to ruin your life.

In discovering his mother, little person would look up with glee and giggle at the water swishing around the toilet.

At this, I would peer into the bowl to see what caused little person such happiness. And what is it that I see? Are those my car keys? Oh, my God! There's my driver's license! Wait, is that my new lipstick?? *¡Ay Dios Mío!* Or, to say it in English: What the fuck?

"Are you having a good time?" Ethan asked.

"How about you?" I said.

A major offer was coming my way. I could sense it. I needed to riffle through the excuse bank inside my brain. And I needed to do it fast.

"You mind if we sit for a minute?" Ethan said.

Shit! I'm too late. I don't have an excuse. I should have left with Alastair.

"Sure," I said, grabbing my former chair.

Ethan's tan was so even I thought it had come from a spraying hose. But no. My earlier assessment of his forearms being forged by hanging from rocks turned out to be accurate. When he wasn't at work in his office in Brisbane (pronounced BRIZ-BON), he was rock climbing somewhere or other with his twin brother, Jake. Together they owned a winery in Adelaide that had been bequeathed to them by their late father.

"Mostly Sauv Blanc. Some Voignier," he said.

At first I thought he might be talking about his other relatives, until Ethan explained they were grapes called "varietals." It was probably the vapid stare that gave me away. Whatever they were, the subject of how crushed grape juice ended up in a bottle bored me to tears, so I changed the subject to something a little more thrilling.

"Where did you learn to gamble?" I asked.

"Dad. He loved taking risks. Jake and I learned to play poker before we learned how to read. How about you?"

Gambling? Money? Taking chances? Taking chances with money? I'd just as soon sit naked on a cactus.

"My gambling experience dates back to a certain roulette table," I said. "That was my first time ever."

"And you won," Ethan said.

I could feel it approaching. Something was building. The more we talked, the closer we would get. Ethan and I didn't have a lot in common, except, perhaps, that we were both from different countries on our way to different countries than our own, and the fact that both of us seemed like decent people. But let's face it. We were sitting out in the sun sipping something frothy, one of us with a bare chest that brought to mind push-ups, though not on a gym bench. We were talking in circles about nothing because we both knew that the moment was fast approaching when the tiny electric waves being passed back and forth between us were going to have to be plugged somewhere. There would come a moment when one of us would make the move toward, at least, kissing.

What I felt for Ethan out on that deck was not lust, though. I'd be lying if I said I wasn't at least curious to explore the rugged terrain in front of me. But my attraction was closer to gratefulness, the way you're grateful for a glass of milk, which is never as delicious as the cookie with the melted chocolate on the side.

What about just conversation? I asked myself. *How about just tanning and no sex? Or, how about sex with a condom? And then what?*

What came to mind after Ethan peeled off the sundress I was wearing and pulled the strings of my bathing suit was a short-circuited fantasy filled with visions of microscopic gaps through which eager sperm swam faster than Michael Phelps at the Olympics until one, the enterprising one who had done more laps, would get to the other end and yell: GOLD! And what was worse, now that my body was issuing the first warnings of curtain call it would be my luck to do both: get pregnant *and* give birth to a sea monster. Except in my fantasy they were triplets.

I was in a kind of prison. A less troubled person might argue that people in prison don't care who they have sex with. But given that my prison was of my own making, I could be as selective as I pleased. Because it's never the sex, is it? It's the next morning you have to worry about. That was the side conversation I was having with myself when Ethan asked me about dinner. I was of two minds at the same time. I wanted to say, "I'd love to have dinner!" At the same time, there was a dry lump in my throat the size of a walnut that made my answers get stuck.

How about a vibrator? Now *that* was a liberating thought. Except that, given my financial situation, I'd have to sell my shoes to spare some change on economy size. And what woman you know wants to throw good money after bad on an economy-size dildo?

"Did you say something about dinner, Ethan?"

"Yes. I asked you if cared to join me for dinner tonight?"

"Uh . . . Hmm . . . What's your cabin number? I'll let you know as soon as I clear something up with my mom."

MASTER YOUR GAG REFLEX

Her name was Nadja. She was from Romania. A large photo of Nadja pointing a long, sharp sword to the tip of her outstretched tongue had been posted on various marquees around the ship. A smaller version of the picture was included in the activities calendar that was placed nightly on our beds. People were talking about Nadja as if they had been her neighbors in Romania, as if they *knew* her in the biblical sense.

On the morning of the day when Nadja was to perform, while my mother and I were having a leisurely breakfast on the veranda, we overheard the couple in the table next to ours.

"Nadja got started at Cirque," said the wife.

"But she loves cruise ships best," said the husband.

Who were these people? And who was this Nadja? Who makes a living sliding steel down her throat dressed in a striped corset? What if she had to sneeze while swallowing that thing? Or had an urge to cough? All of a sudden I wanted rum with my orange juice.

It wasn't difficult to do; to imagine the conversations after her act.

"How do you do it Nadja?"

Obligingly, Nadja would say to the man salivating in front of her, "Oh, repetition is key. You keep sticking it back there until it fits."

"I got something for you to swallow," the man would say.

"Gag me with a spoon!" That's what *I* wanted to say.

"What time is the sword swallower?" My mom was curious now.

"I can't believe my life has come to this!"

The moment the words left my mouth I regretted them. I wasn't in the mood for more lectures about moving on.

"Come to what?" said my mother, archly.

"Hmm, nothing. I was just thinking about what to wear. That's all."

"Apparently, sword swallowing is so dangerous, Nadja is doing only one show."

"So you've fallen for it, too?" I said, staring at my mother in disbelief.

"What are you talking about, Valentina?"

"You're calling her Nadja, like the rest of the people here; like she's your best friend."

Inhaling deeply through her nose, my mother looked at me as if I were a textbook case. Soon, very soon, I expected naval orderlies in white to yank me from my chair and into a straitjacket. But I was not to be rewarded with being taken away from this oceanic nightmare. Instead, Michael Coin's voice reached us from afar.

"Ladies and gentlemen, please don't forget that tonight we have the incomparable Nadja, our sword swallower, at the Odyssey Theater at seven thirty. See you at the show!" he sang, and hung up whatever device he used to short-circuit our peace of mind.

Ha! As if anyone could forget Nadja was performing tonight.

Poor Homer. At least the builders of this boat had had enough sense not to call the theater *The Iliad* and finish whatever was left of the Etruscan civilization. But how dumb of me to indulge these pretentious literary musings. A mere mention of Homer at the Odyssey Theater was sure to sink me into the depths of despair. The moment someone told me that they, too, loved Homer Simpson I'd do a nosedive into the Majestic Mediterranean.

WARNING SIGNS AT THE ODYSSEY THEATER

Warning:

There may be some frontal nudity in tonight's act. If you were born anywhere near the state of Nevada, you may wish for more nudity. However, if you have ever been in the vicinity of Utah, or have any religious inclinations, you may wish to consider our many other entertainment options this evening. If you're French, *votre attention s'il vous plait*: refrain from inviting Nadja to join you for a threesome.

Warning:

Owing to a typographical error by our team member from the Czech Republic, the words *weld* and *lewd* have been transposed in tonight's program. We apologize for the misunderstanding.

Warning:

Due to the dangers involved in sticking sharp blades down your throat, we ask that you refrain from flash photography this evening. It may cause Nadja to gag, or worse. Should an accident occur, we may be forced to take legal action against the flashing party.

Warning:

We had hoped for classier entertainment during this voyage. But the gymnast who was to perform tonight sent her regrets after landing the job of her dreams at Cirque du Soleil in Montreal.

Warning:

If you happen to be male and have any blood coursing through your veins, you may feel the urge to ask your companion for oral sex later this evening. We strongly encourage you to refrain from this as it may impact your ability to enjoy the rest of your vacation.

Warning:

In order to enjoy tonight's performance it is necessary to have prior knowledge of strip joints so that Nadja comes off smelling like a rose by comparison.

Warning:

In some interviews with critics, tonight's performer has been known to use the following words to describe her act: slides easier, down your throat, lubricant, distended throat muscles, cocky, swallow, come, and come again.

Warning:

Despite the fact that tonight's performer shares a name similarity and country of origin as the famous Olympian Nadia Comaneci, the resemblance ends there. We apologize if this is whom you thought you were going to see.

Warning:

Due to the challenges involved in sliding steel down your throat there will be only one performance tonight. To make up for this inconvenience, Neptune's lounge will remain open after midnight.

Warning:

Tempting as this might be, we strongly encourage you to refrain from trying this act at home or anywhere on the premises.

$\Pi = 3.1416$

Does everyone remember the first time they heard of pi? When I was a high school girl in Venezuela, Profesor Platas—the only male teacher in our all-nuns school—wrote this on the chalkboard: $\Pi = 3.1416 \infty$.

These days, whenever I see a trendy restaurant's menu written in chalk, I remember Profesor Platas. I was never into math. But math was into me. It was one of those subjects for which you have skill, and also happen to dislike. I wanted to have the skill to be a painter, but I was terrible at it. So bad was I that the art teacher saw it fit to call my mother one day to tell her how hopeless I was, and to please guide me in a different direction. It wasn't that I didn't understand color, she said. The problem was that I lacked perspective. Can you blame me if after so much artistic discouragement math became the object of my affection? Math offered many rewards, the chief one being that I rarely had to study.

You survived forty-three years with yourself, Max? Why not forty-four? Please explain this to me: how did you come to the realization that forty-four would not be worth your time?

Did you expect too much of marriage? Did I expect too much of you? But what I find really, really troubling is this: what does it take to successfully deceive someone into believing you are who you say you are? What percentage of the time did you have to lie in order for me to believe that we were happily married? Was it something inconclusive, like 15 percent? Or were you lying, say, half the time? We're not making any progress, are we, Max? As long as I keep looking at you through the eyes of a statistician, I'm going to stay stumped. If I were to look at this differently, say, through the eyes of a philosopher, I might get some real answers. Now I can ask you, not "What percentage of the time did you have to lie?" but "What exactly did you take away from me by leaving?" Was it the chance to talk to someone for a couple of hours every night who was not who he said he was?

Please forgive me for saying that sometimes, many times, I felt like a woman shouting, "Operator, operator!" with the hope of talking to a real person at the other end of the line. And that's where we are now, Max. Or, rather, that's where I am. You left me with a pain in the gut and the antidote nowhere to be found. I want to attack what you did head-on, but there is no quantifying pain, no clear governing principle that can connect the forces that are pulling at someone who is pulling apart from the inside; no one system that can tally the fragments of hurt, or chart the labyrinthine turns a person might take in order to offload it. Because it hasn't been invented, has it, an instrument that can accurately measure what it means to be truly disheartened? Even if we do have the gadgets that allow us to chart the ups and downs of a heartbeat. So we are united now, Max, in this shared defeat.

I once made love to a guy who pushed an imaginary lock of hair from the pillow. I say imaginary because my hair was very short at the time, which is to say, there were no locks on that pillow—at least not visible to the naked eye. I don't know who, or what, he was making love to, probably to absence; to whomever he missed, someone who had either moved on or moved away. And when I asked, "Who was she?" he said, "What is it with women?"

I remember sitting perfectly still on that bed. Whenever I smell imminence—say, a fire; a glass vase too close to the edge; a snake—I keep still. With any luck, the thing might miss me.

But suicide is different. Suicide is infinite, like pi. Even after all these years I still can't wrap my head around the fact that the next number is never going to be the last.

Monday, Monday, Can't Trust That Day

"When is the midnight buffet?" someone asked.

As if Nadja had not been enough to fill our plates, now we had to get stuck behind Tommy Bahamas' retarded brother in a floating theater.

Why, the midnight buffet was at five in the afternoon, I was tempted to say. *You missed it! Everyone knows that the word* midnight *is just a gimmick to make it sound more interesting.*

Mercifully, with the promise of more food, the long line soon began to move at the speed of growling stomachs. Near the entrance of the theater I spotted Robyn. She squeezed through the crowds and made it a point to come over to say hello. She was going over to Neptune's, she said. Would she see me there later tonight? I wasn't sure what to say. I had more pressing concerns tugging at my mind, the chief worry being introducing Robyn to my mother. What if Robyn said, "You missed a load of fun at the swingers' party?" Then what? How would I explain to my mother that she had spent all this money to bring me here, only for me to hang out with undesirables ready to pump their friends' hollows while strangers watched?

In addition to her training, my mother has a very sharp nose, which has always allowed her to smell smuttiness the way certain dogs can smell drugs. Euphemistically, my mother refers to slutty women as undesirables. I'm always on the verge of correcting her; tempted to tell her that it's exactly the opposite, that in certain circles slutty women are *very* desirable. So rather than introducing her to Robyn, I opted for rudeness.

"Mamá, weren't you going to finish that book tonight?"

Afterward, Robyn and I walked away together and headed to Neptune's. On the way there I asked her where her friend was, to which she said, "Nicole isn't feeling very well."

Too much cocaine, huh?

This was the question at the tip of my tongue. I wasn't trying to be nosy or anything. Mainly, I was curious as to how anyone got cocaine past the German shepherds at TSA. But my curiosity got turned around by a rug. The rugs placed at the entrance of each elevator announcing what day of the week it was continued to puzzle. What was with reminding people on vacation that today was MONDAY? What if, on entering the elevator, someone had a flash of guilt and said, "It's Monday! I should be in the office and not here sipping blue drinks at eight in the morning."

So instead of asking Robyn about lines of cocaine, I asked her about the MONDAY rug.

"Why do you think they put these by the elevators? Or at all? Isn't that like shooting themselves in the foot?"

"*My* guess," she said, "is so that people don't get disoriented."

Speaking of which, that night Robyn was wearing a formfitting black dress with a silver tic-tac-toe pattern stitched across the front. The temptation to make a move on her torso was very real. *My* guess was that the disorienting experience of playing tic-tac-toe vertically and on a tight dress wasn't going to be corrected with a stenciled rug, no matter what day of the week it announced.

"That's a different dress," I said.

"I know," she said. "I'm into with tic-tac-toe!"

"Really?"

Neptune's was very crowded that night. We made our way through the lounge and right away spotted Larry and Alastair holding court toward the back. A few lounge chairs had been rearranged to accommodate the small group of friends gathered around them. Alastair motioned for us to join them and we soon became part of the lively group.

As Robyn and I were sitting down, the singer from the Philippines hopped onto the stage to an encouraging round of applause. On seeing her, my first thought was that she had run away from the circus. The blood-red lips and the tight black leather shorts over the fishnet stockings made it seem as though she had stolen a random set of clothes during a rushed midnight escape. And yet, nothing garnered more attention than her singing "Piano Man" with a lisp.

Fing uth a fong I'm the Piano man
Fing uth a fong tonight
And the piano, it founths like a carnival
And the microphone fmellths like a beer
And they fit at the bar and put bread in my jar
And fay, "Man, what are you doing here?"

My thoughts exactly. What is *she* doing here? I had someone new to pity. His name was Billy Joel.

CIRCUS LIFE: A DOCUMENTARY

We had been drinking martinis and making jokes about Nadja's performance when in walked Nadja, followed by Marco. She had put on a jacket over her striped corset to come to the lounge. Marco, like every other guy on formal night, was wearing a tuxedo.

"Speak of the devil," said Alastair, his eyes gleaming toward the new arrivals.

Robyn shot him a look through those disconcerting vampiric eyes of hers. For his part, Larry had positioned himself in the direction of the band, but I had the impression that his mind was elsewhere. For one, he was staring at his drink, his gangly limbs almost swallowed by the capacious lounge chair.

"Be right back," said Alastair and left us there to enjoy each other's company. He then proceeded to station himself behind Marco and Nadja, the better to overhear their tête-à-tête. So *this* was how uncertain knowledge was gained, through strategic positioning.

While Alastair was busy playing spy I talked to Robyn, who told me I had missed a great party with Mimi and Thomas. How to make small talk about a swingers' night out? I didn't know what I didn't want to know. But still, I was very curious. There was a brief short-circuit between my brain and my tongue while I reshuffled some questions in my mind. Asking about specifics might be considered rude. So I riffled through other options. Who went first? Or, What was it like doing it with someone like Mimi, who offered so much feedback? Did she nod while you and Thomas were together? Or did she shake her head in disapproval? Obviously out of my depth, I opted for Googling "orgy etiquette" when I was back on land, and decided to ask Robyn about Brooklyn instead.

"I used to live in New York," I said, casually.

"Whereabouts?"

"Brooklyn Heights."

"Brooklyn's changed a lot in the last few years," she said. "It's like . . . hipster central."

"Really? And when did you live in Europe?"

"Couple of summers ago. I worked at a vineyard in the Loire Valley. How about you? Was it Argentina you're from?"

Here we go again! Has anyone seen a world atlas around here?

"Venezuela," I said.

"What's it like down there?"

Hmm, where to start? Should I shock her with the knowledge that Angels Falls is fifteen times taller than Niagara Falls? Nah! She wouldn't believe me. Maybe I should I tell her about the Venezuelan poodle moth, a most unreal-looking creature; as if a teeny velvet poodle had mated with a flying rat. Maybe not. *Animal Planet* doesn't begin to compare with working at a vineyard in the Loire Valley. Or perhaps I should tell her about the new express kidnappings, where thieves take you to an ATM and empty your bank account in less time than it takes to whip up a milk shake at McDonald's. Hmmm, the word *kidnapping* is a little dicey . . . it may dampen her vacation mood. I know! I'll tell about Isla de Plata, an Eden of shimmering sand you'd swear has been sprinkled with silver glitter. Because isn't that what all of us secretly long for, a little escape? Wasn't that what all these people were doing here, buying a little bit of packaged majesty between Netflix binges?

In the end, I didn't have to tell Robyn anything. Alastair was fresh from his snooping expedition and longed to tell us all that Marco Mangini was a famous film director from Sydney.

"Never heard of him," said Robyn.

She was leaning into Alastair's phone screen, and in the semidarkness of the lounge I caught sight of a tattoo on the inside of her arm that reminded me of the doodles I had done in math class back in Caracas.

"Do you buy it?" I asked.

"Which part, dearest?"

"That he's a film director in Sydney."

"I Googled him," said Alastair.

"And?" said Robyn.

"Look," said Alastair. "That's him."

And there he was, Marco Mangini, a trail of films to his credit. In our defense, due to the fact that he was from Australia, we had not heard of a single one. It's also possible that his work had never crossed an ocean because it wasn't any good.

"What about Nadja?" Robyn asked.

"What *about* Nadja?" echoed Alastair.

That's how easy it was to slip into gossip mode.

"What did he want with her?" I asked.

"He wants her to do a screen test for a documentary he's working on."

"A documentary?" Robyn said, almost spitting her drink.

"Not just any documentary," said Alastair. "But a documentary about circus life."

"Very interesting . . ." said Robyn.

"Swallowed a sword, lately, dearest? I swallow a sword all the time."

At this, Alastair picked up the little bamboo sword that held the olives in his martini and stuck it down his throat.

PLAYING WITH FOOD

The food entertainment on the ship was themed. This is why we were about to stuff hundreds of grape leaves with rice. We had to make something Greek because the ship was making a couple of stops somewhere in the Aegean Sea. I got that. What I didn't fully grasp was food as entertainment. This wasn't just because I grew up under the watchful eye of a couple of Freud freaks with an aversion to TV. Or because as a result of my parents not getting the TV memo I never got to binge on the Food Network shows everyone in the cooking class kept raving about. Talk about feeling like the dullest knife in the drawer.

The reason that food as entertainment was hard on my stomach was that growing up, my paternal grandmother used to force-feed us while making constant references to the locust.

"Who's locust, *abuela*?"

"*M'ija*," she'd say, "finish your soup. There's still a lentil there."

And then, wiping her hands on her apron, my grandmother would go on to expatiate about the famine that she and her family, and her friends, and friends of neighbors, and everyone she knew as a child, had to endure because some deviant insects called the locust clung to her childhood memories and could not keep their hungry claws from every single last leaf in the trees in her village. As an adolescent, I came to visualize the locust as enormous and very hungry tree-lobsters. To my shame, I must confess that these locust stories made me laugh and that I have never seen a locust, or bothered to look one up. For all I know, a locust is the size of a mosquito and my grandmother was making it all up so we'd eat that horrid lentil soup she made for us all the time.

tHE CILANtRO CONSPIRACY

Depending on whom you talk to, the world appears to be perpetually divided in pairs: dog lovers versus cat lovers; people who like buttered popcorn versus people who'd rather choke; people who think turtles crawl slow on purpose versus those who think they're simply tired of chasing rabbits. Similarly, the culinary world is carved down the middle between people who love cilantro and those for whom cilantro tastes like cheap soap. For me—who always thought of green bunches of anything as grass—this new knowledge was up there with farming innovations. It took going to a culinary misadventure with a fresh chef from São Paulo and food doyens from around the world to fully appreciate that not all taste buds are created equally.

I had so much to learn.

Owing through the commotion from Ohio and pressure from Alastair I ended up registering for the cooking class in the end. But I had signed up late. This meant I had nothing on my person that qualified me to be anywhere near a stove—no hat, no apron, no recipe in hand, no pen with which to take all-important notes. The half-dozen people around the floating kitchen, on the other hand—having signed up for the cooking class on the day they booked their vacation—were already wearing aprons and chef hats, and were ready to start chopping something, anything; in this case, they were ready to chop off my head for being late.

In my defense, I had not meant to be late. I had forgotten about the class altogether. So by the time I squeezed into a small space between Ethan and Alastair, the chef was already talking.

"Welcome everyone. I'm Chef Paolo. Paolo from São Paulo," he said, grinning broadly.

Through Paolo's chef uniform one could see he was built like a *fútbol* player. He had green eyes that were a little shattered, giving his whole face an allure this side of cunning. If the male universe were made up of heroes, rogues, and lovers, Chef Paolo could have been all three. So good-looking was he that the idea of him having any brains seemed redundant, unfair even. Everyone around the floating kitchen looked at him both attentively and suspiciously. Because, as was to be revealed in very short order, everyone there assumed that having a pepper mill back home made them a superior species. Not only did they pity the hopeless earthworm who had never heard of a lemon zester—me. They were almost daring Chef Paolo to prove that he had the chops to be there. For his part, he was unfazed by the skeptical stares. He seemed one of those people who are game for anything.

"How many people have made dolmades before?" he asked.

Every hand, except mine, went up. I was like, "What?" If you already know how to make this thing, whatever that is, why are you here? I was green as cabbage, and also ignorant of something crucial: These food aficionados were not here to make dolmades. They were here to dissect the differences in textures, cooking times, kinds of rice, grape leaf size, and other boring details about to be hurled our way. What if the grape leaves procured by a professional chef were different, say, from the ones Larry and Alastair got in San Francisco? Or from Ethan's, whose leaves arrived in a jar in Brisbane? And what to make of Barbara, the woman from Portland with the gremlin haircut who had made dolmades with different kinds of rice, which she proudly rattled off.

"I've made them with wild, brown, carnaroli, and jasmine," she said. "Completely different results."

Alison Wood and her mother May, both from London, seemed the two only normal people in the class. They listened politely. May nodded respectfully as Chef Paolo explained how he planned to run the class.

Who were these people? I didn't have to ask. Sooner rather than later, their culinary biographies began to unfold. These were people who had stayed at a Tuscan farm and learned to shape gnocchi while their two-month-old baby rolled biscotti dough with a famous Italian chef. These were people who knew the difference between "grass-fed" and "grain-only," and who spoke of cows as having, or not having, suffered growing up. The class hadn't even started when Barbara asked Chef Paolo if it was too late to sign up for his market tour of the Spice Bazaar in Istanbul. They gave gluttony a great name.

A recipe card was placed in front of every person. Already this wasn't going very well. Without being told to do so, just about everyone picked up the recipe and eyed it suspiciously. They looked like a roundtable of eminent doctors weighing in on a patient's X-rays.

It was Alastair who gave voice to the offending ingredient on the list.

"Cilantro?" he said, in disbelief. "That's a new one."

"My thoughts exactly," said Ethan.

"Interesting . . ." said, Barbara, pondering the cilantro conundrum, recipe card in hand.

May Wood raised an eyebrow. Her daughter Alison's face was unreadable; her amber eyes disconcertingly like an owl's. Larry shook his head, though I couldn't tell if it was at the cilantro, or because Alastair could not keep his opinions to himself. Meanwhile, Alastair looked at me askance, and just because I was standing next to him, his gesture brought unwanted attention to my person. That's when Chef Paolo noticed I wasn't properly attired for the occasion.

"Shall we get you into an apron, *cariño?*" he asked.

In Spanish *cariño* means something between darling and sweetheart. In this case, it also meant, unequivocally: *Cariño,* what are you doing *after* class? Now I was embarrassed. I hoped no one had ever heard the word, and imagined it to mean, "You whore. Why aren't you wearing your apron?" I also wanted to know how come Chef Paolo spoke Spanish when people in Brazil speak Portuguese. I must admit I was a little curious.

Answer the damn question about the cilantro, I wanted to say. But I had so much to learn. And not just about cooking. Had Chef Paolo been Chef Paola, she would have apologized, felt inclined to respond, or otherwise address the cilantro conspirators. But no. Chef Paolo had the heat levels in his kitchen completely under control.

tEACHER'S PEt

A foodie impostor, that's how I felt in the monogrammed red apron. But at least we could get started now. I couldn't believe we were about to spend the better part of a perfectly sunny afternoon prying, boiling, and rolling these oddly shaped leaves that looked like lawn fertilizer. Given the length of the recipe and the steps involved I could not fathom exactly how this was going to happen in two hours. I had visions of the coast guard finding us, a month later, washed up somewhere near Mykonos, wet grape leaves stuck to every part of our anatomies.

To start the process Chef Paolo broke us up in pairs. Larry was paired with May Wood. Her daughter Alison with Ethan. Barbara with Alastair. Or, as Alastair quipped, "Portlandia versus San Francisco," as if this were some sort of race. These pairings weren't ideal, mainly because of what Chef Paolo couldn't know. He couldn't have known that Ethan despised "the arrogant Brits" more than women hate Gwyneth Paltrow. He didn't yet know that Barbara was a little obsessive about rice and that Alastair's flippancy would become her disgrace.

I, myself, wasn't crazy about pairs. Back in Catholic school the nuns used to love to put us in pairs to work on various class projects. Sooner, rather than later, the *tonta* who was going to do all the work got exposed. The nuns called this "natural leadership." Well, Barbara had a lot of natural leadership coming her way in the form of rolling a hundred grape leaves by herself.

"You're with me, *cariño*," Chef Paolo said, eyeing me like easy prey. "We'll get started on the rice while they prep the leaves."

On hearing this, Ethan's eyes became sharp as kitchen shears. It was hard to take the menacing stare he gave Chef Paolo seriously because of the silly hats everyone was wearing. Why was Ethan doing this? Did he want to be teacher's pet? Who could know?

At one point, a steward in full uniform brought in a few bottles of wine and set them on a side table along with glasses. Secretly, I praised Dionysus. I stared at the bottles longingly. The sooner this wine was poured the easier it would be to get through this stretch of camp labor.

"Where's your hat?" Chef Paolo asked, measuring a truckload of rice.

"I took someone's place," I said. "I guess the hat must be in her cabin."

"I can get you one, if you want."

"No, no," I said. "I'd much rather measure rice with you."

"We're just parboiling it," he said.

"Parboiling?"

"*No cocinas*," he said, smiling. It wasn't a question.

All the same, I shook my head to indicate that no, I did not cook. At this, he put his top teeth together with the bottom teeth and scrunched his mouth sideways. It was a hilarious gesture that belonged in some comedy act about kitchen blunders. To add insult to injury, in South America a woman who can't cook is the equivalent of a North American woman who doesn't wear a tampon; something must be seriously wrong with you if you prefer pads.

"I love it!" he said.

"You *do*?"

"Yes, I love having someone here who doesn't know everything, for a change. What do you want to know?"

"I want to know how come you speak Spanish."

"I see . . . Worked in Spain for a while," he said, looking around, visually checking on the others.

"Did you like Spain?"

"*Más o menos*," he said. "We're not exactly welcome there."

"You mean people from South America?"

He nodded, and poured a bucket of water into the rice.

In a little while he went to check on everyone's progress with the leaves and explained that we were going to boil them twice. In a conclusive tone Ethan said that he only boiled the leaves once. Alison Wood turned to him as if he were on parole and wasn't supposed to speak until his officer allowed it.

For her part, Barbara put in that she had done it both ways and that, in her experience, boiling them once was enough if you boiled them five minutes longer. For good measure she added, "unless you're at sea level," as if she were some sort of geologist.

"Whatever works," said, Chef Paolo.

Ethan shot him a contemptuous look, as if for being a professional chef he needed to provide a more specific answer. But Chef Paolo was unfazed. He returned to our rice, turned down the heat, and then told me it was time to chop the cilantro.

"So what's the problem with the cilantro?" I asked.

"There's no problem with the cilantro, *cariño*," he said. "Smell."

At this, he tore a handful of leaves and placed them under my nose, as one presenting a bed of roses. Whether it was the way he underscored this next *cariño*, the expert hands tearing the leaves, or the heat in the kitchen, I was starting to warm up to this culinary adventure.

"Isn't that an incredible smell?" he said.

"A little grassy, no? But they don't seem to think it goes with this dish," I said, pointing to the group with my chin.

"I like mixing it up every now and then," he said, nonplussed.

There was so much glee in his voice I almost thought he had done the cilantro thing on purpose. And perhaps he had. I suspected that as a child Paolo might have switched his parents' shoes, or put coffee beans inside a pillow case, or some other wicked thing.

"You like stirring the pot, don't you?"

"Almost as much as you," he said, and did that thing again with his teeth.

Alastair wasn't minding his leaves. So Barbara was doing all the work. Instead, he was tuned into our conversation like a radio during World War II. He gave me a thumbs-up and Barbara in turn rolled her eyes all the way to Portland. Larry was busy taking notes in a little purple notebook he had brought for that purpose. May Wood was probably a nurse. She had put on gloves and handled the leaves as if they were newborns.

After all the cooling, chopping, and mixing, the stuff that was supposed to go inside the leaves was finally done.

Chef Paolo stuck two spoons into the mixture. He tasted it first and offered the second spoon to me.

"What do you think?" he said. "A pinch of salt?"

Now everyone's eyes were on me. This was my part. I was making stuffing with the chef and was expected to pass final culinary judgment on the finished product. What if I said yes, a pinch of salt, and the little burritos turned out salty and inedible. Why couldn't Chef Paolo say, "Pinch of this, pinch of that. Done."

"It's not that complicated," said Ethan. "Either you like it, or you don't."

Now Ethan was beginning to annoy me. What was the matter with him? Besides all the pressure, now we had to deal with kitchen politics, too.

"Hmmm . . . I think it needs a bit more cilantro," I said, looking straight into Paolo's eyes.

In truth, I had no clue what the mixture needed. I only said it because Ethan was being so ridiculous about it all.

Paolo caught on to this and said, "You know . . . I think you might be right."

Alastair looked at me significantly. I could tell he was proud of me, as if he were the proud papa of my fast emerging rebellious cynicism. Once he deemed the mixture was of the right consistency and taste, Chef Paolo proceeded to demonstrate how to roll the leaves.

"Like this," he demonstrated. "As if you're rolling a cigar."

"Helps if you've ever smoked pot," Alastair put it.

Now it was Alison's turn to turn her owlish eyes into full disapproval mode. Because I wasn't interested in making Greek burritos, while everyone scrutinized every twist and turn of Paolo's hands, I got lost in Alison's hair. She had a chic, modern haircut, and blond highlights coming out of her strawberry blond hair that shone under the bright kitchen light. I wondered who did her hair in London.

Barbara was either an expert roller or had once been a refugee. Before you could learn to spell the word *dolmadakia*—the Greek name for this dish—she had rolled two dozen leaves. She couldn't wait to leave Alastair's side. So she came over to my little corner, took stock of the mess, and proceeded to take over my spread of torn veins, split leaves, and spilled stuffing. I've always been a little put out by overachievers, but thank the gods on Mount Olympus that Barbara was one. If it hadn't been for her, my dolmades would have looked like elephant droppings.

"Wait, wait," someone said. "We need to take pictures."

Phones were at the ready as the little packets were carefully placed in the pots where they were going to take a little bath. This was going to take a while. So Chef Paolo ushered us to a large table where it soon became clear that size mattered, after all.

MY DOLMA IS BIGGER THAN YOURS

"The best time was making paella in Barcelona."

"No. Roasting a pig inside a *caja china* in Hawaii."

"That's in my bucket list," someone said.

"The market tour in India wins hands down!"

"Oh, no. Nothing beats the Grand Bazaar."

"I once petted a crocodile in Gambia," May said.

Dead silence.

Uh-oh. Had May Wood said something she shouldn't? I straightened in my chair, the better to take in the collective shock wave. Everyone looked as though she had stunned them with a river rock.

"That's not food," Barbara said, at last.

Apparently, if it wasn't food, it couldn't come to this party. It seemed that May Wood's remark about sunning crocodiles in Gambia—a little over the edge of water as it was—didn't count, unless you cooked the crocodile. *You dumb woman! Don't you know it's called themed entertainment for a reason? If you want wild life, if it is hippos and lizards you want, feel free to disembark and hop on the next pirogue to the Siné-Saloum Delta in Senegal.*

So after making May feel like croc feces for killing the conversation, they carried on with their list of feats.

"I had the most decadent Carbonara once. Made with pork belly."

"That can hardly be called Carbonara. Where was *this*?"

I was a little surprised to hear the laid-back Larry speaking as if this were a grave sin against humanity—this pork belly substitution. His remark made me think of my grandmother and her talk of locust. I was tempted to ask the table if they had ever had chicken feet soup, which my grandmother made all the time. Nana made soup with chicken feet, not because feet were a delicacy, but because where she grew up, sometimes the feet were all that was available. But after the May Wood throwdown I had a feeling that comparing real hunger to pastime hunger in front of these people might be a little biting.

For all that, the talk at the table was generous and gregarious; their enthusiasm easily transmitted. I was squeezed between Paolo and Alison Wood, who was sipping her white wine contentedly taking everything in. Alison was the picture of a woman on holiday with not a care in the world. In looking at her, I wished I could be that unofficial.

"Speaking of the Grand Bazaar," said Barbara. "Is there still room to join your tour, chef?"

"I believe so," said Paolo. "Speak to the front desk."

After Barbara rejoined the Culinary Olympics, Paolo leaned into my ear and said, "You should come on the tour, *cariño*. I'll save you a spot."

As he leaned into me I caught a whiff of his scent. Paolo's scent was a mixture of roasted wood and pine. There was also a hint of sweet wine on his breath. Our eyes met in silence and I felt as though my nerves were being unscrewed one at a time. *Can someone please catch me on the way down?* To make everything more confusing still, I was, at the same time assaulted by random thoughts of Max. And the thoughts were like an accusation. On the surface, Paolo and I were just talking and drinking wine. But both of us knew that beneath the words and easy flow of wine, a whole other dimension to this conversation was going on between us—the lust dimension.

"I have something on that day!" I blurted out, surprising myself with the lie.

"Do you?" he said. "Do you even know when the tour is?"

Paolo was nobody's fool. That's one of the things that made him so attractive. He knew who was who, and what was what. I started biting on one of my nails. Paolo noticed it, and I noticed that he did. Embarrassed, I hid my hands under the table.

"It's just that . . ."

"Ahh . . . You're here with someone."

"Uh . . . no. Well . . . not exactly. But yes. I think so."

He cocked his head and frowned. Now he was a little puzzled.

"I didn't mean to put you on the spot," he said.

"You didn't," I said. And then, "I wish you did."

Where did *that* come from? I laughed nervously and reached for my wine. The entire mess of my discomfort was packaged in that awkward gesture.

All around us the lively conversation continued—the smiling, the head bobbing, the "you did?" and "how was that?" of a shared language. Coming here had been a mistake. I saw it clearly now. I lacked the vocabulary to be among these food enthusiasts. And Paolo's unflinching gaze made me feel my heart was about to leap out of my chest.

"I have to go," I said, getting up.

"Restrooms are at the end of the hall," Paolo said with a wink. "We'll wait for you to get back."

This is what I should be doing. This is what I need to do. I am here at a cooking class. You tell yourself these things and then proceed to think about the chef pushing you against the table.

Why was I betraying Max in this awful way?

SLEEPING IN OUR DREAMS

The ship's library was only slightly bigger than a closet. There was a brown leather love seat by a boxy window that overlooked one of the decks, and on that particular day, the ocean. The squatty bookshelves were crammed with an assortment of books in several languages, and the side table next to the love seat was stacked with magazines from various parts of the world. The table held a small lamp, too, presumably for the odd sleepwalker. Cozy for one, crammed with two people, but as hiding places go, it was ideal. People barely noticed the small space on their way to the casino. Despite all that, Alastair managed to find me.

"Talk about hit-and-run," he said by way of a greeting.

"What are you talking about?"

"You add cilantro to the dolmas and leave us to get food poisoning. Is that it? Everyone was wondering where you went."

"Please! No one even noticed I was there."

"Now, now," he said, "Are we throwing a pity party?"

"Whatever. Were the Greek burritos any good?"

"Well . . . I haven't thrown up yet. And it's been, what, a couple of hours?" he said, checking the time on his phone.

"You're totally wasted, Alastair."

"You haven't seen wasted, dearest. What's that you're reading?"

"Oh, some Australian magazine. Something's up with their prime minister."

"I'm fascinated. Please don't stop. I love it when you talk Aussie politics on the way to Istanbul."

"Shut up."

"So. Are you coming on the tour?"

"I think I'm done with culinary adventures for a while."

"Well, I wouldn't hire you to roll my cigars, necessarily. But I'll bet Paolo will be more than happy to show you the hidden spots of the Grand Bazaar."

And just like that, I burst into tears.

"What. Is. Going. On?" he said. "I can't stand it when people cry."

The love seat wasn't very big. So when Alastair came to sit by me I had to move my handbag to the carpet and uncross my legs so he would fit.

"It's no-thing," I said between sobs.

"Bells. Bells. Bells," he said. "When a woman says it's nothing there's a whale in the room." And then, patting my knee, he said, "I don't want to pry, dearest . . . But do you want to talk about it?"

Did I want to talk about it? I didn't know. Where to even start? The ship was moving ever so slowly, so much so in fact that I thought we weren't moving at all. I trained my eyes outside and saw another ship not too far from us. It, too, looked as if it were parked there, in a surreal parking lot the color of asphalt. Were it not for that, Alastair and I might have been sitting at a coffee shop somewhere on land.

"It's Max," I said, drying my tears with the back of my hand.

"Who's Max?"

"My husband."

"You never said you were married."

"I am. Well, technically, I was . . . I guess."

Alastair was a most focused listener. It was this trait, more than anything, that allowed him to amass vast amounts of gossip about so many strangers. From that point forward he didn't ask any more questions; he just listened. So I told him about my mother kidnapping me to come on this cruise and how come I wasn't interested in going on tours, or any other adventures, for that matter. But besides knowing what I *didn't* want to do, I had no idea of what I wanted to do. That was part of the problem. I was very stuck. At one point, after telling him the whole story, or most of the story, I reached into my handbag.

"This is him," I said.

"In a bottle of Advil . . . ?" he said, a little surprised. "Well, I'm glad I haven't come down with a headache yet. I might have swallowed your hubby by mistake."

"Alastair Douglas . . . what am I going to do with you?"

"I could give you some ideas," he said. "But in the meantime, the more interesting question is what are *you* going to do with Max? Forgive the prying, dearest, but was he malnourished? It's hard to believe that a whole person would fit in a bottle of Advil."

"Well, this isn't all of him."

"If you don't mind my asking . . . , where's the rest of him?"

"My mother vacuumed him," I said. "It wasn't even accidental, Alastair. I think she meant to do it. And that's part of the problem . . . This is all I have left of him."

"Dearest . . ." he said, looking tenderly into my eyes. "That's not true. Those who are dead are not dead. They're just sleeping in our dreams."

"Oh, Alastair . . . that's so beautiful."

"Is it?" he said, turning toward the window. He didn't know what to do with his face. He stood there for a while reliving something; not so much as one facing a death, but as one facing a life before he was ready for it. By the time he found his words, his voice was dim.

"I'm one of death's celebrities, dearest."

I went up to hug him, but I missed my chance. In mid-hug, Alastair returned to his usual, flippant self.

"Maybe we can put your Max to rest on a nude beach along the way. Would he have liked that?"

"Only if the women are ugly," I said, forcing a smile.

"We'll check out Mykonos," he said. "You may be in luck. Every nude beach I've ever been to, everyone who's naked should not be, and the other way around."

"What does that make you, Alastair? That's like saying that every drug deal you've ever handled has had some kind of glitch."

"My dearest Valentina, you are such an innocent," he said. "I'm headed to the Sky lounge. Wanna come with?"

I shook my head.

He got up to leave but his feet remained firmly in place.

"Alastair . . ."

"Yes, dearest?"

"I'm worried about your liver."

"Oh, you're just jealous!"

Invariably, Alastair's departure from a room left an enormous void behind. Long after he left I stayed on that love seat staring out to sea. Max would have liked what I saw. The ocean seemed infinite and peaceful; the horizon a straight line cut with glass. And it was as I contemplated that gray line in the distance that I came to a decision: wherever I end up, wherever I may go, it would have to be open and peaceful like this. I knew that the world could never be as straightforwardly beautiful as what was now in front of me. And that as far as decisions went, this wasn't much. But the idea was fluid; at least it contained movement. It was also a parting of sorts; a farewell to the sorrows that had threatened to swallow me whole.

ALI BABA

It took a brief detour and another strike in Greece to drum up a few childhood prejudices and to find out the truth about Ali Baba once and for all.

In much the same way that some innocents believe that all Latin people are named José, dig ditches in pairs, and say, *"Qué?"* through dumbfounded, illiterate brown eyes, I had grown up with the mistaken notion that everyone in Turkey was a bearded thief. And who could blame me? An imported cartoon called *Ali Baba and the 40 Thieves—Alí Babá y los 40 Ladrones*—was a childhood favorite of mine. Because I wasn't allowed to watch TV at home, I used to catch Ali Baba and forty other barbarians steal jewels on horseback at my friend Cristina's house. Like mine, Cristina's parents were both doctors who, more likely than not, needed to have their heads examined. Both surgeons, Cristina's parents were always in the operating room, which in turn meant that they were never home to explain to us that Turkish men are far more handsome than the Italians and that what they really want to do, more than anything else, is not steal your jewels, or snatch your purse, but to sell you a carpet patiently woven by a sister named Sultana somewhere behind the busy stalls of the Grand Bazaar.

We were no longer in the Majestic Mediterranean. The waters left no doubt. We were now in the filthy and congested Bosphorus, where ship traffic was such as to merit popping a little Cymbalta to calm your nerves about the very likely possibility of a shipwreck. Due to this water traffic we had to wait to get orders from someone or other before we could dock in Istanbul. This didn't mean, however, that people waited patiently in their cabins for the go-ahead. Every single last of the eight hundred passengers appeared to be standing somewhere—the front desk, staircases, corridors, and atriums—impatiently looking at the time. To distract us from our prisoners' plight, M.C.'s unwelcome voice piped through the loud speaker to describe the magic that awaited us in Istanbul. He had no idea that his announcement was making it worse; that mentioning the word magic to people trapped in a cage will make them hate you! Permit or no permit, I feared a stampede. People didn't want to hear about magic. What they really wanted was to go shopping at the Grand Bazaar for costumes.

On leaving Istanbul there was to be a themed party called "Ottoman Nights," presumably where all of us would sport swords and turbans to celebrate the rape of young odalisques and the massacre of all those debauched Romans. But all that tragedy had happened a while back. So maybe it wasn't so fresh on people's minds. A little question to ask the wonderfully creative activity coordinators on board might have been, "Have you Googled the word *Ottoman* lately? Or ever?" But who was I to throw the first stone? I had my own prejudices to ditch about these Turkish thieves.

And so, while we stood impatiently on atriums and corridors, M.C.'s voice continued to fill the airwaves.

"Ladies and gentlemen," he went on, "did you know that Istanbul is the only city in the world that sits in two continents?" While he was busy with his little monologue, I found it hard to believe that Michael Coin's vacant eyes could locate two continents on a map, let alone know what they were called. But he carried on, reading from his Nsta-history app, perhaps.

"One side of Istanbul sits in Asia and the other sits in Europe," he said. "You are more than welcome to head to the Asian side once we're allowed ashore. But please remember we sail off at five on the dot."

"Puhh. When have we ever sailed from Istanbul on time?"

This CNN alert was brought to us by the woman who was standing by herself next to my mother. My mother, never one compelled to address people speaking to the air—rhetorically or not—didn't move a muscle in the woman's direction. At any rate, who were these people who visited the same place over and over? I'm so easily bored I can never imagine doing anything more than once. On hearing the woman's quip about Istanbul, though, it crossed my mind that the brochures my mother had used to seduce me into this majestic adventure were pure fiction.

Eventually we were allowed to dock. Once we obtained permits and forms were signed, moods improved. But as I had feared, there was a minor stampede toward the gangway. People ran through the ID scanner and practically stormed into Istanbul.

BUS PEOPLE

The air outside was balmy, almost tropical. And the noise was grating. Famous writers like to call that kind of noise "a cacophony of sounds." But I'm not a famous writer, so my description will be a little less cacophonous. How about: Outside, the sounds of the city came together in one crescendoing growl; passersby hissing at pickpockets, buses expelling exhaust, and street merchants peddling pity under a sky clear as absolution. Istanbul was a furious and frenetic city were smelly pigeons ruled like kings.

At the bottom of the ramp there were two empty tour buses waiting to be filled.

Being the most popular, it took a little while to board the bus headed to the Grand Bazaar. The second bus was booked for a tour of the city—really a tour of traffic.

As I set foot on the last step inside the bus headed to the Grand Bazaar I was surprised to be greeted by Paolo. He was standing next to the bus driver in the yellow overalls, chatting with him about some logistic or other.

"That was a long bathroom break, *cariño*," he said, staring me up and down.

To add to the awkwardness, my mother was standing behind me, waiting to get in.

"Uhh . . . something came up," I said. "But I heard the food was delicious."

At this, Paolo raised both eyebrows and made a grand gesture with his hand to let me pass. He wasn't buying a word.

A little more quickly than we would have otherwise done my mother and I walked toward the middle of the bus, where we grabbed the first two empty seats we found. Sitting next to my mother meant what it meant: I had to listen to her indignation. There's a saying in Spanish used to spurn people who are too familiar. I was about to hear my mother launch the expression on Paolo.

"Why did that man call you, *cariño*?" she asked. "Does he think the two of you played marbles growing up? Why, Valentina? Why do you allow a vagrant to treat you like a common whore?"

"Hmm, I don't know, Mamá. I don't know why I do that. I'd much rather be treated like an *uncommon* whore. Would you help me buy classier makeup at the

Grand Bazaar? Maybe it's the eye shadow that gave him the wrong idea."

"You've lost your mind," she said.

"If you must know, Mamá, I was tempted to tell him I was a widow. But then I remembered that back at the salon in Scottsdale you told me I had to change that."

"Who is he, anyway?"

"He's the ship's chef."

"*¡Qué horror!*" my mother said.

The horror, indeed! The only thing worse than Paolo's familiarity, was that he was someone who wore a uniform to work. My mother has always maintained— a belief not shared by the millions who watch the Food Network, obviously—that uniforms are for postal workers, firemen, policemen, and people who earn a living by the hour. In her words: bus people.

What was to be done? It was becoming pretty obvious pretty fast that travel did nothing to expand anyone's horizons. This air-conditioned tour bus was bursting to the last seat with our unshakable little prejudices. Me and my bearded thieves. My mother and her bus people. The woman's husband by the pool and his fears that Turks were really Arabs about to shoot him. As for our fellow bus passengers, they had wild notions entirely different from ours. Some believed, for instance, that everyone in Istanbul was named Muhammad, wore a turban, and tortured people named John in a stinky jail as a pastime. The truth was the other way around. People named John did torture people named Muhammad. But this happened somewhere else entirely, in a place called Abu Ghraib, not anywhere near sunny Istanbul and its gorgeous red tulips. If there was something the people of Turkey desperately needed, it was an ad agency from New York to help them rebrand. If only I moved back to New York, what couldn't I do with this account. *¡Dios mío!*

The last two people to enter the bus were Ethan and Michael Coin, who was to lead half of us through the wares section of the Grand Bazaar while foodies followed Paolo around the market area. It crossed my mind to tell my mother that to some of our fellow passengers Paolo was practically a demigod for owning a set of knives and for having his name sewn on a chef coat. But I quickly abandoned the idea. What if in the middle of my story about the grape leaves, I missed the thieves and the killers we were on our way to meet?

As for Ethan, there was no denying the man stood out, and not just because he was the last man standing. No matter where he was, Ethan was always the dominant presence in a room. Also, it didn't hurt that the white linen shirt rolled up to the forearms was designed to show off his even tan.

"Sorry to interrupt," he said, as soon as he spotted me.

How dare you interrupt! I was tempted to say. *This is my lesbian lover. And we were about to kiss.*

"Mamá, this is Ethan," I said, instead. "He's from Brisbane. Ethan, this is my mother, Serena."

Already, this was going so much better than our miserable run-in with Paolo. I could tell by the relaxed features on my mother's face.

"It's a pleasure, Mrs. . . . ?"

"Serrano," said my mother.

"A pleasure to meet you, Mrs. Serrano. Are you going on the tour of the Spice Bazaar?"

"No. We're not," I said. "I'm looking for a lamp."

"A lamp?" my mother asked in disbelief.

"I'd better go grab a seat," Ethan said. "I'll see you later, I hope."

When she next spoke, my mother could hardly keep the delight from her voice.

"Now *that's* a gentleman," she said. "What's wrong with *him*?"

"Nothing that I know of," I said. But I knew what she meant. She meant, "How come you haven't mentioned this wonderfully polite eligible bachelor with intriguing eyes whose voice lulls with the sounds of an offshore bank account?"

Let's face it. Hands down, it's always better to make out with a gentleman than with someone wearing a cheap uniform. And that's because, if you ever got pregnant from a gentleman, the bumps ahead would be that much smoother. While seeing the pregnancy to term, for instance, at least the gentleman will be better attired. And the brand name alone can bring such a relief to labor pains.

Now I prayed that Paolo had a nasty tattoo somewhere on his body—something gang-ish and indelibly inked. But it was impossible to tell through the body-hugging black T-shirt he was wearing that day. An invisible tattoo would not be tormenting enough to my mother, though. Never mind the tattoo. I was suddenly inspired by spices. I longed to touch cinnamon sticks and take in the fragrance of allspice while my mother trailed behind me at the Spice Bazaar. It was the opportunity of a lifetime, a chance to show my jailer what it felt like to be trudged and trundled like wet cement in a wheelbarrow.

My lamp could wait.

A TALK WITH NANA (AKA THE MARBLES ARGUMENT)

M'ija, never mix whites with colors; the maid doesn't know what she doesn't know. Put them in separate heaps for her. Socks go to the *batea*, the stone out back. Never scrub them yourself. Your husband doesn't want rough hands. Be sure to soak black beans overnight. On Sundays at church, sit like a lady. People are watching. You can't get a husband if you sit like a common whore. Never walk barefoot. Your husband doesn't want rough feet. Cover your mouth when you laugh. I know how you like to laugh, *m'ija*. But your husband will think he married a common whore. Never chew with your mouth open, either. Or walk with food in your hands. Only whores walk and eat at the same time. This is how you take a hem. This is how you iron a man's shirt so it doesn't have any creases. Start with the neck. You don't want to embarrass your husband in front of other men. No creases on the pants, either. See? Hold the iron this way. Never leave a cut papaya out. If the maid does, you have a serious talk with her. The maid doesn't know what she doesn't know. Fresh fruit harbors flies. She may come from a village where women are sluts. Never squat when playing marbles. You're not a common whore. This is how you set the table. This is how you set a table when your husband has company. Your husband always sits at the head. Use camphor oil to cure a chest cold. Rub it on your chest, but never in front of your husband. You are not a common whore. Always tuck bedsheets under at the corners. You don't want bad spirits crawling inside your marital bed. Show the maid how it's done. She may come from a village with no bedsheets. This is how you hold a broom. You need to show the maid. A maid doesn't know what she doesn't know. She may forget to sweep the corners. This is how you love a man. This is how you punish a man for not loving you. But don't go looking for lipstick stains on his shirts. You don't want to find out what you don't want to find out. This is how you strain milk to make *suero*. The maid should know how to strain. Villagers always know how to strain. Always inspect the chicken. You don't want to kill your husband with chicken. The flesh should be pink, not yellow.

But, nana, what if the butcher won't let me inspect the chicken?

What if the butcher won't let you inspect the chicken? You mean to tell me that after everything I've taught you, you're bent on becoming the kind of woman the butcher won't let near his meat?

I wondered what nana would make of Paolo. Nana had raised my mother. It was safe to assume she wouldn't approve. Ah . . . Paolo . . . I could play marbles with Paolo. But how to do it under my mother's reproving gaze and my grandmother's ghost whispering in my ear at every wrong turn. Perhaps I might squeeze a wish from Aladdin. I was headed to the Grand Bazaar, after all!

tHE EVIL EYe

Arriving at the Grand Bazaar will always be painted in my memory in vibrant hues of red. The beds of red tulips lined up against the red Turkish flag were so vivid they seemed to have been created by a computer animator. Seas of tourists from all over bounced and sprung out of every corner of the place. Among those of us in the bus there were to be two groups. The foodies would follow Paolo. The shoppers would follow M.C.

Michael Coin held up a white sign with a navy blue anchor imprinted on it. Paolo carried an identical sign. An identical sign shaped in the form of a tall tent was also placed by the entrance of the fish market. This was in case anyone in our group missed that we had come here on a boat. The giant letters MEET HERE on the tall sign were in sharp contrast to everything else around us, which was rendered in gold curlicues with lots of dots and squiggles. Was this Arabic?

"If you get tired, or just want a break," said Michael Coin, "meet here." Paolo looked on, happy to let M.C. be the one to strain his voice.

Tired? I supposed that after a while one could get a little tired of the flies. A thing I noticed right away was that no one in Istanbul was in receipt of my grandmother's memo, "Don't eat while you walk." I was surrounded by common whores!

At that early hour in our adventure my mother was still under the impression that the two of us would follow M.C., so she inched forward toward the shoppers' line. As yet, she was unsuspecting of my plans. For her sake, I hoped she wasn't thinking we were headed to Nordstrom's semi-annual sale. Or that anyone here would offer her a glass of Chardonnay while she assessed the latest fashions from Paris and Milan. Michael Coin's job that day was to guide people through the part of the Grand Bazaar where they could feast on stretches of stalls stacked to the brim with shiny objects, counterfeit goods, clothespins, cracked wooden doorknobs, rusted ice tongs, and legions of evil-eye bracelets and pendants. It was going to be hard work, combing through this catacomb of treasures.

After being momentarily blinded by so much that shone and beckoned, and after stubbing your toes a few times on uneven cement floors, your eyes could finally adjust to the real riches. Isn't there a special delight in picking up a baseball cap so far away from New York, emblazoned with the New York Yankees' logo in fake diamonds?

"It's a real fake," a proud merchant bellowed.

"Made here in Istanbul. Not in China!" his cohort echoed.

They were practically salivating at the sight of us. In very short order it became obvious that we were headed to a patent lawyer's paradise. As for me, I tried to break the news to my mother as gently as I possibly could.

"Mamá, I see the people from my cooking class. I think I'll go to the fish market with them."

I might as well have told her she had snot on her chin. Dressed in yacht-white from head to toe, my mother had a hard time putting the words *fish* and *market* together.

"The fish market, Valentina?"

Wasn't this why she had brought me all this way? So I could appreciate interspecies sex? Was it rat urine that gave that rare and cloudy yellow to the lobster tanks? A thick and sticky smell wafted through the air, mixed in with the smell of rotting fish. Was that bus exhaust, or was it bunker fuel from the boats? No. It was pigeon shit sticking to the lining of our lungs.

"See you at the boat," I said, waving like a dumb tourist.

No amount of evil-eye pendants, bracelets, or key chains could protect me from the look my mother gave me.

tHE MAN IN tHE LIttLE toWER

Once upon a time, a very wise man, perhaps great, great, great, great grandpa Abdul, discovered the magic of a cone. And when this Abdul had judged his son, Abdulito, old enough to grasp such things as a Turkish lira's value of geometry, he said, "Allah, bless the cone!" And so it was decreed. And then he said, "Son, if you shape it into a cone, it will sell."

And so it was for all time.

Mountains of cashews. Mountains of apricots. Mountains of spices. We were surrounded by mountains of Turkish Delight that put Whitman's Sampler to shame.

I was particularly enthralled by the mountains of pistachios that looked like parakeets' beaks shaped into a cone. I wondered what held them in that shape; pistachios being a little uneven, and all. The thing to know right off the bat was that no one—except the cone maker—ever touched these cones. But how was I supposed to know this? My ignorance probably boiled down to having lived in North America far too long. In the United States, if you are not supposed to touch something, there are signs everywhere that read, "Please don't touch. If you do, our lawyers will be in touch."

Well, directions weren't all that clear in Istanbul. If you wanted to buy, say, a kilo of cashews, the merchants produced them from the back of their stalls in bags which had been prepackaged and premeasured elsewhere. This wondrous discovery and the disaster that followed were still ahead. The whole day, in fact, more enchanting than I would have hoped for, was still ahead. For now I was enthralled, if a little disoriented, by the effect of conical everything. A genie with golden slippers upturned at the toes was probably behind all this magic.

And then there was Paolo. Just by looking at him the inside of my legs turned liquid.

I was standing toward the front of the line feeling a little lightheaded about being so close to him. I was pretty sure he knew exactly where I was standing; there were just a handful of people between us. I looked away, trying to let go of the invisible string that pulled me toward him. Or maybe I was trying to avoid being perceived as a common whore.

"Paolo. Chef Paolo," groups of Turkish men saluted as he walked by and waved.

It was obvious he had led this tour many times before and was regarded like something of the foreign mayor of this burgeoning bazaar. On our way to wherever Paolo was taking us we passed mats of dark, Mediterranean hair and covetous merchant eyes.

"Dearest! You came, after all."

Alastair surprised me on the left.

"Cute dress," he said, grabbing my hand and giving it a little squeeze.

It was my favorite blue dress with tiny white polka dots and had seen me through a host of scorching Arizona summers.

"It's older than this place," I said. "Where's Larry?"

"Where else? Working."

"Somebody has to pay for your vacation, I suppose."

"I'm a bitch for complaining, aren't I?"

By the time I ran into him, Alastair had already come and gone. He had been through the other part of the bazaar and had run into M.C. and a group of people shopping for "Ottoman Nights" costumes.

"You should take a little stroll and get something wicked for the party."

"What's in the bag?" I asked, ignoring his suggestion.

"A Turkish hammer," he said.

"What's a Turkish hammer?"

"What else could it be, dearest? It's a hammer made in Turkey."

Later that evening I would discover that there was no Turkish hammer in the bag. In the meantime, though, our little side conversation earned us a couple of irritated stares. I felt I was back in Caracas about to be whacked with a ruler by a frigid nun. *¡Por favor!* As if this were a physics class; we were strolling through a stinky flea market where leering men bellowed "real fake" in unison.

"These stalls have been passed down for generations from father to son," Paolo explained in a deeply sonorous voice that carried over the din of the bazaar. He didn't need to explain that no stalls had been passed from mother to daughter. It wasn't that there weren't Turkish women at the Grand Bazaar. They just weren't to be seen.

At one point, Paolo caught my eye and gave me a salacious smile that gave my stomach a squeeze. The feeling was surprising, like a pounce, and also complicit. My mind ran away with fleeting images of bare bodies and searching forms, along with an ever-changing repertoire of rhythms.

"This is turmeric. This is cumin. This is smoked *pimentón*," Paolo said, pausing every so often for people to take it all in and snap pictures of the cone-shaped marvels.

Ethan was strolling around, quasi-independently from the rest of us, but somehow keeping an eye on our group at the same time. I also spotted Alison Wood looking disinterestedly chic and in her straw hat, her handbag hanging casually across her torso. Barbara, our grape leaf roller in residence, took everything Paolo said with great seriousness. How boring was this? Easily, you could get all these spices from McCormick without the flies or the bugs. By now it had become abundantly clear that we were far from lettuce that came with little tags that said, "I've been washed three times. So you don't have to."

Despite the unappetizing sights, though, I was getting hungry. With all the drama about getting or not being able to get permits to go into Istanbul, some of us had forgotten to eat breakfast that morning. I looked around trying to find something to eat that wouldn't give me dysentery. That's when I spotted the tallest yet mountain of pistachios.

"How much are they?" I asked, approaching the man who was guarding it.

Now he was eyeing my wallet.

"It depends," he said.

"Depends on what?"

"On how much you want."

"How do they stand so—"

The words were barely out of my mouth when I heard Ethan yell, "Valentina, no!"

And just like that, by grabbing one miserable, insignificant pistachio, the entire tower came tumbling down and began to spread in earnest through every nook, every corner, and every recess of the place. They rolled and rolled, kept rolling, and dispersed some more as everyone around me watched in disbelief. And then, all of a sudden, as if someone had yelled, "Bomb!" hundreds of people threw their bodies facedown on the ground.

Had all the Abduls gotten on their knees to pick up the falling pistachios? I was so embarrassed.

"Oh my God!" I said.

"Oh their God!" is what I should have said.

As for Paolo, after surveying the mess I had made, he did that funny sideway scrunching gesture with his mouth. He probably wished he had toppled the mountain of pistachios himself.

"Please forgive me, dearest," said Alastair. "But this one could go viral."

While the man who owned the stall was prostrated, praying to Allah for my slippery soul, Alastair was making a video of it all with his white phone. He walked around with great concentration, as if he were a cinematographer working on a documentary called "Falling Cones during Call to Prayer." When he deemed he had caught enough rolling pistachios for his little video, and while everyone else remained on their knees facing Mecca, Alastair turned the phone in my direction and said, "Wave."

I didn't wave. I rolled my eyes instead.

In a little while, order was restored and everyone went back to work as if nothing out of the ordinary had taken place. And perhaps, for them, this was routine. Not for me, though; I kept thinking: So *that* was the famous muezzin call. I don't know what I was expecting. So I couldn't say that it wasn't what I expected. Still, it begged the question: What is a muezzin?

As far as I could tell from my brief acquaintance with the situation, a muezzin was an unemployed man, hopefully not too tall, hunched inside a conical closet called a minaret, counting the hours until the time came to redeem his next life in Candy Crush, or until the next call to prayer, whichever came first, because for centuries and centuries the calls have been based on the sun's position in the sky. As for the actual call to prayer . . . well, I couldn't tell what he was chanting because he was chanting in Arabic. I'm assuming that melodious language in which the muezzin beckons believers to prayer is Arabic. It was, as any self-respecting writer will tell you, a cacophony of sounds. But these weren't ordinary sounds. They were sounds rich with meaning, unchanged by history, haunting, sublimely delivered five times a day, lest anyone forgot we are all goingggggggggg to hellllllllll.

Because I don't speak Arabic, I have taken the liberty of translating the muezzin's call to prayer and rendering it into English so that those not fortunate enough to go to Turkey on a cruise can get a feel for it. Their God? My God? It hardly matters. Owing to this virtuous translation, I'm going to heaven either way. So here it is: the call that brought all those faithful to their knees. And here I thought the commotion was my fault for spilling the damn pistachios. Catholic guilt is so hard to shake.

Your're goingggggggggggg to hellllllllllllllllllll. Your're goingggggggggggggggggg to hellllllllll. Goddddddddd dammmnnnnnnnnnn youuuuuuuuuu. God dammmmmmmm youuuuuuuuuuu. You're goinggggggggggggg to hellllllllllllllllllll. Your're gogoingggggggg to helllllllllll. Goddddddddddd dammmnnnnnnnnnn youuuuuuuuuu. Goddammmmmmnnn youuuuuuuuuuu. Godddddd dammmmmmnnnnnnn allllllllll of youuuuuuuuuuuuuuuuuuuu.

Now, if the people of South America only had a pinch of discipline. If we could stop drinking rum for a couple of hours, drop everything we're doing, and get on our knees, Catholicism could easily outstrip Islam in a decade, at most. I'm no Nostradamus, but that's my prediction, in any case.

ALADDIN GRANTS THREE WISHES

"What are you making for Ottoman Nights?"

"I think," Paolo said, looking pensive for a minute, "that I should make something with pistachios."

"Nice of you to rub it in."

The body-hugging T-shirt he was wearing was becoming more and more distracting by the minute. Now that Paolo's job was done, people had dispersed and had gone shopping on their own. The two of us were walking in the opposite direction from where we had come. I had no idea where we were headed. Wherever Paolo wanted to take me, it was evident by my feet that I wasn't going to protest. It was also obvious that he was taking his time getting us there. I might have asked. But I wasn't about to reveal myself a common whore and ask: "In which of these places are we going to bare it all?"

Not too far from that lusting corner of my mind there still beat the good intention of buying an Aladdin lamp for Azucena. My sister collected antiques. I wasn't sure that an Aladdin lamp made at the Grand Bazaar by the thousands counted as an antique. But there were no other options. If I got Azucena "a real fake" of anything—say a Coach handbag—she would stop talking to me.

I mentioned the lamp to Paolo and he said he knew just the place. Those shattered green eyes that burned for trouble seemed to say, "You can postpone it all you want, *cariño*. But sooner or later . . ."

Desire that made you dizzy; ruthless and insistent, it was the kind of feeling that turned everything into shapes, made your lips dry, and made you crave a bucket of water *now*. Alongside the urgency of this lust, the very recent past kept knocking on my head. Muddled thoughts and loose limbs; I was headed for trouble.

On our way to meet Aladdin we passed a leather shop where all things leather hung—jackets, skirts, gloves, pants. The three men standing outside the shop looked like triplets.

"Leather for the lady?" one of them asked.

Paolo approached him and said, "We're looking for an Aladdin lamp."

"Aladdin! Yes. Follow me."

And this was part of the magic of the Grand Bazaar. Imagine if everyone at Macy's on Thirty-Fourth Street in New York were related to one another. This Abdul turned out to be the third cousin of the other Abdul, who, don't you know it? sold Aladdin lamps in every shape and shade of metal.

"This is my cousin, Abdul," Abdul #1 said, smiling greedily.

"Abdul, they are looking for Aladdin. Give them good price. Then you come try leather jacket. Yes?"

At this, Abdul #2 ushered us inside his shop, where hundreds of Aladdin lamps were lined up, stacked, shelved, and otherwise displayed.

"This one has kismet," he said, grabbing a lamp at random.

"What is kismet?" I asked Paolo.

"It's special," he winked. "It will bring you luck."

¡Por favor! This was total bullshit. Aladdin treated all his wishers equally, didn't he?

Thousands of wishes were waiting to be released from inside Abdul's shop.

Going along with the charade I admired the lamp he offered. Having grown up in South America I was an expert haggler. I had a grandfather, a father, and seven uncles who had taught me haggling etiquette; they would have been very much at home here among the Abduls. To haggle properly, you had to feign disinterest and also be able to walk away with a tad of indignation if necessary.

"Maybe that one," I said, pointing to a slightly larger lamp in silver. I was pretty sure Azucena would have found the gold one kitschy.

"Twenty Turkish lira," said Abdul #2, placing the new silver lamp in my hands.

"We'll give you fifteen," said Paolo. "Look, it has a ding."

This, too, was part of the haggling. We all knew the ding was as much fantasy as Aladdin himself.

"Ding? You say ding? These are handmade. Of course it has ding!"

"I know this other guy down the—" Paolo started.

Abdul #2 didn't even let him finish. The mere suggestion of our walking away caused a third lamp to materialize. In truth, they were all identical. That one, too, he placed in my hands. But this time he said, "Aladdin will give you three wishes."

"Only three?" I said. "How much for this one?"

"For you, fifteen Turkish lira."

"I'll give you twelve," I said resolutely.

Max was in my purse. I wondered if he would have been proud of me or disgusted by the haggling. But I was following standard haggling procedure. Emily might have called it SHP because most people in North America don't have time to go beyond an abbreviation.

Abdul #2 gave my offer some thought. He stalled. He looked around. He considered it. He stalled some more.

"Very well," he said. "But you try leather jacket with my cousin, Abdul. Yes?"

"You have our word," said Paolo.

Nothing of the kind was in our future. I knew this. Abdul #2 also knew this. But it was part of haggling, letting him save face after agreeing to our lower price. Now that our exchange was deemed complete, Abdul #2 proceeded to wrap the lamp in butcher paper and placed it inside a black and gold plastic bag with squiggles and snaky little characters that probably said in Arabic: Have a nice day, sucker!

"I just remembered," I said to Paolo. "I have to buy my mother a present."

"*Buena idea*," he said. I wondered if Brazilian mothers were as high maintenance as other South American mothers. Who knew? Brazil was a former Portuguese colony. Were the Portuguese not as high maintenance as the Spaniards?

Whenever Azucena traveled, even if it was for a one-day business trip, she had to bring my mother a present. Oftentimes, more than one. This was to appease her. All Latin mothers need to be appeased with presents. The more rare or expensive the present, the quicker the offense—whatever offense or sin you may have committed—will be erased from her memory. Yes, I realized that my mother, *too*, was at the Grand Bazaar. I realized that she could have bought herself a present. But it wasn't the same thing. The moment we parted, even if it was for a few hours, I was considered to be "traveling." And besides, given the tension during our parting, I feared arriving back in our cabin empty-handed. In looking at Azucena's lamp—which my mother would end up carrying all the way to Caracas in her luggage—she might say, "Where is my present?" Showing up empty-handed also might earn me a tribal sneer. The scorn of choice depended on my mother's mood. Or she might say, "Only common whores travel and don't bring their mother a present."

In the end I bought my mother a silk scarf. I didn't even haggle. My mother would have rejected any object subject to a price reduction.

The heat of Istanbul was warming up us considerably. Now I had something else to fear: *looking* like a common whore after spending an afternoon with Paolo.

52 STONE STEPS TO SIN

"Do you know where that dress would look good, *cariño?*"

I shook my head.

"Floating underneath the cisterns."

"How far are the cisterns?"

By then Paolo and I were nearly consumed with lust. We were also surrounded by richness and magic. It was almost a sin trying to take in the marvels of Istanbul in one afternoon. Thousands of years before Paolo suggested removing my dress on holy ground, water had been purified for the inhabitants of the palace that used to sit above the Basilica cisterns.

The cisterns were within walking distance from the Blue Mosque and the magnificent Hagia Sophia, another mosque. By now it was becoming pretty obvious that conical minarets, always taller than the mosques they adorned, were pretty much standard construction procedure around here. What was not standard were the gildings, trimmings, and frills on the minarets themselves. A minaret being considered a gateway to heaven, it was also a way for ambitious architects to show off on earth. And what a boaster the Blue Mosque was! Architectural uniqueness aside, the onion domes of the mosque itself were painted in the most fetching hue of IKEA blue. And while Islam maintains that man should not compete with God or nature, in looking at the blue domes while standing in line at the Basilica cisterns, I thought, "What's wrong with giving God a little competition?"

This guy—it had to be a guy three thousand years ago—had done a pretty good job of forecasting that inside large blue buildings there might be something on sale. He wasn't that different from Michelangelo in that regard. At one point, some high-ranking cardinal at the Vatican had said, "Mico, we just want you to paint the ceiling." And by the time the cardinal returned from his afternoon prayers, Michelangelo had gone a little overboard with angels and clouds at the Sistine Chapel.

There was a long line of people waiting to go into the cisterns. But for us it didn't feel like much of a wait at all. This might have had something to do with the fact that while I mused on the excesses of ancient art, Paolo kept running his hand from my neck to the middle of my back, and up again. His touch was sensual and unpredictable, and after a while, my vision became so blurred I wasn't even sure I was standing anymore.

Dark, moist, and inviting; these were the words that came to mind once we finished descending the fifty-two stone steps that led us down below. At the bottom of the steps we came to a pool of shallow water framed by elaborate arches that gave off a golden light.

Someone in Scottsdale needs to build a spa like this, I thought. It turned out this wasn't as original an idea as I thought it was. *From Russia with Love* (the famous James Bond film) had been filmed on the very ground where Paolo and I now stood. You didn't need a tour guide to come across this information. For one, people going down the steps kept repeating this again and again, as if they had to keep repeating the mantra in order to believe they were actually here. Rather than admiring the incredible pillars of Medusa, most were snapping photos of themselves pretending to be James Bond in the film.

I, too, was a little distracted. I was taking stock of Paolo's tower of a body, so the architecture of the turrets and pillars of former Constantinople hardly stood a chance. Suddenly, I hoped for a small miracle: I prayed the cisterns were a bed. This line of reasoning is only possible if you've been raised Catholic. When, as a child, adults whom you trusted took you to dark and dank places to tell you that a man named Christ would grant you anything you wanted, you grew up to think of Christ as a human vending machine. If Christ could turn water into wine, couldn't he turn this cistern into a bed to make what was about to happen a little more comfortable?

Before I could blink again Paolo leaned into me. He descended on me so swiftly that I had no time to register what was happening. Pretty soon he began walking me backward, his strong grip firm and unyielding, until my body was pinned against Medusa's pillar. Paolo was a serious kisser, sensual and totalitarian. It was easy to give in to him. He placed one hand on the pillar above my head as his free hand moved slowly up and down my legs. "There are peop—" I started to protest. He bore his eyes into mine and pushed me into him.

I no longer cared where we were.

Ours was an instinctive connection, instantly primal. Paolo's searching fingers trailed my body as if they had been down those curves many times before. We kissed, searched, and tasted each other; my hips rising and falling until our rhythms became one. It was freeing to give into abandon for a change. After a while Paolo grabbed my arms and stretched them high above my head. He pinned them there while he continued to explore the rest of me. His was a touch so frank I thought

I might weep. To be touched like this was such a novelty. It was also a gift.

By the time we came out of the cisterns, Istanbul seemed to have changed colors. It was as though we had gone on a vast and grand journey and on our return everything around us had been magically touched by the intensity of what we had known. For a while, we walked in silence, yet in a heightened state of awareness. In the distance, the imposing Topkaki Palace seemed grandiose. The minarets of the faraway mosque looked particularly expansive pointing toward heaven. The entire city, in fact, appeared magnified. And this is saying a lot, because Istanbul was already magnificent.

"What are you going to do with your three wishes, *cariño*?" Paolo asked.

"Nothing," I said. "The lamp is for my sister."

"You can always steal a wish. She'll never know."

That was true. Azucena would never know. But in a world where everything was meant to be broken, the last thing I wanted to do was to steal a wish from my little sister. Yes, it was tempting. It was tempting to become a wish thief. It was also tempting to believe in Aladdin. There was a seductive allure to returning to the bustle of the Grand Bazaar to get another lamp. But I didn't have three wishes in me. Only one.

"I wish—" I started. But Paolo hushed me with a kiss.

The late afternoon call to prayer carried throughout the entire city. It was a haunting sound that meant nothing to a couple of tourists, except that we were going to be late.

"*Ay Dios mío,*" I said. "We're going to miss the boat!"

"Run!" said Paolo, grabbing my hand.

We ran and ran and ran, darting and dashing, skipping around the faithful kneeling on the ground, Paolo never letting go of his tight grip on my hand as we ran toward the afternoon, the sights and sounds of Istanbul sweeping before us. The Galata Bridge looked small and blurry in the distance, and echoes of the ship horns announcing their departures reached us as we gasped for breath. We had a ways to go yet. We had to get there before they pulled up the gangway and before Michael Coin's voice announced his final and conclusive "all aboard."

No doubt Paolo would lose his job. As for me, staying behind in the holy city with a Brazilian chef—now *that* was a common whore. If we didn't get back in time my mother would chop off my head on a butcher block. So we ran and ran. And ran some more.

PARLEZ VOUS OTTOMAN?

If there was ever a heart full of premeditation, it was mine as I started to get ready for Ottoman Nights. Paolo had told me that themed nights were the busiest for the kitchen. He also said he'd be running around all over the place. So I knew the chances of seeing him again were slim. Still, the evening was barely under way. Standing before the small mirror in our cabin I ran my fingers through my lips. They were sore from Paolo's kisses. Just thinking about the intimacies of the afternoon was enough for the warmth I had felt earlier to start spreading through me again. But something very like guilt gave my heart a squeeze. I was about to put on some lipstick when I remembered that Max was still in my handbag.

"It's just for tonight, Max," I said, returning the bottle of Advil to the shelf. "Something tells me you won't like this party."

In the end I should not have feared that Ottoman Nights would be the second fall of Constantinople. The evening wasn't that far from combination fried rice at a bad Chinese restaurant. Maybe a little worse. The menu had been announced on that day's events calendar as "Chef Paolo's Ottoman Menu." When had Paolo had time to cook? He had been with me all afternoon. As a matter of fact, the two of us had been the last to arrive, just as the ship's security officer was giving orders to pull up the gangway. I didn't care much about food. But as I was putting on my earrings I did wonder if we would be having Turkish TV Dinners by Sea Stouffers.

The events calendar offered two dress options for that evening. Either you went Ottoman (whatever that meant), or you went formal.

Alastair had decided on both: an Armani tuxedo accessorized with a red velvet imam's hat. That hat turned out to be the supposed Turkish hammer he'd been carrying inside the bag when I ran into him at the Grand Bazaar. He looked striking in his East-meets-West ensemble. People's admiring stares were not lost on him, either. His foxy gray eyes shone like jewels against the red velvet, and for a passing, covetous instant I thought about what great fun it would be to go on a real date with Alastair.

Groups of strangers who had by now sworn to lifetime friendships for sharing an afternoon in a foreign land were huddled around the bar. The rare assortment of turbans, tunics, and gold chains made any Halloween party on land seem lame by comparison. A little gold cuff here, a little plastic shackle there, and the massacres of the past were soon replaced by a sultan's fashion nightmare. But the thing that truly gave Ottoman Nights their place in modern history was the Greek music. Now one had to wonder if the Turks played Greek music and smashed plates on the ground as they proceeded with the genocide of millions of Ottoman Greeks.

The people I felt truly sorry for, though, were the wait staff.

Waiters were wearing what looked like shorn pillow cases clumsily wrapped around their heads. They were so busy running around that some of their head pieces had partially unraveled. Their eyes were smeared with black makeup, presumably to make them look authentically Turkish, or just fresh out of a gang fight at the docks. For their part, the women were made to dress like harem girls, even if some of them were fighting (and losing) the battle of the bulge. Whether in ancient or modern times, some bellies simply are not meant to be bare.

"He's trying to start a jihad," Larry said, looking at Alastair's imam hat.

"Oh, you're just jealous it didn't occur to you," Alastair snapped.

Larry's only concession to the evening was a purple cummerbund with matching bow tie, two small embellishments to his otherwise conservative tuxedo. Like me, Larry had decided that formal dress would be the most sensible option that evening. I was wearing a white silk white dress accessorized with dangling gold earrings that I thought would have passed for exotic anywhere. But our choice of glitz turned out not to be nearly as Ottomanish for Alastair's taste.

"Both of you," he said. "Don't you realize you won't be able to wear an imam's hat to Costco once we disembark? Tsk. Tsk. Tsk."

"As if. As if there's a Costco in San Francisco," I said. "It's probably illegal."

Larry smiled paternally at my remark.

A petite waitress holding a round tray containing little packets lined up on a plate approached us and asked us if we cared for an appetizer. Each of us in turn grabbed a little packet and took a bite. I felt a pang of pity for Paolo after the first bite. But the feeling didn't last long.

"Are these leftover dolmades from our class?" said Alastair.

"I wouldn't know," I said. "Remember, I left?"

"Larry," he said, "is that cilantro I taste?"

Larry took a bite, considered what he was chewing, and said, "You know, I think you might be right . . ."

Had we done all the work for Paolo? Is that why he'd been able to take the afternoon off without a care in the world?

A couple of buffet tables were set up nearby. Alongside so-called Turkish meatballs, gyro platters, and green sparkling something or other, our only worry should have been whether or not there was a doctor on board for the upset stomachs that would follow the party. What made the buffet truly authentic, though, were the printed cards before each item, announcing what it was. Otherwise no one would have been able to tell a Turkish meatball apart from one at the Old Spaghetti Factory.

"I almost forgot," Alastair said, speaking to Larry. "Wait till you see this!"

Now he was busy retrieving his white phone from his tuxedo jacket. He then did that searching thing that people with chic and smartphones do with their fingers, and proceeded to show Larry the pistachio fiasco at the Grand Bazaar.

Unfortunately, Larry wasn't a man of big gestures. That's probably how you kept your CEO job anywhere, by looking interested yet without judgment at every piece of paper placed in front of you. "Oh, we lost a million dollars last month." And then, "What's on my schedule for this afternoon?"

Staring at the screen placed before him, a nearly imperceptible upturn of the lips came to Larry's face when the tower of pistachios came falling down. Hard as I tried, I couldn't see the two of them together. Alastair, like me, was expecting something a little bit more expressive by way of reaction. Something along the lines of "Alastair, you have a future as a film director!" Or maybe, "Valentina, was it sooo awful, all those strangers staring you down while you made a giant pistachio pyramid tumble to the ground???"

Sadly, nothing of the sort happened. Larry sipped his Kir Royale and offered us a kind smile this side of patronizing. Seeing that his pistachio documentary had gotten him no Oscars, Alastair put his phone away without further comment. This wasn't the viral reaction he had expected. Not in the least. And when Alastair was disappointed, hurt, or simply bored stiff, he did what came most naturally to him: he picked up his toys and left the room.

"Coming with us, dearest?"

"I promised my mother we'd have a drink before dinner," I lied.

What I was really thinking was, "Where is Paolo?"

My eyes darted in every direction. Running into him wasn't so far-fetched a notion when you considered that there is only one place where a chef can be on a busy night, and that is in the kitchen. There was a kitchen behind the lounge.

In the meantime, while I had been busy learning history at the cisterns, my mother had made a friend. The two of them were chatting animatedly at a small table not too far from where Larry and Alastair had been standing. For her Ottoman attire my mother chose the silk scarf I had bought for her at the Grand Bazaar. It was olive green embroidered with a subtle paisley pattern in black. I thought the green complemented her brown eyes beautifully.

Her friend's name was Lydia and she was from Lima. What better luck than to meet another woman from a sister parallel so that together they could indulge their hemisphere's favorite pastime: talk of deviants and dictators.

I slipped into my seat quietly so as not to interrupt their reverie.

"*Oh, sí. Los años de Fujimori en Perú. Terrible.*"

"*Sí. Sí.*"

"*¿Y los años de Pinochet en Chile? Qué terrible.*"

"*Sí. Sí. Terrible.*"

"*Pero los años de Chávez si fueron terribles. ¿No?*"

"*¿Y qué me dices de Fidel?*"

"*Ay sí. Terrible. Qué cosa tan terrible.*"

"*Pero no tan terrible como los años de Somoza en Nicaragua.*"

"*No. Eso sí fue terrible.*"

It was tempting to suggest they start in alphabetical order, so they'd get through the entire hemisphere a little faster. How about starting with Argentina and running quickly past Bolivia, spending a little more time in Chile, and naturally, Cuba. Then off to El Salvador, an obvious pause in Nicaragua, then rushing through Uruguay and Paraguay, and ending in Venezuela during the carnival. Everyone from South America knew that Brazil didn't count because of *that* linguistic glitch. As for Costa Rica and Panama, the two rarely featured in any serious political discussions. You could hardly use the word *terrible* when talking about Panama or Costa Rica when instead of dictators these small countries had tourism directors who were always on hand to greet people from North America during spring break.

What if I joined their deviant tête-à-tête and told them that in my adopted country the most that citizens feared from their rulers was a blow job under the presidential desk? Banal fears, if you ask me. Blow jobs are harmless. To my knowledge blow jobs have never stopped a country from running. As a matter of fact, while the president zipped and unzipped his pants in Washington, imports from China continued to arrive on time at Walmart outlets in fifty states. No one got hurt. Or to put it in a way that *all men* can understand, inch for inch a blow job and an express kidnapping are simply not on the same scale.

But I was only half-listening to their conversation. My eyes were busy darting back and forth from the flapping doors behind the bar where members of the waitstaff appeared and disappeared like actors behind a theater curtain.

That's when I saw them.

Paolo and the waitress who had brought us microwaved dolmas were engaged in a heated argument. She was considerably smaller than him, so she was looking up, her face contorted. She looked very upset. Maybe she had messed up the buffet display and Paolo was letting her have it. That was, in any case, want I wanted to believe. But no. After stroking her hair, he further calmed her down with a significant kiss and a bonus pat on the bottom. This sent her on her way, allowed her to pick up her tray and to return to the job of continuing to amuse the rest of us.

"What is your specialty?" I heard Lydia ask my mother.

Schizophrenics, I wanted to say. *Her specialty is schizophrenics who carry ashes in bottles of Advil halfway around the world. Her particular specialty is* tontas *who make out with butchers in three-thousand-year-old toilets sold as cisterns to tourists while wishing that Aladdin would grant her an impossible wish. That's her specialty.*

Why bother to deny it? After spotting Paolo and the waitress I was as deflated as a party clown who had failed to bring laughs. The talk of doomed countries and wicked dictators didn't help, either. The live music failed to enchant. After meeting Paolo I had the child's faith that everything would be all right. When it wasn't, my disappointment was doubly freighted. Every person wants a life that moves toward some form of happiness, or at least a life free of unpleasant truths. At that moment I wanted very badly for Max to come back. But was I only wishing that because I'd been disappointed? A few hours earlier, at the beginning of the evening, I had wished for something else entirely. My stomach started to churn. I felt guilt-ridden. Poor Max. He didn't deserve this cheap betrayal. He didn't deserve to be left behind on a bathroom shelf like an afterthought. And what would bringing him back mean, exactly? Bringing Max back from wherever he had gone, would mean that he would have to return to face whatever nightmares had chased him away in the first place. And what kind of person wishes that for a loved one? For the better part of a year I had tried to imagine his line of vision. What did he see on his last day? I was there, too. But for whatever reason Max didn't see me. Or if he did, it didn't help. The news that he was gone hit me like a thud.

I placed my palms on the armrest and tried to get up. But I felt as though a wounded bird were nailed to my chest. I wanted to take off, to fly elsewhere. My mother gazed at me. Silently, she was asking: Are you all right? I looked away and then back. I didn't want to have to answer. So I tried again, getting up. The time was slowly approaching when I would have to let go. Not let go of the idea that Max wasn't coming back. I had to let go of the wish. But the thought of forgetting Max and all the promise of our life together was debilitating. What would I have left once I forgot? Memory is a shifty mix of reality and wistful imagining. I didn't have enough steam to go all the way back, to remember the bad times. That's why I missed Max. I missed the wistful imagining part of our marriage.

It Didn't Taste Like Chicken

The following evening my mother asked Lydia to join us for dinner in the main dining room. I was grateful for this new friend of hers. For my mother, a new friend usually meant a brand-new head in which to conduct new experiments on why grown humans insist on lying to themselves; believing, for instance, that you could find fresh deer in a floating dining room at sea. For me, Lydia's presence meant that I was no longer my mother's full-time charge in the Majestic Mediterranean. I knew nothing about this woman. And yet I loved her!

Lydia had alert eyes that stood out from a wide forehead. Her hair was always pulled back in a small bun at the nape of her neck, and her makeup was always perfect, if a little severe. My guess was that Lydia had probably perfected this look by hosting fundraising dinners back in Lima.

As for dinner in the main dining room, the way this was touted and hyped you would have thought we were going to have dinner in Paris. So much puff was built around the main dining room that by the time you took your seat at one of the tables, the only acceptable food groups would have to be truffles or caviar. Or better yet, truffles on top of caviar. No chef could live up to the bogus promises typed at the last minute on the allegedly daily-changing menu. But least of all Paolo, who by now, it had become clear, hosted classes where excess food made by expert foodies would later appear as his own with a different sauce on top.

The three of us were led to our table by the maître d' from Romania, whose given name was so complicated, apparently, that his name tag read: Eddie. The visual aid name tag was a very considerate touch. Except, the moment Eddie opened his mouth and you heard the accent as thick as lava, you knew he was born to a name chock-full of consonants, one vowel, at most.

As for me, all it took was to open the menu for my stomach to turn on seeing the words: Chef Paolo's Daily Special. We were on our way to Mykonos. Now that we had left all things Ottoman behind, Mykonos was the new Holy Grail. In all likelihood the strike Ethan had spoken about had been subdued with a few Trojan arrows while everyone was busy shopping at the Grand Bazaar. Either that or our captain had bribed some port authority somewhere so they would now let us enjoy the rest of the Grecian delights in peace.

There were many delights ahead, and a couple of surprises as well.

Chef Paolo's specialty this evening was the chicken in Champagne sauce. Really? A safe bet was that the Champagne was probably water from the cisterns. After handing out menus and taking our drink orders, Eddie asked us if we had any questions. I wasn't hungry at all. But all the same, I was curious about the fictional Champagne sauce on the chicken. This is something that women the world over seem to enjoy doing. Once a situation comes to a close for obvious reasons, we like reliving it a little longer in our minds by continuing to torture ourselves with the reruns. Sometimes we opt for torturing the offending party. Sadism versus masochism—it depends on the day. It depends on the woman. That night I was in the mood for both.

"How is the chicken prepared?" I asked.

"We bring it on plate," said Eddie.

On a plate? Don't you know? I straightened my back against the faux-velvet chair, the better to take in this intricate preparation. *Valentina, keep calm. In just a few more days you'll be sitting on a cactus again. It isn't Eddie's fault that he left his family in Romania to serve chicken of the sea to bitter Venezuelans.*

"Sounds delicious," I said. "That's what I'll have."

After me, it was Lydia's turn to have her puzzling questions answered.

"What do you think of the salmon?" she asked.

At this, Eddie lowered his head as if he were at a funeral and said, "Bigg meestake."

The salmon must be tripe for the maître d' to call it a big mistake, I thought. Now what? The composed Lydia beamed her pageant smile at all of us.

"Thanks for your candor," she said. "I guess I'll have the chicken, then."

In the end, the three of us ordered Chef Paolo's Daily Special. I could hardly wait for this special chicken that was going to be brought to us on a plate. By then we had learned to expect abrupt language from most of the staff, not because they were rude or ignorant, but because they were translating from their native tongues and had few verbs in their vocabulary.

While we sipped our cocktails and waited for dinner, Eddie returned to our table holding a bottle of wine.

"We didn't order any wine," I said.

"From the gentlemen," he said, leaning in conspiratorially.

On Eddie's behalf I would offer that he had much to recommend him. But his dumpster breath was not it. *Did you, by chance, have rotting carp a week ago and forget to brush your teeth?* All I could do on such short notice as he leaned into me to tell me about the wine was to urgently pick up my napkin and pretend I had a virulent cough that would not abate.

Mercifully, my cough encouraged Eddie to turn his gaze in the direction of our benefactors. As I followed his gaze I noticed that a few tables down from ours, Ethan and Marco were having dinner and enjoying a wine bottle of their own. So busy was I stewing in my own juices that the only thing I seemed to have noticed that evening was Paolo's name on the menu. But not to worry, my mother was aware enough for both of us. When she realized who it was, she bowed her grateful head in Ethan's direction. As for Lydia, she exclaimed, *"¡Qué amable!,"* which in Spanish means, Why didn't I bring my daughter?

"Pour the entire bottle on Chef Paolo's head."

This is what I wanted to tell Eddie as he proceeded to rotate the bottle in front of me several times. Where had he learned this? I had to imagine that eventually the rotation would have to come to a stop at the label on the front. And so it did. Where was Azucena when I needed her most? I had no clue if this wine was or wasn't liquid plumber. But this mystery was soon to be resolved. As soon as I noticed the year on the bottle I looked nervously at Eddie and hoped he would not spill it. After the ceremonious opening of the wine, he poured me one sip into a new glass and asked me to taste it.

"Will dekkant it off curse," he said.

"Ah, yes, please decant it."

Certain that I had ingested hundreds of dollars in that one sip I made an obliging little wave in Ethan's direction. I really wanted to like Ethan, the Aussie rock climber with a taste for expensive wines. An heir to a winery, no less! Someone who taught me to play roulette and insisted I keep my chips. Ethan was beyond good-looking. He was a striking exponent of the male species who also knew what was going on in Greece. As a bonus, my mother liked him. That fact alone, right there, confirmed me as the schizophrenic I really was. No. I wasn't as sick as all that. No doubt what we had before us was an unprecedented case of stupidity. What was wrong with me that I had ignored his gracious invitations? Given that Christ had failed me at the cisterns I was entitled to a second miracle. Now I wanted for Christ to turn our table into a couch so that my mother could tighten the lose screws inside my head.

"Doctora Serrano," I would ask, "why did I fall for the player when the nice guy was handing me the chips? Please explain."

So we toasted. We took tiny, careful sips of our holy wine. When I lifted my glass in Ethan's direction his wide grin showed how obviously delighted he was. By way of returning the favor I meant to yell across the dining room, "Ethan, whatever you do, don't order the salmon!" He had been gracious enough to warn me about the tower of pistachios, after all. But my mind was elsewhere. My thoughts returned to Paolo's chicken. I wondered what it would taste like. As fowls go, chicken is always present to mind.

Say you're in Kenya. An hour or so under the sun in the plains and you ask the jeep driver, "How's the giraffe?"

"It tastes like chicken."

In China, "How's the cat?"

"It tastes like chicken."

Now you're in the Amazon.

"How's the crocodile?"

And the guy with the lance says, "Looks a little angry to me."

So what did the real deal taste like on your way to Mykonos?

Let's just say that a cage-free chicken, the kind that is petted, fed fresh corn, and sung to before it's killed, well, that kind of chicken, this wasn't. For her sake, I hoped Barbara from Portlandia was dining elsewhere this evening. The chicken we had that night tasted a little stunned. It had probably been bludgeoned on the head from behind. After the first bite, I had the spooky suspicion that whatever was on our plate had never been allowed anywhere, except possibly near a lamp. As for the Champagne sauce that wet its limp wings, all I could say was "I demand to see the chef!"

Azucena did this all the time. As the editor of a prestigious magazine where her readers trusted her to bring them only the best, my sister was always eager to call the chef out of the kitchen at her restaurant of choice, if only to watch him melt under her scorching gaze.

Nana had warned me about the butcher, hadn't she? Hadn't she said to inspect the meat? Hadn't she said the flesh was supposed to be pink? I poked at the lifeless bird with my fork this way and that. I cut another piece. But I didn't take a bite. Instead I took another sip of wine and proceeded to replay the afternoon one frame at a time. Yes, the urge to ask Eddie to call out the chef was almost irresistible. But tempting though it was to go back for a second peek under the kitchen hood I knew the only thing I would find there was lard.

PART IV
ANCHORS AND TIES

GRECIAN DELIGHTS

Leaving behind the Golden Horn—an inlet of the ship-jammed Bosphorus—and returning to the Majestic Mediterranean meant that everyone was to become straight again. You didn't have to be a cruising connoisseur to know that the new faces around the ship hadn't been hiding in their cabins. Back in Istanbul we had picked up a fresh boatful of innocents in pairs. Well, as it turned out, some of them were not so innocent.

Yes, Mykonos was in the air. So was Corfu. So was Mylos. So were the Grecian Delights. An alluring young woman sporting the job title *Future Cruise Consultant* was stationed by the front desk offering deals on the upcoming Grecian Delights. The concept could not have been simpler. If you happened to have robbed a bank in Istanbul, or found four thousand dollars under your mattress, the eye-popping consultant in the low-cut dress would let you stay on board as we treaded calmer waters. By then, the LGBT label had been removed from the brochures and replaced with a new label: MDTA. These new passengers in blissful pairs consisted for the most part of Men Dating Their Assistants.

Gone were Nadja and her sword. A new wave of entertainers had joined the ship in Istanbul. In the next few days the entertainment was to become slightly more conservative, easier to swallow by couples who were in love. I was in no way prepared for what awaited me at the Sky lounge that evening. My eyes had to adjust a little in the dark.

"Alastair," I said, "I think I'm seeing things."

"Have another martini, dearest. Then you won't care what you see."

"I'm serious, Alastair. I think that man sitting over there is Max's old business partner. His name is David Warren."

"I'm listening," said Alastair. At that point he stopped playing with his white phone and set it on the lacquered table in front of us.

"But it doesn't make sense," I said. "What would David be doing here all by himself? He has kids in school and everything."

Up until this point, Alastair had been listening while looking straight ahead. Now he turned to face me. For good measure, he lowered his gaze to prove how daft I was.

"He's not here all by himself, dearest. Everyone knows that the Greek Isles are the perfect place for a business off-site."

"He is, too!" I insisted. "Look at him. I'm going to say hello."

"Leave your drink here. Something tells me you might spill it."

PEOPLE WHO NEED PEOPLE

"Is that you, David?"

"Uh . . . hmm . . . Valentina. This is a surprise. What are *you* doing here?"

"Me? What are *you* doing here? Where is Ann?"

"Ann? Right. Ann. Well, Ann is busy."

"I see . . . So. How are the kids?"

At this, a person of college age appeared before us and served David an accusatory look. Her whole face looked like an angry question mark, in fact.

"Uhh . . . Jordan," David said, getting up. "This is Valentina, an old friend."

Jordan eyed me from head to toe.

"An *old* friend. Yes. I can see that."

"Valentina, meet Jordan . . . my assistant."

"Nice to meet you, Jordan."

What was that silly shrug supposed to mean? Did the girl have special needs? Was she stuck in high school?

"So you're in real estate, then?" I asked her.

Jordan's voice was very high-pitched. She reminded me of a cheerleader. Or maybe it was the long ponytail that reminded me of a cheerleader.

"David's helping me get my license," she said.

For some reason, David saw fit to stem the flow of adoring remarks about to be hurled in his direction.

"Listen, Valentina . . . I'm truly sorry about that business with Max . . . But I'd really appreciate it if you . . . you know . . ."

No. I don't know. I have no idea what you're talking about. That business with Max? Was suicide now a business?

So wise of Alastair to tell me to leave my drink behind. The choice would have been a difficult one: pour the contents on Jordan's miniskirt, or on David Warren's balding head?

"There's nothing to explain," I said, leaving him in midsentence. I wasn't in the mood to hear Ann was busy with the kids.

By the time I returned to Alastair he was talking to Jean-François, the aviator from Montreal whom I had met by the pool deck in Santorini.

"I got you another drink," Alastair said, looking up. "The other one got a little wet."

"Did it?"

A giant "Well?" was written all over his face. Unfortunately, beyond what Alastair had already surmised, I had nothing of substance to report.

There's this involuntary tic I have, this thing I do with my index finger sometimes, a kind of wiggle. It happens whenever I spot someone who needs a new haircut, or any change in their appearance. Say I'm talking to a woman. The moment I meet her I try to figure out what part of her looks she needs to update in order to achiever her best self. While I work to figure this out, though, my index finger goes up in the air, wiggling to and fro. *Tone down the shimmering blue eye shadow*, I might be thinking. *Either that, or ditch the bright pink lips—the two together are a little much.*

Many times in conversation I get deeply absorbed in these imaginary makeovers. Sometimes I want to write some ideas down for the grooming-challenged and hand them out at the end of a conversation on index cards. I suppose it's inevitable. When you're the daughter of psychiatrists you're doomed to see the world through the eyes of a repairman; thinking that other people need to be fixed, that they're the ones who need to change. I always start with the physical appearance. It's far more efficient to start from the outside in; the inside could take years. At any rate, that's precisely what happened when I looked at Jean-François that night at the lounge. I wasn't aware of wiggling my index finger until Alastair said, "What's with the hummingbird finger?"

"Oh, I'm sorry. I was just thinking of something," I said, lowering my hand.

As soon as I sat down, I said to myself, *I know what it is. It's the mustache! This man doesn't have enough testosterone in his system to produce a proper mustache.*

And it was true. The top of Jean-François's lip looked as though a handful of albino ants had feebly decided to crawl on it but were about to retreat to get some leaves elsewhere. It crossed my mind to offer him one of my razors. What was with everyone in this boat changing their look at every port of call? Some transformations were more difficult to believe than others. Take, for instance, M.C. That evening, Michael Coin had miraculously transmogrified from snarky cruise director to professional announcer. Microphone in hand, his blond hair was slicked back. Well dressed and neat, he looked almost respectable.

"Ladies and gentlemen," he beckoned. "Please put your hands together and help me welcome the incomparable Sly."

For now, at least, the entertainment had returned to favorite American Classics. This was to delight the new honeymooners who had not yet OD'd on "Piano Man" sung with a lisp. People clapped. The incomparable Sly herself had ditched her black leather shorts and cheap fishnet stockings and was now wearing a blue sequin dress that did better justice to her image and her lovely figure. At first, I didn't recognize her. It was the voice that gave her away.

"Take it away, Sly," said Michael Coin.

The delight in his face was obvious. This kind of evening was Michael Coin's first love. His voice was keener, his manner less pedantic than when he said, "All aboard at Five. On. The. Dot." He should move to Vegas, I thought.

Out of the corner of my eye I watched David and Jordan getting up to leave. I wondered if their Grecian getaway was now ruined. Meanwhile, Sly's voice echoed throughout the place. She was ready to take everyone to heaven. And then:

Peeper who need peeper
are the rockiest peeper in the werld.

Now it was Alastair's turn to shake his head in disbelief.

"Poor Barbra," he said.

"Who's Barbra?"

"Streisand, dearest. She might drown herself in Mykonos, if she heard this. Do you even know what this poor girl is trying to sing?"

I shook my head.

"People who need people are the luckiest people in the world. It's a classic."

"Never heard of it," I said, getting up.

"Come on," said Jean-François. "It's not as bad as all that. You're not leaving us. Are you, Valentina?"

David and Jordan were halfway across the lounge when I went after them.

"David, wait!"

He looked around awkwardly, the way some guilty people do. As for Jordan, she rolled her eyes as if another cheerleader had stolen her lip gloss.

"What is it, Valentina?"

"It's just . . . You know . . . The past year has been really . . . I guess I just have to ask. Did Max ever say anything to you? I mean . . . he didn't even leave a note."

"Oh, he left me a note."

"He did? What did he . . . ?"

"He left me a big, fat note from the Bank of New York," David said. "It's taken quite a while to clean up the mess."

The simmering rage in David's voice was wholly unexpected. David had always been overly polite, his words and manner as measured as a politician's. I never trusted anything he said. Once, joking about it with

Max, I had asked him if David rehearsed everything he said in front of the mirror beforehand. Besides phony, he was also incredibly self-absorbed. It didn't even cross his mind to ask me if I was traveling with anyone.

"I see. Is that why you never came . . . ? I mean, how come you never said anything about it?"

"It was business between me and Max, Valentina. I just took care of it. And besides, you had your own mess to deal with."

"How did Max seem to you? I mean, those last few days . . . ?"

"Listen, Valentina. You need to understand that whatever I might say is nothing but speculation. The one thing I know for sure is that it wasn't just the money. Max and I had lost money before. We'd seen the markets come and go over the years. So it wasn't just about that. This was different."

"Different how, David?"

"Hell, I don't know. This probably isn't what you want to hear. But have you ever disappointed yourself to the point that you've no idea how you got there?" he asked, running a hand through his thinning hair.

I'm sure you're speaking from experience, I thought, eyeing Jordan.

"I'm not trying to imply anything here," David went on. "But it's the everyday catastrophes that get you in the end. It's the picked fights, it's the truth bombs; it's the wife who checks your mileage and wants copies of every receipt..."

"Oh, not *this* again," said Jordan, walking out.

"Best of luck, Valentina," David said, rushing after her. "Jordan. Jordan, please come back!"

Best of luck? Did I hear him right?

This was way too demeaning; wanting to get answers to the point of ambushing someone like David Warren in the middle of a sea date. The only reason I went after him was that, even after all this time, everything was still murky. I suspected there was something David knew that I didn't. And I'm not talking about a simple, morbid desire to know about some secret Max might have shared with him.

There's a terrifying inevitability in the aftermath of suicide: that you'll go on wondering forever and ever and ever, and every waking moment after that. I was terrified that through his choice Max had released me into a state of permanent chaos with a longing that would remain forever unrequited.

Up until actually running into David, I had believed that if I called him, met him for coffee, or went to his office to ply him with questions he might give me an explanation that made sense. Now I realized that in those early weeks, and the blurry ones that followed, I had lived inside a fantasy, the fantasy that one day I would actually *know*. Way back when there had been so much I had thought of asking David. But to my complete surprise and later disappointment, he never came to Max's service. It had been Ann, not David, who had come to pay her respects. Duty-bound and mindful of protocol, Ann had offered some excuse or other for her absent husband. To be fair, if giving condolences after a normal death makes a few people speechless, well . . . condolences after a suicide render most people inert. At the time, I had believed Ann's excuse. But I won't lie and say it didn't hurt. Max and David had worked together since before I met Max. Was their friendship not as deep as I had presumed it was? Was it a business-only relationship I had mistaken for friendship?

In the end, the explanation was probably far simpler than I could have imagined. David didn't come to the service because he was busy having an affair. That he was selfish and inconsiderate was a lot easier to swallow than: David didn't come to the service because he knew something he didn't want to tell me. But it's never easy to substitute an alternative explanation for the one you already have. Now that he had insinuated something else—that there was more to it than money—I didn't want to believe it. I especially didn't want to believe it from someone who was on his way to Mykonos with his girlfriend while his wife helped their kids with homework. Had David been talking about Ann? Was she the cliché jealous wife? So it wasn't that Jordan was taller, thinner, *and* younger; it was that Jordan didn't obsess about receipts. I felt like going after him again. I felt like screaming: "So what was holding your marriage together, David? Was it Play-Doh?? Was it Silly Putty?? Or a combination of both?"

Our exchange left me a little lightheaded. I felt that queasy feeling that you get when someone just broke up with you and you didn't see it coming. But for once I was the lucky one. I didn't want to be Ann.

PLUTO: PLANET NO MORE

This wasn't what I expected to hear, especially from a five-year-old.

In the years that I took to the desert to help Max raise Rosemary's babies, my friend Joanna, with whom I had worked at the ad agency in New York, had met someone, gotten married, and proceeded to get pregnant. I hadn't met the husband. I hadn't gone to the wedding. As it so often happened when Max's kids were growing up, life got in the way. As for Joanna, it was the pregnant part that made me feel a little betrayed. Joanna and I had been the career women, the ones with ambition. Work was life's work for us; not the other way around. As far as I could recall, Joanna and I were the last two renegades who weren't going to fall for the trap of mommyhood. Isn't that strange, how a friend's situation can spookily illuminate your own as if she were shoving a flashlight in your face?

I met Joanna's son when he was five years old. And the one thing I could say about Jake is that he was a liar. Well, there was more I could say. In a pinch, there's always a lot more I can say.

As for my friend, the Joanna who had been affectionately called a "ball buster" behind her back at the office, she had changed; except the change wasn't physical. Even as she shushed away my compliments, she was still lean—her arms were defined, and her butt didn't jiggle when she walked to the kitchen to get us some water. It was the other changes in her that caused me to clutch my purse. Focused as a heat-seeking missile, Joanna was now a spent puddle of womanhood, defenseless before this all-consuming experience, the near obliteration of the self that ensues upon becoming someone's mother. She now worked a few times a week, but she did so from home, the better to be stumped by Jake and his devilish maneuvers.

Max and I were in New York to visit his brother, Ira, and after much discussion about how, when, and where to meet Joanna during this brief visit, I ended up sitting on her couch while she kept three eyes on Jake and one ear in our conversation. If there was ever a body divided, Joanna's was it. The setting was far from ideal. Certainly, it wasn't my first choice. What person sane of mind would choose mom *and* kid, versus mom alone? *I shouldn't have come. I shouldn't have come*, kept running through my mind, as I tried to calmly sip my water. In very short order it became clear that sitting quietly nearby while the person he owned—physically, spiritually, longingly, exclusively—talked to a stranger, wasn't working out for Jake. After a series of menacing stares in his mother's direction, Jake literally took matters into his own hands and proceeded to slam his Lego trucks against the wooden floors.

"What did we say about slamming?" Joanna said.

"Is his dad very strong?" I asked, by way of normalizing the violent demolition. "What's he like, your husband? I can't believe I won't get to meet him this time."

After a few imploring and useless stares that failed to soothe the now-enraged Jake, Joanna looked at me and said, "Would you mind if we went to his room? That way he can play, and we can actually talk."

Would you mind if I left right now? I wanted to ask. *Here you go again, Miss Accommodating. Now you get to go play with Jake the Madman!*

The entire ordeal brought to mind a story about the dad who took his son to a park where two dogs were humping.

"Daddy, what are those dogs doing over there?"

"Let's see, Johnny . . . Well, the dog on top must have hurt his two front paws and that dog on the bottom is helping him home." To which the kid said, "It figures, every time you help someone out, you get screwed."

I was about to get screwed; to be locked up in Jake's POW camp. The way I saw it, the farther into the house from the front door we traveled, the more difficult it would be for me to leave. Joanna's voice was full of anxiety, and something else, besides—a kind of bizarre fear, as if Jake were Hannibal Lecter and she were his helpless victim. Jake's intensely blue eyes were trained evenly on his mother. If we didn't get up and go to his room *now*, I half-expected him to say, "Bowels in, or bowels out?"

It was with a touch of weariness that I left my safe corner on the couch to follow the two of them toward the back, through a long and narrow corridor that led us to Jake's playroom. I stood by the door and leaned against the frame, reluctant to take another step in, lest running away went from mere daydream to mission critical.

Jake's playroom room was a paean to the inevitability of Toys 'R' Us. Amid hordes of soldiers, towers of Legos, a bright red fireman truck the size of a bike, and a ladder that went all the way up to the ceiling, really, the only place to stand was by the door. So I was safe where I was. Until Joanna waved me inside. Never had such a harmless gesture spelled doom so clearly. I had no choice but to go in, which I did, taking nervous geisha steps toward the first thing that caught my eye on the floor—an enormous map that doubled as rug with pictures of the sun and other things galactic. While Jake assessed his new prisoner, I looked down into the rug and in an effort to engage him I asked him if he knew his planets.

"I know them in Spanish," I went on, and proceeded to rattle them all.

Mercurio
Venus
La Tierra
Martes
Jupiter
Saturno
Urano
Neptuno
Plutón

This tender, if fugitive moment, was the only time during my visit when Jake smiled. Actually, he giggled.

"Do it again!" he said.

I was about to, but a second glance at the rug told me something was amiss. So I said, "Jake, your rug is wrong."

"My rug isn't wrong," he said.

"Yes, it is," I said. "Pluto is missing."

"Pluto isn't a planet," he said, smugly.

Hmmm. Public school was a mistake, I wanted to say. But it was Joanna who corrected me.

"Jake's right," she sighed. "Pluto's been demoted."

"Since when?"

"Oh, I don't know . . ." she sighed. Joanna sounded exhausted, but it was the resignation in her voice that really spooked me.

"Jake, do you want a smoothie, sweetie?"

"Noooo. I want her to leave."

It took me a few seconds. But I got it: Her was *me*.

"I'm sooo sorry," Joanna said. "He hasn't had his nap today."

A nap isn't what he needs, I wanted to say. *Have you tried electric shock therapy?*

Now he wailed.

Vestiges of innocence, the culprit, puke and piss, rude, little dictator, tic-tac-toe, uh-uh, oh oh, tick tick tick, oh fuck, jam on the carpet, splitting headache, slaughtered bugs, 666, 911, please stop Jake, please STOP, Jake. Mommy you are mine!!!!!!!!!!!!!

This jumbled list of minor horrors kept running through my head. But the one word that came to mind while Jake continued to wail, devastated by the unexpected loss of his mother to a stranger, was: smackable.

Now that Pluto was gone, I took it as a sign. Pluto's galactic departure was definitely a sign for me to take my leave as well. I was startled by the random noises and wails. I was also rattled by this unexpected planetary amputation. Who had decided this? After years and years of Pluto being a planet—a fact that had been printed in the textbooks of my childhood—my solid education was now in question. Other doubts would soon begin to trickle in as well.

If Pluto no longer revolved around the sun for lack of gravitational pull, then what of the more impermanent things on planet Earth, like marriage, for instance? Up until the day when I glimpsed my friend's foreseeable future demolished by a five-year-old, I had believed steadfastly in the permanence of planets. Now that one of the stars of my childhood was reduced to swirling in clouds of black and haze, I felt like stardust of neutronic proportions. On the way to the subway to meet up with Max, the all-consuming drama of life in progress pulsed between my temples like one of those songs you can't seem to get out of your head.

My mind was cluttered with images of Pluto floating aimlessly around, unable to clear the universal neighborhood, like some trans-Neptunian object without a home. Why was I so rattled about some random planet's demotion, anyway? People got demoted all the time. Was Jake's piercing wailing what made my head feel like it was about to split? Or was it seeing Joanna's doomed future behind bars that brought on this sudden panic?

Reluctant step after reluctant step toward the subway, I began to fall apart under the weight of the loss of our mutual, utopian dreams of emancipation. It was odd how that happened; how Joanna's precarious position vicariously reinforced my own. After seeing her, I could no longer deny it; the years had passed, quickly and so many. In the interval, Joanna and I had failed to become the people we had envisioned. Worse still was the realization that we couldn't go back to fix it. I felt like I was digesting thorns. A terrible sense of disappointment began slowly to descend into me. Perhaps I needed a little coaching about how to revive my ill-fated future married to someone who had an ex who mistook her kids' hands for ashtrays. Scarier still was the thought that Max might be as busy debating with himself as I was. What was I supposed to tell him when he asked: How did it go with Joanna?

At some point during our lives some of us might say, Shoot me. But sooner or later, we come to our senses and see the wish for the venting valve that it is. Except, some people mean it. Did Max slip through the cracks of our marriage because I was caught up in my own private dilemma? What signs did I fail to recognize?

One thing was certain: Pluto was now a dwarf planet, an astronomical label for planets that couldn't cut it.

A BUNCH OF FLOWERS

The day before the one that would be his last, Max brought me flowers. It was a colorful bunch of daisies, lilies, sunflowers, roses, and carnations. I hated it. I don't know if Max knew I hated flowers. It's possible that he knew and was trying to say: If you don't like this, wait till tomorrow. It's also possible I never got around to telling him why I didn't like flowers. What probably happened was that we were so busy with stomachaches, swinging moods, and ear infections that the opportunity never arose to tell him about my floral dilemma. I didn't mind them at the botanic gardens, in hotel vases, or in other people's houses. But I've never been one fond of maintenance, especially of living things. Changing the water, opening those little dusty packets that look like powdered sugar, and watching scattered petals on surfaces you're later doomed to clean—that's never been a personal ambition of mine.

Coming from the airport as he was after visiting his brother in New York, the only thing I could say was "Max, how thoughtful of you!"

But maybe this bunch of flowers wasn't a romantic gesture. What if Max was trying to apologize in advance? What if he was saying, though not in so many words, "Valentina, please forgive me for what I'm about to do. Remember the flowers, not what came afterward."

I've never thought of a bunch of daisies and lilies as a potential preemptive strike. Men tend to give flowers *after* the fact; after they've screwed up your day, or after they've screwed your best friend, an apology for all that is vexed in them.

Constricted. Tormented. Devastated. Stumbling. Confused. Disappointed. Bitter. Unhappy. Overwhelmed. Exhausted. Defenseless. Selfish. Was Max any of those things on that fateful evening?

Naturally, these thoughts were far from my mind as I went into the kitchen to arrange the flowers in the vase. These ideas didn't come to me until much later. That's probably because after a time committed to the institution of marriage one struggles, one learns to be tolerant, one learns to stop asking silly questions, such as: What are these for? One learns to silence the disappointments; to hush the expectations placed upon such a doomed endeavor as trying to know another person.

There was no forgetting those flowers, though. There was also no forgetting the moment when I became convinced of two opposite things at once: that the voice at the end of the line was speaking a truth as cold as ice, and that what he was saying was also impossible.

All of us, without exception, pledge ourselves to a cause. And by this I don't mean worshipping Wicca the Witch, the prophet of the pyramid, or the ewe up the mountain. Whether we worship ten infrangible commandments, or a bottle of gin, there is nothing truer than that to which we pledge our lives. And there is danger in this. Because anything to which we pledge our lives will begin to decide for us, will infiltrate our thinking, will determine what has and doesn't have value. If you pledge yourself to love, you have also pledged yourself to loss. If you pledge yourself to youth, you will die a thousand deaths with the advent of every wrinkle. If power is what you worship, you will awaken every day in fear it might be taken away. What struck me about the unexpected encounter with David Warren was a different kind of truth; the truth of choice, the only truth there is: to decide what to worship; knowing that all worship is insidious because of how easy it is to be consumed by it. And once that happens, whatever your choice of deity, it will begin to decide for you, consistently, repeatedly, until your own capacity to discern is all but annihilated. David had chosen Jordan and the consequences of Jordan, whatever those might be. And me? At some point I would have to stop thinking that for leaving the way he did, Max also made a choice for me. Eventually, I would have to separate "him" from "me" and "me" from "us." I just could not fathom how. There were times, most times, when even the thought of it felt like chopping my own arm in half with an ax.

Whenever something inexplicable touched our lives the priest who came to say Mass at our school on Fridays bribed us with faith. He leafed through the Bible. He preached of rebirth. We knelt. We got up. We knelt again. He said God blessed those who believed without seeing.

Now that I had come to a stretch of road that might stretch on forever, I suspected that what the Friday priest might have been trying to say about faith was something else entirely—not the faith of believing in floating angels, or pitchfork-bearing demons, but faith as a blessing of sorts. Faith is a virtue precisely because of how arbitrary it is. Actually *knowing* would vitiate its grace.

As for suicide, the beast seemed to have a hunger that might well be insatiable. I could keep feeding it. I could keep trying to figure out what the flowers meant. I could continue to ask if in the rush to get home to me after a week of traveling, Max forgot to pin a note on those petals. I could also choose to rehash what David Warren had said about there being more to it than money, until I was swallowed whole by it. Or I could choose to give David's speculation some room for doubt.

tHE BEGINNING OF tHE END

#49
1 of 1
4/4/2013
1:17 PM
Medium
****

Printer 1 - LAG
C: Roy
Check: 23067

Every life has its own topography.

In time, the topography of our marriage lost many of the jagged edges that prick the getting-to-know-you stage of many relationships. In turn, these edges were replaced by the nearly flat landscape of routine. That is, until the day Max decided that routine was for him no more. Afterward, there were sharp edges again. But not for Max. A sharp plunge. Then the abyss. Except Max could have no memory of it.

Before going to work that last morning, Max had coffee, but not cereal. Only later would I find out he wasn't going to work. Max always had cereal for breakfast. As for me, despite years as a transplant in the cereal-loving North America, I have not been able to make up my mind as to which of the hundreds of colorful boxes on display at the grocery store are worth the risk of what might be inside. Assuming that kind of risk could take years. So I have toast for breakfast, instead.

That day Max was wearing a blue linen shirt I had given him for his birthday. Blue was a beautiful color on him. Max had alert, brown eyes and long lashes I used to envy. His brown eyes stood out even more when he wore blue. Was this an intentional choice, or did he just grab that shirt out of the closet without thinking?

Right before leaving, Max pulled out a receipt from one of the pockets in his sport coat and set it wordlessly on the kitchen counter next to the barely touched bowl of cereal. That receipt had been handled. It was wrinkled, smeared, and stained; it had passed through several hands before making it into the pocket of Max's sport coat. Despite its sorry condition, though, that receipt went on to become a prized possession of mine. That little piece of torn paper became part of a jigsaw puzzle that had more missing pieces than I could count. Beyond Max taking it out and leaving it behind on the kitchen counter, I paid no particular attention to it that morning. At the time, it looked like what it was—another travel receipt. But afterward, through further handling, the receipt became an almost holy object for the mystery I could not unravel. The mystery was hidden in the word: *medium*. The rest of the receipt was fairly simple to figure out.

On April 4, 2013, my husband placed a single order of something at 1:17 in the afternoon, New York time, at the LaGuardia Airport. LaGuardia being so busy, there were 48 other orders before Max. His was number 49. On that particular day—which would become eventful for me, but only in retrospect—there had been 23,067 checks, receipts, or orders, placed at that particular eating establishment. The cashier's name was Roy. So this Roy at LaGuardia was one of the last people to witness what Max put into his body before getting on the plane. For a while, Roy kept me awake, colonized my dreams, and periodically visited my nightmares. What did Roy look like? Did he say to

Max, "Have a nice day!" Or was he rude in that passive-aggressive way some people have? Did Roy still work at LaGuardia? Should I go to New York and ask Roy if Max mentioned he was married to someone named Valentina? Did Roy make small talk? And what was Medium? For a while I felt I might be crushed by the weight of so many unanswered questions.

Unfortunately, part of the receipt, which was printed on Printer 1, got chopped off. So I have no idea where Max ate one of his last meals. Did Max order a burger, medium? Or did he buy a medium drink? Was it tea? Was it water? Was it lemonade? Was he hungry or impatient while he waited for #49 to come up? Or was it one of those places with some promise of "under five minutes, or your order is free"?

Unfortunately, again, there was no price. So maybe this wasn't a receipt. Maybe this was just the little order ticket Roy brought to Max's table along with the food. If so, where was the real receipt? Was this why Max took it out of this coat, as a reminder? That morning, the breakfast conversation that would be our last, went something like this.

"Busy day at the office?"

"I think so."

"Would you be home for dinner?"

"I'll call you later."

After that, he gave the bowl of cereal a tiny push forward. I took a bite of my toast.

I might have noticed more. I could have noticed more. We can all stand to slow down a little, to pay a little more attention. But to what end? I remembered his lush eyebrows, the nearly imperceptible crinkle of his brow when he had a question, his strong forearms, and the way he stirred sugar in his coffee, clockwise; a few absentminded rotations before putting the spoon down. Could I have saved Max by asking, Why the extra sugar this morning? Is the occasion of life really so frail as to hang on an unasked question about a teaspoon of sugar?

I'll never know.

Max was patient, quiet and had a way of wisdom. Did he? Did he leave carrying a grand secret of what it means to be alive? He was also adventurous. Max liked to explore uncharted waters and uncharted territories. He was the one to suggest the where and how of our vacations. In the end, he had his own map. It was a map of a place of unsettled borders, a most rugged landscape shaped through his attention and particular needs. Whatever its seasons, its attractions, its wonders, they were known only to him. There were no signposts, nor was there a place where I could locate myself amid such arid vastness.

After all this exploration, after everything that's happened since, afterward, and in between, I still can't answer the question: What should Max have done? Seek therapy? Talk to a friend? Take another pill? The only thing I can say with any certainty is this: I wish he hadn't.

Did I love Max?

Did he love me?

Knowing how the end would come, would I marry Max all over again?

The best I can say for myself is that I would want the good times we shared, the memories of our wedding day, the times we read side by side, and the jokes we shared. But life doesn't let you distill the bad days from the good. In the end, love guarantees nothing. And yet, despite the trickery, despite the land mines, despite the seismic shifts, people still fall in love.

It's hard to believe.

ILLUSIONS

Along with hundreds of others, Jordan and David were in line to go ashore in Mykonos. What with its fluorescent waters and multihued sunsets, this was the place where Homer should have set his sights. In the end, though, Homer had a bigger odyssey to fry than the discreetly idyllic Mykonos. That is, in any case, how I remember the lovely Greek Isle: as discreet. But it's possible that my memory of Mykonos is colored by an unexpected find.

I was standing by myself a few paces behind David and his supposed assistant. That day, Jordan was wearing blue fluorescent sunglasses and a halter top in a striped orange pattern. Her ponytail was tight and perfect. Her skin was supple and young. While I won't deny that David's face glowed younger in Jordan's presence than when he was with Ann, he looked much older than I remembered him. But that was an illusion. Like me, he was barely a year older than the last time I had seen him. I was just seeing him in a different light. And it wasn't very flattering.

Nearby, Lydia and my mother were talking animatedly while waiting in line. It has always been my mother's unwavering belief that every lunatic has a theme. Had she discovered Lydia's theme yet? Was Lydia compulsive about pencil sharpeners? Were *pirañas* her pet peeve? Was she obsessed with dust particles? Was Lydia, too, confused about the march of dimes?

Humankind came in such freaky flavors. I suspected my mother was having her own private Grecian delight.

After running into David and Jordan at the Sky lounge the night before, I had cried myself to sleep. I wish I could say that my tears were for Ann. But, to give due credit to my mother, we are all selfishly self-absorbed with whatever our favorite self-centered theme happens to be. At first, seeing David had made me feel nostalgic for Max. Watching David sit there by himself brought Max back whole. But the discovery that he wasn't really "by himself" was a wake-up call with a very loud ringing tone.

All those years I had thought that he and Ann had the perfect marriage. Ann was the perfect wife. Trey and Dana the perfect kids. I was the oddball. I was the South American *chica* with the North American stepkids whose husband ended up blowing his brains out in his ex-wife's kitchen. I was positive. I was positive that I was the only one *not* living the American Dream.

On closer inspection, though, everyone's lives were an illusion. The time had come to admit that Max, too, had been an illusion. It was time to accept that for years I had shared a bed with someone I barely knew. So after smearing the pillowcase with black mascara, I had decided that Mykonos was the place where I would let go of Max for good. These blue and enchanting waters were the place to say goodbye to my one and only wish to Aladdin.

Alastair had wanted to go check out the nude beach together so that we could get a good laugh. He promised it would be a good laugh, and not at all the paradise of beautiful models on holiday I had envisioned. When I told him what I had planned to do instead, he said to come knock on his door afterward, never mind what time it was.

Ethan had dropped a note under my door, inviting me to spend my roulette winnings at a spirited Mykonos taverna his brother had recommended.

While standing in line, Robyn and Nicole said they were headed to the monastery on the mountain. It was supposed to be "breathtaking," said Robyn. Did I care to join them and a few other people on that tour?

Nude beach. Spirited taverna. Mountain monastery. Had I not been busy with my own concerns, of all the things to do in Mykonos, perhaps I would have gone to the monastery. I had grown up surrounded by some of the most glorious beaches in the world. But I had never seen a monastery on top of a gorgeous beach.

In the end, I went into Mykonos by myself. Max's ashes were in my purse.

SIGNS

There are untold advantages to being a Catholic. One of them, one that makes us stand apart from the less fortunate who practice lesser religions, is our ability to read signs. By this I don't mean ordinary signs in bright and obvious yellow, such as SALE. Catholics can read those signs, of course. But we can also read more interesting and telling signs, such as, if the water in your fish tank turns a little cloudy, it might mean your goldfish is about to die. That's a sign. If a person has a coughing fit at a Greek restaurant, it might be a sign that he swallowed an olive pit. Or, if while you are strolling down a narrow street in a foreign country a dog's bark seems out of control, it's possibly a sign to run. The dog might have rabies.

So I strolled, paused, walked and walked some more, waiting for a sign that would tell me how, when, and where to part with Max's ashes.

A young woman with long, honey-colored braids was standing outside a boxy white square too small to be called a shop. Both her arms were lined with bracelets. On seeing me approach she extended both arms in my direction. She told me she was selling the bracelets and asked me which one I liked. I was standing before a human bracelet display. Did they hire her because of the long arms? I wondered. Greek women don't come with long arms. Where did they find her? As it turned out, my initial, if unspoken assessment, was right on the money. She was from Dubrovnik. Was that a sign?

It was. It was a sign that I needed a bracelet. So I bought one from her for five euros and kept walking, in search of more signs.

The day was bright and full of promise. The couples we had picked up in Istanbul strolled hand in hand. In fact, Mykonos was packed with couples who looked like extras in a foreign film to be shown at Cannes. Seeing so many couples was a sad sign. I was by myself in a glorious place with no one to kiss. Briefly, I remembered Paolo.

In the distance, a man who belonged in a brochure sat inside a giant boulder that had a whole blown through the middle. Probably some ancient volcanic rock that now looked like a modern sculpture. Dressed in white from head to toe, the man appeared to be lost in the impossible beauty before him. It crossed my mind to walk up to him and say, "Buddy, you mind if we share the rock?" This had been done to me once at a coffee shop in a place called Boulder. I remembered wanting to spill the coffee on the guy. What is it about us humans that we can't leave peaceful enough alone?

On my way down yet another cobbled street, I waved at a few people I had seen on and off during the past week, and kept on walking until I came to a little cavernous place that reminded me of the old pharmacies in Caracas. The little cave turned out to be an alchemist's shop. In addition to perfumes, dried flowers, potions, and lotions, the place sold tiny bottles and tiny boxes, presumably for stressed-out travelers to carry their Xanax.

The only reason I entered the cave was the fleeting memory of home. I had wanted to see if this, too, was an old pharmacy staffed by an old man holding a cane. But then, on seeing the tiny glass bottles—a giant sign if there ever was one—I had an idea.

DID YOU SAY: GREEN MELON MOJITO?

The swarthy taverna owner was equal parts muscle and discreet. Thirty, at most, he wore a day-old stubble like a second skin and a hand-woven shirt I had seen in many of the shops, which turned out to be the Greek man's answer to hundred-degree heat.

He was attentive without hovering and after offering me the best seat in the house within a toe's touch of the water, he asked me if I had come here "in ship."

No. I swam here, I wanted to say.

Hanging out with Alastair was having a definite harmful effect on my already unstable disposition. But it wasn't as dumb a question as I thought at first.

"Yes," I said. "That big one over there. Can I please have the mojito?"

"Great choice," he said, and walked away.

I didn't expect much. I mean, a mojito in Greece? *¡Por favor!* But what did I have to lose? I had already lost everything I thought mattered to me. After my mini epiphany, I was ready for an adventure. I was here to start over. I was here to become someone else. A green melon mojito hardly counted as a risk. While I waited for my drink to arrive I took out the bottle of Advil and set it on the wooden table. I then put on my sunglasses and proceeded to stare at the water for what seemed an eternity. The sun was constant and unsparing. It made the already sparkling water look fluorescent.

The tavern owner came back after a while and placed a gorgeous creation in front of me.

"Headache?" he asked, pointing to the bottle.

I shook my head and he took his leave.

The tall glass contained a handful of lime slices wound around the glass as one with tiny mint leaves sprouting between them. It was tempting to admire it as a liquid bonsai, but after the first sip I considered moving to Mykonos instead. The sweetness of the green melon in contrast with the mint was a revelation. Had I been the kind of person who wants to replicate at home concoctions from the road, I would have asked, "How in the world did you do this? Or, in short: Recipe, please."

When Max and I exchanged our vows I never imagined that one day in the future I would be sitting by myself halfway across the world, taking him out of an Advil bottle and trying to pour what was left of him inside a tiny glass bottle bought at an alchemist's shop in Greece. It's the things you can't imagine that turn out to be true. It's a green melon mojito in Mykonos that turns out to be the true Grecian delight.

The transfer of the ashes must have looked clumsy. Because out of the blue, a tiny silver teaspoon, the ones used to stir sugar into cappuccino, was placed quietly on the table by my side. An hour passed. Perhaps two. That afternoon, time passed the way it's supposed to pass in hot yoga, except mine wasn't a planned meditation. After transferring the ashes from one bottle to the other, I fell into a sort of trance that lasted quite a while. But who knows? It's also possible that two shots of ouzo had been stirred into my drink. Whatever the case, when I finally came to, I asked the taverna owner for the bill. As I was getting ready to pay, I learned from him that Mykonos was an incredibly sophisticated place, notorious for its nightlife, and that during the day it was mostly dormant. Wealthy people came from other islands very, very late at night and expected only the best. When I praised the mojito, he assured me that it was nothing. Apparently, coming "in ship" was vastly different than coming "in yacht."

That green melon mojito turned out to be something of a personal legend for me. It wasn't a sign of anything, though, other than what wealth can buy. A quick look around and you knew that melon trees did not grow behind this tavern.

"Your office has a great view," I said, finally getting up.

He closed his eyes and nodded sagely.

I was about to leave when it occurred to me to ask him if he knew of a good place to leave someone's ashes. The man barely blinked. He had obviously wandered far and wide, had likely seen as many broken hearts as he had seen drunken fools at his taverna. The two of us walked in silence to a little inlet full of strangely shaped rocks covered with the greenest moss I had ever seen. The place looked like a coral reef in miniature.

"How do you say 'thank you' in Greek?"

"*Efkharistó.*"

"*Efkharistó,*" I said, meeting his eyes.

A quick nod and he was on his way.

In looking back, he was the perfect person to have asked. To someone from Greece, a land rich in gods, legends, and tragedies of epic proportions—to say nothing of the insufferable strikes—a tourist asking for a place to leave some ashes was probably small pebbles. In all probability the taverna owner had grown up saying, "For Helen's sake!" as he dispatched hundreds of toy horses in his backyard.

tUMbLe HoME

I was about to reach one of life's inarguable stops.

A light wind feathered through my hair and water lapped gently through my ears as I walked the length of the inlet and back, trying to find the perfect spot for Max. Inside, though, between my ears, the sounds of the wind were a great deal more violent. I was having a private thunderstorm. I was trying to make peace with returning to a house that would be filled with commonplace noises, the ticks of the refrigerator, the buzzing of lightbulbs about to give out; a house that also would be empty of a voice that at one point had given it character. From now on that voice would be absent; not for a day, not while Max was at work, or away on a business trip. But *all* the time.

Max loved to snorkel. So after all the pacing back and forth I decided on a turning corner that was surrounded by oddly shaped rocks covered in green-as-in-dreams moss. Tiny, tiny fish were swimming round and around. They seemed to be having a good time swimming in circles. So that's where, after much deferment and anguished hesitation, I decided to tuck the tiny bottle—between two of those rocks. Standing side by side between what I once had and had no longer, I knew that two lines had intersected, and that one of them had reached a vanishing point. And although the goodbye threatened to swallow me the way the sky above threatened to swallow the land, I knew that the landscape beyond this moment contained new life.

Without being aware of it, I had spent the better part of the past year in shock. It was the kind of shock that wraps you in a haze that makes you feel you're looking at everything from a distance. Staring into that cove I remembered being aware of people's kindness, of their hugs, and their gestures. I also remembered being courteous and polite. That's because, for all purposes, these condolences were being offered to someone who was numb as a block of ice. I wasn't actually present but was made to witness everything nonetheless.

Leaving the cove was very different. By then the numbness had thawed, so now I experienced my own departure at the sharpest possible physical level. My back was pelted by a storm of sun rays spilling their glow on the hurt that had been quietly constant, but which now had reached the inarguable intensity of irrevocability.

It would be a lie to say I was entering an overcast world. The sky that day was the purest blue. The cotton clouds perched above matched the white of the boxy houses that dotted the hills. It was as bright and beautiful a place as there is likely to be anywhere. And yet, I couldn't leave Max there. I hadn't taken a dozen steps back toward the taverna when I was overtaken by a wave of panic. What would Max do here, in this foreign place for the rest of time? Had Max been standing in front of me, the terror of never seeing him again would have felt exactly the same.

So I turned around.

For the longest time I could not manage to take my eyes off the tiny bottle tucked between those rocks. The longer I looked at it, the more the panic spread. The sunlight raking on the sparkling waters of the shallow inlet made me feel as if I were experiencing a flashing exposure to light. The finality of it, that Max would not be there again to talk to, or to say good night, tricked me with its mock impossibility all over the again. This had not happened. This could not be. This wasn't Max. And this wasn't me. It hit me all at once: the dry heave, the choking sobs, the wetness on my cheeks. I knew I could not leave him. I just knew. I couldn't.

And then I did.

"Bye, Max," I said. "I don't know what you were expecting. I hope . . . I hope you'll like it here. I know this isn't what I had in mind."

UNSTABLE ON TWO WHEELS

Perhaps the biggest fear my mother was never able to overcome was the fear of bicycles. To her, bicycles were two-wheeled monsters that would launch her daughters into a hospital ward somewhere and turn them into kale.

For his tenth birthday my cousin Frasquito got a bicycle. There were only a few things my young cousin could not do with his bike. So agile was Frasquito that he was able to stand up on the seat with only one hand, among other acrobatics. On seeing his many feats, my mother would exclaim, *¡Niñas, qué peligro!* and would yank us away, squeezing our wrists until she cut off our circulation. This was lest Azucena and I decided to pull the ribbons from our braids, tear off the ruffles from our white socks, and say, "Frasquito, move over; it's our turn." But no matter, watching other people riding bicycles was *un peligro*, a deadly danger in and of itself.

Things could have easily gone the other way. For instance, I might have learned to ride a bike and become a circus performer behind my mother's back. Instead, when the time was right, I escaped to another country and chose therapy in a second language. There was, though, that time in Sedona when Max taught me to ride a bike. It wasn't a full-on lesson on how to beat the people riding in the Tour de France or anything. But as lessons went, it was enough to know what I didn't want to know.

Sedona is called Red Rock Country for a reason. You trained your eyes in the distance and the sight of the enormous red sandstone monoliths that surrounded the city was enough to make you believe in energy vortexes, spiritual discovery, and concepts like positive energy fields. For the less spiritually inclined, the imposing red rock monuments and hundreds of acres of rugged terrain said: This is the place to learn to ride a bike. So that's what we did. Max rented a couple of bicycles and taught me how to feel unstable on two wheels.

"Maybe we should all live in grass huts," Max said, contemplating the landscape. "Not touch so much of the earth."

What? Was I hearing things?

"Really, Max? That's what you do all day, stir the earth."

"Look at this, though. It's so beautiful, so peaceful. Sometimes I feel we're ruining it for everybody else."

"We?"

It wasn't like Max to go all schmaltzy and philosophical. Mostly, I remember him as a very practical man. And yes, there was that side of him that came out when we were on vacation, when we were closer to nature, as we were that day in Sedona. So perhaps his musings that morning deserved further exploration. But they were so unexpected I was too baffled for words. I didn't know what else to add to these random ruminations about ruining the planet for future residents. For one, there was a real and present danger right in front of me. It was called a bike.

"These are your controls," Max said, twisting and turning the front of the bike this way and that.

"Max, wait! Where are the little wheels in the back?"

"You mean training wheels?"

"I don't know what they're called. But I need them. Otherwise, my head might split like a coconut."

"Do you trust me, Valentina?"

"Hmmm. Maybe . . . Maybe it's the bike I don't trust."

"I'll be your training wheels," Max said.

I felt the anxiety brewing at the pit of my stomach. And my heart was about to leap out of my chest. After a couple of tries, I finally managed to get on that bike.

For a few yards Max trotted behind me, saying encouraging things as if I were a child.

"Go. Go. You're doing great!"

"Max, it's going too fast."

"Turn the handle. Just turn the handle one notch."

"What handle, Max?"

"On your right."

"I can't stay up here forever, Max. Make it . . . ssstoppp."

Boom! I landed on a tree.

"Are you all right, Valentina?"

"I think so," I said, getting up.

My badge of honor was a greasy tattoo, a stencil of a bike chain imprinted on the inside of my calf. Tiny trickles of blood threatened to ruin this perfect design.

"Let's try again," Max said, encouragingly.

"I think the bike isn't up for it, Max."

If ever there was a real miracle in this world it was that I had agreed to get on a bike. But once was enough to find out that I didn't want to do it a second time. So we cut our biking adventure short and decided on a leisurely walk through the historic town nearby, which turned out to be all things as promised.

Despite the voodoo view of sports at our household, somehow Azucena still managed to learn to play tennis. Given that there were yellow balls in my immediate future, I should have been more amenable to my sister's entreaties to go with her to the club from time to time to hit a few tennis balls. But I simply didn't have it in me. I was a natural-born klutz. To my great surprise, there was tennis in the Majestic Mediterranean. But I was innocent of this fact when my passenger card was scanned by the ship's security officer on my return from Mykonos. How was I supposed to know there were tennis courts on this boat? A real cruise ship vacation worked like this: Gamblers to the casino; sun worshippers to the pool, shoppers ashore, and the clumsy to the library. I had two days to finish Ellen DeGeneres's memoir I had been carrying around.

After leaving Max's ashes in the dreamy cove, I had meant to take Alastair at his word and knock on his door. Larry and Alastair's suite was on a different deck than mere mortals' cabins. I was on my way up to that deck when I was stopped by a mini-revelation: I had nothing to say to Alastair. Whatever was left to be said on the subject of the ashes had passed quietly between me and the school of fish I had enlisted to keep Max company. It was done. Or, in the words of real experts like Dr. Phil, after a year of cross-dressing and dragging my feet in someone else's Italian shoes, I finally had "closure."

So I turned around and took the atrium stairs back down.

That's where I ran into Ethan. He was at the bottom of the stairs, by the front desk, returning a bunch of forms that had to be filled out before we disembarked in a couple of days. As soon as he spotted me he asked if I had filled out my forms yet.

"What forms?" I asked.

He quickly riffled through them and showed them to me. I had never seen them before. My mother, with her hyperactive responsibility gene, had probably filled them out ten days ago.

There was much to like about Ethan. But what I especially liked about him was that he wasn't dense. Yes, he was a little insistent. But he wasn't dense. I was grateful that the first words out of his mouth on seeing me weren't "I guess you didn't get my note." Or, "Did you like the mortgage wine I sent you the other night?" Instead, he said, "How about a game of tennis?"

I burst out laughing.

"What's so funny?"

"Nothing," I said. "I guess this is the part where you tell me your bed is a tennis court."

"Wouldn't dream of it," he said, smiling. "The tennis courts are on deck nine."

"I don't believe you. There are no tennis courts on this ship."

"Then meet me there in ten minutes. And you can see for yourself."

CALYPSO (THE NYMPH)

Sailing away from a place like Mykonos didn't require spectacular entertainment. The only potential competition to the island might have been fireworks reflected on its crystalline waters.

I headed to my cabin to change for our game of tennis, which really meant taking off the copper sandals and putting on the silver pair. Really? Did Ethan think I owned a pair of tennis shoes? I was going to treat him to a game of Venezuelan tennis—a dress in feminine floral patterns and dainty silver sandals. But the moment I entered the room, I got sidetracked. Looming like a bomb under the dinner table in a Hitchcock film was the blessed events calendar. Setting eyes on the piece of paper on top of the bed was enough to get me sweaty palms. *What should we do tonight?* I might never recover from that question. So much to do, so little time left in this majestic bubble bath.

A small photo of a woman who played the flute graced the events calendar that day. Her hair, long as a theater curtain, concealed half of her face. The only thing that really stood out from the picture was the flute. Perhaps someone in Michael Coin's staff had dreamt up one of those cunning sirens who had derailed Odysseus in the *Odyssey*, which might explain why, in the end, Odysseus had washed up at a bar in Ithaca, New York, and not in the island of Ithaca, where his wife, Penelope, was worried sick and had no option but to pass the time consorting with her wooers.

I could almost hear the conversation: "Michael, I have an idea! How about a flutist dressed as a mermaid after Mykonos?"

But maybe that's giving M.C.'s staff way, way too much credit. That would mean they knew the difference between the *Odyssey* and that reality show where a handful of people are dropped on an island, naked and afraid they'll never find their Nike dry-fit shorts again. So maybe the flutist after Mykonos was a coincidence. Either that or they simply could not afford a second sword swallower.

In the meantime I had to hurry. I had to change for a tennis match.

30–Love

"Sorry I'm late," I said. "I got sidetracked."

Was that Poseidon in front of me, or Rafael Nadal?

"Wow," I said, pretending it was the view. And there was a little truth in that. Seen from the very top of the ship, Mykonos was a sight. *I should move here*, I thought. Meanwhile, attired in regulation Wimbledon tennis whites, Ethan was a sight all his own.

It had always been Azucena's dream to go to Wimbledon. Maybe after my mother gave her the Aladdin lamp, she might get her wish. When we were teenagers, Azucena's favorite pastime was to torment us with her tennis racket. Her many tennis outfits had to be washed by hand by a long line of ever-departing maids. Thanks to my sister I knew many tennis celebrities by name. I also knew what they were supposed to wear; how short was too short for shorts, how long for a ponytail. Thanks to the lovely Azucena I was well versed on the etiquette of the game and its related penalties. It was my understanding that a moody Russian girl whose name was Maria wasn't supposed to be wearing jewelry on the tennis court.

None of this, however, meant I actually knew how to hit a ball over the net.

Despite the jewels on my silver sandals, I was fairly certain that Ethan wasn't thinking Maria Sharapova when he saw me. He probably thought I was trying to play some sort of joke on him. Ethan couldn't have known that a sundress and sandals was as sporty as it got with me. In the end, the joke was on me. As it turned out, Ethan couldn't have cared less about any of this. He was in a world of his own creation, a world that was very foreign to me. Apparently, there were people out there whose personal philosophies ran pretty close to this: I don't care what I do, as long as I do it with you. This was an especially difficult concept for me to grasp, seeing as I was always busy trying to change everyone, aiming my wiggling index finger in every direction. To me, this vast and wide world was populated by deviant and imperfect people—many of whom were my mother's patients—who must be whipped into shape by normal people such as myself. Ultimately, that might have been the trouble with Ethan; there was nothing wrong with him. With his offbeat philosophy of the world Ethan was about to put me out of a job.

"Let's get some water," he said.

At this, his fit and tanned self walked toward a large blue cooler located by the side of the tennis court, extracted two bottles of Evian, and handed one to me. How he knew this cooler's location and that it contained bottled water remains a mystery. As a bonus, unlike the water in Volos, this French water was free.

"Ready to get started?" he asked.

"Where should I stand?"

"Behind the white line over there," he said, nonplussed.

I was pretty sure I was holding my tennis racket like a witch broom.

Unlike the many courts where I had seen Azucena play, the thing to know about this particular tennis court is that it was surrounded by nets. Not just the obvious net where the balls are supposed to cross over, but giant, invisible nets that were meant to keep the balls from going into the ocean. I didn't know this at the beginning of our match, though. Because, as I said, the nets were invisible; the better to feed you the illusion that you were playing tennis at the top of your penthouse overlooking the Greek Isles.

The challenge, from my limited vantage point, was hitting straight; the goal being not to lose a bag of yellow balls in five minutes. So rather than holding the racket sideways, the way Ethan was doing, I held mine above my head and proceeded to hit the ball *that* way.

Needless to say, that didn't work so well. When Azucena and her country club friends played doubles, they made this look a lot easier than it was. For his part, Ethan was unfazed by my ineptness. He kept producing balls from a magical wonderland and throwing them in my direction as if I were Roger Federer having a bad day at the court.

Ethan didn't have to work at the NASA of Australia to realize this was my first time standing on any surface the color of green Kool-Aid. A few times, I barely managed to get the ball over the net in front of me. But mostly they hit the other net. The first time, I thought it was a magic trick, the way the balls didn't go into the ocean. That's because the afternoon was supernaturally bright; the sun was as blinding as the flash in a camera, making every surface look as though it had been sprinkled with fairy dust. In no time we were sweating like construction workers, so Ethan suggested a break and we went to sit on the blue cooler.

It was very cozy on that cooler. So tight was the space there was barely room for our water bottles. I didn't want to be scrutinized at such short range. Clumps of wet hair were pasted all over my face. I was pretty sure I looked like a used kitchen rag. For his part, Ethan looked like what he was, a victorious tennis player gracious enough to sit down before humiliating his opponent.

"So what did you think?" he said, taking a swig of water.

"I'm a little wiped after the U.S. Open," I said. "But I'll recover in the next set."

Ethan turned his generous smile into the oasis that was Mykonos.

"Where in the U.S. do you live?" he said. "I'm in San Francisco quite a bit."

"How come?"

"Jake sells our wines to restaurants. Australian wines are big in the U.S. Maybe we could meet there sometime."

"For the rematch? You can't stand losing, is that it?"

"That's one way of looking at it."

"By the way, thanks for the wine you sent us the other night. Was that a good wine?"

"You tell me," he said. "You're the one who tasted it. I was surprised they had it on their cellar. It was a Petrus 1983."

"Whatever it was, it was wasted on me. I know nothing about wines."

"Let's see . . ." said Ethan, leaning into me, "sometimes there's a little taste left on the lips of the person who tasted it first."

"Is that a fact?"

CAPTAIN KURTZ MAKES A SPLASH

The captain's farewell was one of those time-honored cruising activities that made going on a cruise different from any other vacation. I had imagined it as a stodgy affair where a line of supplicants waited to shake the hand of a man in uniform; someone who ought to be reading his radar rather than drinking Champagne.

"We're going to meet the captain!" people said with glee in their voices.

"We're going to meet the captain???" I said, with alarm.

While getting dressed for the much-anticipated farewell I was nagged by a recurring thought. And it was this: if an airplane pilot were to leave the cockpit to toast the passengers, more than one person might get up and say, "No. Really, please go back to your seat." But of course, keeping steel afloat is so much easier than keeping steel up in the air. So Captain Kurtz could afford the luxury of relaxing and taking a little time for a toast.

My first impression of Captain Kurtz was that he was built like an ice rectangle. Everything about him was chilly. He had cold platinum eyes he used to appraise everything and everyone, giving the odd impression that they never blinked. He certainly wasn't my idea of a party host. Why didn't his PR handlers keep this sad man in the boiler room? As so often happens between us, my mother had the exact, opposite view. No sooner had the captain shaken her hand than she pronounced him a true gentleman, which is to say, the true gentleman I had failed to meet. We had time, though. There might be one day left on our Majestic Mediterranean adventure, but there was work to be done before the eminent Doctora Serena Serrano could peel off the CLINICALLY DEPRESSED sticker from my forehead. Earlier in the evening, on the pretense of applying lipstick in front of the bathroom mirror, she said in the most natural-fake tone she could muster, "Maybe you'll finally meet someone decent tonight."

This was the ultimate, if unstated, goal of this majestic adventure. This was why she had flown halfway around the globe and spent all this money. At the captain's party, she was planning to locate a creature who owned a penis and affix him to my person with Velcro, preferably with Crazy Glue. Why bother to deny it? The women in my family took marriage very seriously. My grandmother was proud of saying, "Three daughters, all married off before they finished college." As if my mother and aunts were ripe papayas at the market and any day after sophomore year they might start to rot, and by then it would be too late for anyone to buy them. Never mind that two of them were doctors, and one of them turned out to be a famous economist.

As for the other side of the family, my paternal grandmother finally exhaled peace when her one daughter married, at long last, at the rotten age of thirty.

"Well, we finally got Lupita married off," she said.

There was such relief in her voice you had to meet my aunt to realize she wasn't deformed.

It was with these unrealized, well-meaning desires that we left our cabin in search of reliable masculinity. As we were to discover, though, the time-honored captain's toast had suffered a metamorphosis of Kafkaesque proportions. Shortly after greeting the captain by the pool entrance, we spotted a young redhead reading on her Kindle on a pool chair.

"Look at the mermaid," my mother said, in case I had missed this sequined specimen of life aquatic. There was no denying it. The mermaid with the blue sequin fins was very theatrical. Had I been her handler, though, I might have said, "Hey, Dolphina, don't you realize mermaids are illiterate? Put that Kindle away."

What else could we be possibly immersed in after the juggler, the sword swallower, and the flutist-cum-muse? It seemed expectations had gotten so sophisticated that nothing short of a live mermaid was going to make a splash for these coastal culture seekers. There was plenty of liquid to go around, and already some people had a hard time enunciating the name of what they were drinking as they requested refills. Many were snapping photos of the mermaid. I seemed to be the only one afraid that her Kindle might break the illusion that she was Neptune's niece.

To better get everyone excited about the party that was just beginning on one of the decks, an activities host circulated through the crowd offering various prizes for whoever was brave enough to dance to the percussions issuing from a poolside stage. There were several hundred people lined up on the various decks, looking into the stage and the lit pool. One of them was Zoe, the widow from Connecticut. That night she wore a necklace that shone like real diamonds under the pool lights. They probably *were* diamonds. She was standing by herself holding a drink, an ecstatic look on her face. I made my way to her slowly, full of purpose, and after leaning casually into the rail I reintroduced myself and asked her if she was enjoying herself.

"I love it. I simply love it!"

It wasn't difficult to picture Zoe as a young woman saying these exact same words to someone else.

"About your friend, Fannie . . ." I started.

But the wise and seasoned Zoe was several steps ahead of me.

"Dear, sometimes an illusion is all a person has left. Who are we to enlighten anyone?"

After that, she let the matter drop and inquired after my mother.

"Is your sweet mother enjoying herself?" she asked.

I nodded that yes, she was. But I really didn't know.

It was after Zoe's question that it occurred to me that it was probably about time to leave the cracked world inside my head and start noticing a little more about the world I had forsaken after Max. Yes. The time had come to set sudden widowhood aside. A pool deck in the middle of nowhere was as good a place as any to kiss self-absorption goodbye. After my watery epiphany I made it a point to ask my mother if she was having a good time, even if my first assumption about her always was: If there are lunatics around, she's happy.

I was busy with my resolution when all of a sudden a loud and suspenseful drum roll began echoing from the poolside stage.

Toodroommmmm

Toodroommmmm

Toodroommmmmm

As if on cue, hundreds of people aimed their cameras in the direction of the show of lights below. On one side of the pool the former Kindle reader was suspended upside down from an aerial hoop. The lights shifted across her fins in scintillating hues of various colors, while a shirtless man whose abs you could count sprung out of the pool and joined her up a pole that they both began to climb as people gaped in disbelief.

Captain rectangle and the ship's first officer looked on from one of the decks as two bored bystanders who had seen it all before. They looked like two coworkers on a lunch break. On every deck, the party was barely getting started. People were dancing, shooting drinks, and shooting photos of various scenes. Chains of laughter echoed intermittently before getting lost inside the whooshes and splashes of the ocean.

My mother, too, looked slightly more animated than usual.

"Are you having a good time?" I asked.

She smiled as much as it is possible for an introvert to smile without the smile coming across as the result of physical torture. I took it as a resounding YES!

"Hold this," I said, handing her my drink.

Fueled by the pulsating rhythms and the foursome belting live music from the stage, I peeled off my sandals, made a run for the deck below, and jumped into the very pool where the Kindle mermaid had been contorting her fins a few minutes before.

Sometimes, the only way to get a therapist off her couch is to do the unexpected and make a splash. In all likelihood my dash into the pool ended up in someone's Instagram feed; another anonymous stranger in a world that more and more demanded to be shared in order for the sharers to believe it was actually real. But there was something more to it. Jumping into the water was the cold shower I had needed all along to wake up from the stupor. In the end there were no penises my mother could affix to me in these majestic waters. But I had to admit she had been right in her diagnosis. In all that time, it never occurred to me to ask for help, or to talk to anyone. That's because, all along, I had known what was wrong. Someone had left unexpectedly. No pill could help. No friend could cheer me. No one could reverse the course of events. There isn't a cure for a problem that can't be fixed. The gift my mother gave to me, though, was her genius for devotion. It is also true that she knew how to untwin one person's story from another's; how to turn the howling sadness she encountered at my doorstep into memories we must transcend—that we may continue to live.

And I had so much more for which to thank her, besides: mermaids who could read, chefs who could not cook, gay men who could go either way. There were also merry widows and the escorts who asked them to dance. To say nothing of the unexpected friends I met along the way. What with the Friends of Dorothy, the Friends of Bill, and the Friends of Jesus, these real-world friends might possibly rival my friends on Facebook.

Who could ask for more from an unwanted vacation?

ALL BECAUSE OF A MOSQUITO

I can no longer remember how many security lines we had to go through to get from the port of Piraeus back to firm land. But how to forget the conversation I had with my mother before we went our separate ways?

We were at the airport waiting for our respective flights. She was headed back home to my dad, to Azucena, to her schizophrenics, and to the grandchildren I knew she missed more than she dared say in the presence of one who was "clinically depressed."

"Thanks for the trip," I said. "I know you probably had better things to do back home."

"*Hija*, did I ever tell you what gave me the idea for the cruise in the first place?"

"No, Mamá. But I've been meaning to ask."

"Your cousin Isabella got dengue fever. But first, her fish died."

Hmm. Was this a sign? Was Isabella the Antichrist? Or was the fish?

As bad luck would have it, one day out of the blue Isabella became bedridden with dengue. Isabella, a successful corporate lawyer in Caracas, lived by herself with a cat named Pancho, a nameless fish, and two hamsters. Unfortunately, her getting dengue was preceded by a series of untimely deaths.

My mother has always had a thing against hamsters. She's always referred to them as rats. As soon as she mentioned the hamsters, I could tell that they had something to do with my being whisked away to eat prison chicken in the Majestic Mediterranean.

You have to have been born in the breezy tropics to fathom dengue fever. This is no ordinary temperature increase, say from 100 to 106. Besides the fever, dengue hits your bones as if a cement truck had dumped its contents on your body. Therefore, you are unable to move. There are also massive headaches involved; the kind where you feel your head is about to split. And then, on the second day, you begin to hallucinate. The moment her head hit the pillow, Isabella knew what was coming her way.

Like many busy professionals in bustling Caracas, Isabella had a maid. Her name was Flor, which in Spanish means: ignorant as a flower. It was Flor who locked Isabella in her bedroom and began to pray in earnest, vowing not to open the door until all the spirits were gone.

What caused the well-meaning Flor to lock my cousin like a white-collar snitch in her own bedroom was that the week before Isabella was knocked out by the dengue fever her fish died in the fish tank and then vanished. The day after *that*, Pancho, the cat, died. And the strangest thing happened—one of the hamsters disappeared, too. Any person who knows how to read signs would conclude that after eating a rotten fish and a hamster, Pancho died of ordinary food poisoning. But not Flor. As it turned out, Flor was reading completely different signs. And it was this supernatural reading that caused my cousin to be locked up in her own apartment fishless, minus one cat, plus one hamster.

On the day Flor found Pancho passed out in front of the washing machine, she made a sign of the cross and explained to the washing Gods, *Eso significa que viene una muerte.* To translate for those unfamiliar with superstition: three animal deaths precede one human death.

"I wonder who it will be?" Flor mused out loud.

From Flor's point of view, a death in the offing meant it would be either Flor herself, or Isabella. So after her little prediction, Flor locked Isabella in her room so my cousin would not die. The logic behind this being that Flor, herself, could not die because she was busy praying outside, and death isn't smart enough to get through a wooden door. In Flor's beautiful flower mind, she had all the bases covered. As for my cousin, on realizing her predicament, Isabella, smart lawyer that she is—dialed a few phone numbers. No answer at her office. No answer at her mother's. In the end she called my mother to save her life.

"Do you realize rabies, Valentina?" my mother asked, trying to see if I got the point already.

"No, I don't realize rabies, Mamá. Please go on."

Now that one fish, one rat, and one cat were dead, the talk of rabies began. Had the dead rat/hamster bit Isabella before meeting its fate? Had the leftover rat/hamster that was still alive chewed Pancho to his death? This had to be resolved somehow. In order to find out how much at risk Isabella and Flor were with one rat still among them, a rat pathologist had to be located. And pronto! It would fall to this doctor to confirm, or deny, if the leftover rat/hamster posed any harm to Isabella. To the rat pathologist, only Isabella's life mattered. A real doctor in the tropics cannot be concerned with the lives of people named Flor. Had

Pancho died of rabies? The pathologist had to figure this out, too.

"And if that weren't enough bad news," my mother went on, "all this happened during carnival week."

"Oh my God!" I said.

"*Hija*, do you realize how hard it is to find a doctor, any doctor in Caracas, during carnival week? Let alone a pathologist!"

"No, Mamá. I don't realize. In the U.S. you can Text-a-Nurse from you smartphone and she will text you back from the comfort of her rickshaw in Mumbai."

I'd be lying if I said that all of this didn't smell a little fishy to me. The whole thing reminded me of that movie, *A Fish Called María*.

To make my cousin's predicament worse, during carnival week superstitions count double; a kind of superstition double jeopardy. So my mother had to hurry. If she wasted another minute, Isabella might die from both dengue *and* rat poisoning. While waiting at the pathologist's office, my mother picked up a magazine. And it was while she was waiting for her name to be called, as she blithely turned the page, that she saw the ad. It was a sign: A luxurious megaship gliding across seas so blue that it made Aristotle Onassis's yacht, *Christina*, look like a tin boat.

And the next thing you know, she's knocking on my door in Arizona. So in the end, I shouldn't have thanked my mother. I owed the cruise to a dirty parasite. Everyone knows that dengue fever is caused by a mosquito that doesn't drink bottled water. Beyond that, all the talk of dead fish, dead rat, and dead cat is pure fiction.

So here's my advice. If you've been itching to swim around the world's unpopular coastlines with ex-cons from former war zones, I highly recommend typing two little words into your device of choice: swimming lessons. I certainly wouldn't entrust my vacation to an expired magazine left behind at a rat pathologist's office downtown Caracas. With so much water to go around in the oceans of this world, you don't want to end up in a place where they might charge you for the water.

To quote someone I met on that majestic adventure: "That would be a bigg meestake."

Bon voyage!

EPILOGUE

Given the short time that we spent together I was surprised to find how often I thought of Ethan, and how tenderly, once I got back. But the person who came to mind most often was Alastair. If there was someone I expected would return my emails, it was him. But he never did. Alastair, it seemed, went from port to port collecting acquaintances the way other people collected postcards, or souvenirs. In the end, he was part of the illusion—that after sharing blue drinks for a couple of weeks in faraway places you had made a new set of best friends.

A couple of times I thought of Paolo, though never tenderly. Paolo was like a delicious chocolate soufflé. It was impressive when they brought it to the table. But in the end a soufflé is nothing more than chocolate full of hot air.

Ethan was different. I wondered what might have happened had I taken him up on his offer to meet in San Francisco. A couple of times I imagined strolling down the vineyard in Adelaide where he said he and his twin brother Jake had grown up. The invitation to go to Adelaide had been genuine, and the idea of walking through vines sounded idyllic, if not downright romantic, even if I could never claim to be one with the countryside.

More than once I told myself that there would be other opportunities; that as soon as I was settled and sold the house, someone like Ethan would come along, maybe someone even better than Ethan. Do I ever cross your mind, Ethan? And what do you think about? It took a journey halfway around the world and multiple detours to get to where I was; I didn't want to cheapen the struggle with regret.

One day, as I was getting ready to meet Emily for lunch, the phone rang. I was tired of people calling me directly about the house. Why couldn't they call Marilee Lewis, the Realtor of record whose number was listed on the sign outside? Some people were impulsive like that. They'd be driving around the neighborhood and a house caught their eye. They Googled the address, and if they were lucky, the phone number was listed. I considered getting it unlisted. But I wouldn't be in Arizona for long. In my heart of hearts I knew I couldn't die in the desert, among sneaky spiders, random shrubbery, and whining doves.

"Yes. This is she," I said, picking up the phone.

"Valentina, how are you?"

"How am I? How did you get my number?"

"Guess."

"You bribed M.C."

"Guess again."

"You Googled me?"

"It wasn't that hard."

"Then how?"

"Your mother gave it to me."

"I don't believe it. This has now escalated to the level of full-blown conspiracy."

"The reason I was calling . . ."

"Yes, Ethan?"

"Have you ever heard of Bondi Beach?"

"I can't say that rings the bell. No."

"It's the Miami of Australia. I was wondering if you'd want to meet me there."

"Unfortunately, Ethan, I have lunch plans already. But I have to admit that a beach sounds very tempting right now."

"I'm taking that as a yes."

MIS GRACIAS

Sometimes, the inspiration for a work can seem as mysterious to the writer as it is to the readers who ask: What inspired you to write this?

I owe a debt of inspiration to writers who trekked the serious humor road before me.

In particular, I want to thank David Sedaris for his essay "Ashes," which inspired Valentina's carrying of Max's ashes in the bottle of Advil halfway around the world.

To the inimitable Jamaica Kincaid, I owe my thanks for penning *Girl*, which inspired Valentina's memories of a talk with her Nana in Istanbul.

Before shipping out to the high seas myself, I received a copy of the late David Foster Wallace's story "Shipping Out" (*Harper's Magazine*), later retitled "A Supposedly Fun Thing I'll Never Do Again." The keen eye with which Wallace observed life in an inescapable environment remained present to mind throughout the writing of this story.

As for funny, moving, and true, this is a hard thing for any writer to pull off without coming across as one of Serena Serrano's patients. I'm indebted to Arnon Grunberg for penning soulful elegies that glide effortlessly from absurdly funny to devastatingly heartbreaking. His lucid body of work is always humbling to read. *Phantom Pain*, in particular, informed many a detour in Valentina's whacky odyssey.

Jessica Anya Blau, writer extraordinaire and champion of my work, *Merci, madame, et gros bisous!* Because doesn't everything sound better in French?

And, first and foremost, thanks to my husband, whose belief in my work despite my tired protests to pursue more sensible occupations shines through like light through a window, and whose absence from my life would certainly be the death of me.

AUTHOR'S BIO
MARISOL MURANO

Valentina Goldman Ships Out is the sequel to the best-selling *Valentina Goldman's Immaculate Confusion*, and Marisol Murano's third work of fiction. Among other honors, Murano's work has received the Latino Book of the Year award, was an Original Voices selection, and has been translated into several languages.

VALENTINA GOLDMAN'S IMMACULATE CONFUSION

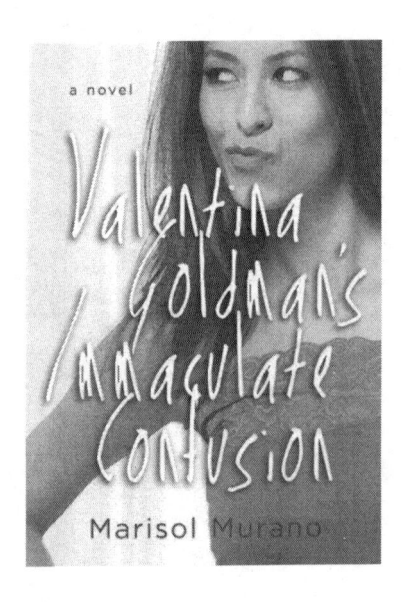

If you enjoyed this book and would like to embark on the series of detours that led Valentina to the high-seas, get *Valentina Goldman's Immaculate Confusion*—her quirky take on life in America.

Made in the USA
Middletown, DE
26 June 2015